THE SIGNAL
For The
STORM

I0682394

Robert Walters

A Pencarian/Bankes Edition

ISBN-13: 978-0615957425
ISBN-10: 0615957420

DEDICATION

THIS BOOK IS DEDICATED TO LEIGH JACKSON.

"And to fight for a cause they've long ago forgotten,

then she'll be a true love of mine."

"Scarborough Fair - Canticle"

Simon and Garfunkel

CONTENTS

In Memory of Those Who Have Passed On. . .

Katherine Lee Walters, my wife.

Edward and Dorothy Walters and Evelyn Woodle, my parents.

Jack B. Sowards, native Texarkanian, former television and

motion picture screenplay writer, who upon reading the first

chapter of my book saw some potential in my writing and in

me as a writer.

Larry Crabb, and to the former World Import Jewelers; jewelry,

trays, good music, and many, many laughs!

Betty Taylor Hines, now truly my guardian angel.

Jerry L. Atkins., jazz saxophonist, radio host, author, and life

mentor, who taught me almost everything I know about modem jazz and about style and good taste in music.

Flem and Ouida Ferguson, my Gerald and Sara Murphy. "That's

God's Music."

and

Jeanne Maxwell. and the former Bagatelle

and Les Saisons Restaurants in Dallas, Texas.,

> *and a once in a lifetime experience in jazz.*

PROLOGUE

Art and Laura Lee Wilcox were parents of Budd Wilson's best friend, Mikie They were twelve years younger than Budd's parents, and they were of a totally different era and had a totally different value system than Edgar and Mildred Wilson had.

Budd's parents were the serious young couple involved in classical music that grew out of the Depression and were rigid and austere in their moral values. They lived in the old part of town. Budd's father did not serve in the war.

Art and Laura Lee Wilcox grew out of World War II, and they were one of many young married couples of the Eisenhower post-war boom era. They listened to Bebop and modem jazz on wired-together, individual high fidelity components, experimenting with stereophonic sound, reel-to-reel tape and long-playing L.Ps. They were people of the Chevy Bel Air convertible era who lived in rows of new, identical tract houses that they were buying on installment plans that were labeled "the suburbs," each house with an antenna that gave service to the new recreational and informational device inside, television. Also each tract house had air-conditioning, another feature of the post-war boom in the Southwest. Art and Laura Lee Wilcox's house was just like any other north of town only it was bigger and cost more, and they had a Pontiac convertible rather than a Chevy. They lived beyond their means in the affluent suburbs where young married couples lived, loved, procreated, and were usually faithful to and had long-term monogamous relationships with their partners. Yet sometimes some of them were unfaithful and either kept their secrets or divorced, depending on the financial ties to and of each mate and or the degree of passion . . . or love.

Quite often an indiscretion was just forgotten and lived with by both partners, especially if it was for the best interest of the children. Divorce became a common place occurrence for young middle-class couples of the 1950s, and Alfred Kinsey kept a record of it all in The Kinsey Report, a survey of the sexual behavior of young post World War II adults.

Art and Laura Lee were physically active as were many of the young couples of their day. They swam and they jogged, and they raced sailboats together and he raced sports cars in amateur sanctioned S.C.C.A. races. He was the first person in Texarkana to have a Triumph TR-3 roadster and he was constantly under the hood adjusting the carburetors of his Volvo PV544. Art and Laura Lee hung out in coffee houses and in small, intimate jazz clubs when in Dallas. They were drinkers and also experimented lightly in marijuana and other drugs. Laura Lee Wilcox was a young, beautiful and seductive woman who used her sexual charms with and over men, sometimes dashing men, and later in life, young, much younger men and her husband Art, not knowing what to do about it, and a shy and gentle man, chose to ignore her extra-marital behavior.

They had met after the war in New York during all the partying after V.E.-Day. He had graduated from Texas A.& M. in 1942 with a degree in mechanical engineering and was immediately shipped to England and was put in charge of one of the crews responsible for patching up wounded, returning B - 17 bombers that had been hit but made it back to England from bombing runs over the European continent each day. It was his job, along with the crew he supervised, to make sure those planes would be able to fly out the next day to make another day's bombing. Laura Lee's first husband had been a fighter pilot and had been killed in a dog fight over Europe. She had never really gotten over it.

When Art met her it was love at first sight as far as he was concerned, and he brought her home to Texarkana and married her. Art's parents had money, which influenced Laura Lee's decision and they offered the new couple an auto dealership after they married. Art, feeling he didn't have the personality for sales, rather decided to open one of the city's best auto diagnostic and repair garages. He quickly gained a reputation for being one of the best auto repair and trouble shooters in Texarkana, as he had in England during the war. Art and Laura Lee continued to lead somewhat daring lives in the 1950s and sixties, into their thirties and forties and beyond.

Laura Lee would face her older years as a true eccentric, at home in her eccentricity. They brought four children into the world. In terms of real involvement with her children, Laura Lee was, more or less, a part time parent. She was more involved in her own life, and each time the pieces would shatter after a broken affair, Art would pick them up for her, for their four children, run a house and run a business too, as Laura Lee would retreat to her bed, locked behind closed doors in an induced grog brought on by the abuse of prescription drugs or anything else she could get her hands on. When she was in bed with her self-pity she was apart from any reality, engaged in a dangerous, self-indulgent, self destructive state as Art would desperately try to find any pills in the house and get rid of them, terrified of her own possible self-destruction and feeling responsible for it. Their children, as a result, would become very independent. As young children and even later into life, they had no supervision nor guidance.

They could go and come as they pleased, anytime they pleased and they could make their own decisions based on their own observations and needs Budd loved the freedom of the Wilcox house.

At his own home, conversely, everything was controlled. Art and Laura Lee were right out of a Jack Kerouac novel; young, free, experimenting with life, and always restless and searching. They had the money to pay for their addictions, sail boats and sports cars. They were part of a sexual revolution that was echoing in the bedrooms of young married couples in the suburbs of America in the 1950s and early 1960s. As a couple they were roaming, unfounded and unsettled. And in keeping, their children would become the flower children of the 1960s, experimenting with drugs and sex.

It was just after Labor Day, 1963, and Budd was now in junior highschool. When school was out on Friday afternoon he and his best friend Mikie Wilcox jumped on their bicycles and made the week-end trek to the Wilcox's home. Summer had been too short, and they were ready to seek new adventures for the week-ends, especially the pretty young girl, Nickie White, who lived down the street from Mikie, and whose mother had a new Thunderbird Landau.

The boys were already having strong feelings for girls and they were crazy about automobiles, and they weren't quite sure if they wanted to be with Nickie or ride in her mother's new Thunderbird, or both. When they arrived at the Wilcox's home, completely to their amazement, sitting in the driveway was the most low slung, aerodynamic automobile they had ever seen. Budd had been reading about the revolutionary machine in "Road and Track" magazine, but he never in his wildest imaginings thought he'd see one sitting in the Wilcox's driveway. It's fish mouth front end would set the trend for design of automobiles around the world for the next fifty years. It was so low slung that it barely hovered above the pavement, and it had wire wheels and dual chrome pipes, and was the most revolutionary automobile Budd had ever seen.

And there it was, right there in front of him, in the Wilcox's driveway. It was the most orgasmic automobile Budd had ever encountered, and it created a sexual response in him that no automobile had ever created before or since. It was a brand new Jaguar XK-E coupe. Art came out the side door of their house and out onto the driveway.

"What do you think of it? It's a beauty, isn't it? It's the first E-type to come off the boat in Houston. I decided I had to have one. So I ordered one direct from Coventry. Get a good look at it. We're going to race it."

"Wow!" said Budd and Mikie in unison. So much for the Thunderbird They realized then they had out-classed the whole junior high school in terms of parents' automobiles. Nickie would have to be put on hold for another week-end. This week-end they had more pressing matters.

"It's a real cat, isn't it?" Art was proud of his new purchase. "Gus Johnson also ordered a new Chevy Corvette Sting Ray. We're going to race them as a team. Andrew Jerome, Gus and I. What do you think of that?" Again, Wilcox beamed with pride.

"Dad, it's neat. It's really neat."

"We've got to get ready for it. Our first race is Sunday, November, 24th. Get in. Let's take a tear down Potomac Street."

Mikie got in the passenger seat, and Budd crawled in the hatch. The Jaguar roared into action. Art, Andrew Jerome and Gus Johnson would take their cars to an abandoned World War II Air Force field outside of Hope, Arkansas, every day and put the cars through simulated trial races to test the cars' and drivers' abilities in preparation for the first upcoming S.C.C.A. race. They would push the cars through trial curves and then hammer down on the straightaways testing the strengths and weaknesses of the men and their machines. Also at least once a week, Art would get up at sunrise, drive to Hope, and on the longest runway of the old field

bring the Jag to its highest speed only to top brake on the long, straight surface to get the feel of the front end under pressure. The men were learning the feel of their automobiles at top end, flat out, then braking for curves, then pulling through 'curveyhen' accelerating back to top speed -- not unlike jockeys as they learn the strengths and weaknesses of fine thoroughbred horses as they prepare for a derby. The Jag was proving to be a thoroughbred.

The first big S.C.C.A.,Grand Prix style race was to be held in Stuttgart, Arkansas, on Sunday, November 24th, 1963 on an abandoned World War II air field. Their practice in Hope had not been in vain, for the terrain in Stuttgart was much like that of Hope. Art Wilcox would be head pit on this race. They had also practiced and timed pit stops, cutting time for each stop as much as they could. Gus and Andrew had pre-registered the 'Vette and the Jag, as they would be driving. Art, in addition to being head pit crew leader on the first race would serve as a relief driver, if needed. As head pit crew leader, he would be putting the lessons he'd learned in England during World War II to use in a creative, exciting way. The Stuttgart S.C.C.A. field was set-up with straight-aways and curves making it like a simulated Grand Prix track. As Mikie's best friend, Budd would be going to this first race. All Budd could think of was the race. He could not think of anything else, much less, school His thirteen year old mind was fluttering. On Friday, November 22, 1963, Budd asked to stay home from school.

He said he didn't feel well, but his mind was really on the race, and it was racing faster than any of the cars. He felt he needed to stay home to relieve the stress of anticipation. His parents thought the race at Stuttgart might be good for Budd, good for his mind and ease the anxiety he was enduring now that he was an adolescent.

x

Neither of them really knew what to do about Budd's recently occurring onset of anxiety attacks. It was thought he should see a psychiatrist.

Perhaps it was just his age. Never-the-less, if Budd was to stay at home he would have to help his father rake the yard. Budd played at helping rake the side yard, but his mind was on the race.

"CBS was rushing a flash to Walter Cronkite in New York, while officials were calling for a cut-in on all CBS affiliates throughout the country. The announcement read, in Dallas, Texas, three shots were fired at President Kennedy's motorcade."

It was a little after twelve noon. Budd's mother quickly raised the side kitchen window.

She was hysterical. "The President's been shot! I heard it on the radio! Edgar! Edgar! Come quickly!" she cried.

Father Richard Thomas, of St. John's Episcopal Church in Texarkana often went up to reflect at the alter alone. He was standing at the alter this Friday, praying, when his secretary, Eloise Powell, came rushing up. "Father Thomas, President Kennedy has just been shot in Dallas! I just heard it on the radio in the office. You must come now!" Father Thomas dropped to his knees and began to recite the confession.. She helped him up and they both hurried down to the office.

Mrs. Rachel Mitchell, English teacher at F. Ben Pierce Junior High School in Texarkana had just gone to the principal's office before beginning the class's daily reading of Charles Dickens' Great Expectations. She returned with tears streaming down her cheeks. "You must all go home. You must go home, now. Something terrible has just happened. The President has been shot. We must all be careful. Something awful has occurred. Go home, now. We must be careful. I 'll call your parents. If I cannot get them, I will take you home. Something awful has happened."

"Father Oscar Huber had been the only Catholic priest to see the Presidential motorcade on Lemmon Avenue as it headed towards downtown Dallas. After returning to the rectory to eat his lunch of plain fish he was told by his assistant, Father Thompson, 'The President has been shot, Father.' I don't believe it,' said Father Huber. He could hear the voice on the television. He could hear the excitement in it. 'Several shots. . . No one seems to know... Parkland Hospital.' Father Huber tugged at his young conferee, "Get the car, Jim. You drive.

Parkland Hospital is in our parish. Come on, now. Hurry."

The two priests arrived at Parkland and hurried inside. A priest had been requested..

"Father, please pray for Jack." Father Huber agreed. "'To do Penance and to amend my life..."

Edgar, Budd and Mildred Wilson were glued to the television in the living room. Cronkite was on the air. The news was from Dallas.

"From Dallas, Texas. The flash—apparently official—President Kennedy died—at one p.m., Central Standard Time, two o'clock Eastern Standard Time—some thirty eight minutes ago."

It is said that this was the only time Cronkite lost his composure on the air. Budd saw him bite his lip and noticed his eyes filled with tears.

Father Richard Thomas, at St. John's Episcopal Church in Texarkana buried his face in his hands on his desk and openly wept as he silently said "Father forgive them, for then know not what they do."

The world reeled: Budd's entire world reeled.

"I need to find out if there is going to be a race! I need to find out if there going to be a race! I'm going to the Wilcox's!" Little did he know then that the events of the last hour would shape his life as it would a generation of his peers for many years to come, as it would for almost every adolescent boy in East Texas and across the nation who wanted to solve in their own souls the crime that happened in Dallas that day. Budd sensed some guilt -- feeling that somehow they could have stopped it.

"Where are you going? Please be careful, Budd.. Anything could happen now. Be careful."

"I will. I promise " He got on his bike and rapidly made the trek to the Wilson home, peddling as fast as he could.

Art and Laura Lee were sitting up against pillows propped against the back of their bed. Their children were all sitting around them on the sides of the bed. Budd sat on the floor. Laura Lee showed no emotion at all as she sat there smoking cigarette after cigarette, with a large ashtray beside her on the bed to catch the ashes as they watched Judge Sara T. Hughes swear in Lyndon Baines Johnson as the thirty-sixth President of the United States upon Air Force One at Love Field in Dallas, late in the afternoon of Friday, November 22, 1963.

"I wonder if we're going to have a race," Art pondered; he saw Budd out of the corner of his eye, looking for a clue. Early the next morning, he got the word from Gus Johnson. The race was on.

Mikie nudged Budd, and Budd quickly went home to prepare for the trip. He got his official Boy Scout sleeping bag and a pillow. The three of them were to sleep on the track with the cars that night in Stuttgart. Art and the boys loaded up the Volvo as soon as they could that Saturday morning and left for the trip. Andrew and Gus, the drivers, left not long after in the day in Chevrolet pick-ups pulling the sports cars. They drove faster than Art and beat the three of them there. When Art, Mike and Budd arrived in Stuttgart they got something to eat, then they went to the track to meet Jerome and Johnson with the cars. The cars were unfastened from the trucks. Art and the two drivers conversed for a while, then the drivers left to seek lodging and get a few hours sleep before the next day's race. Art fired up both cars and listened to them as he had listened to B-17s in England. Satisfied with what he heard, he went over the pit equipment. Then he and the boys made camp. The pavement was hard, and the air was cold, but the boys and Art Wilcox slept with the cars on the concrete, what little dreamless sleep could be gained that night. The wives and other friends of the team would leave Texarkana very, very early Sunday morning in a two rave new American Grand Touring automobiles that had just hit the market, a new Buick Riviera and a new Studebaker Avanti.

Behind the pits were parked some of the private vehicles that belonged to people who were there to see the race. Interspersed with ordinary cars like Chevrolet station wagons and pick-ups with people sitting on the roofs to get a better view of the race, were more exotic vehicles that belonged to a more sophisticated crowd; a Morgan; several Jaguars, an XK-140 and several 3.8 sedans (they would be raced later on) and a1957 Mark VIII sedan; an Alfa Romeo Giulietta Veloce convertible; a Mercedes 190 SL; and a vintage Bentley sedan that towered over the other cars parked behind the pits. There also was an assortment of Triumphs, Austin-

Healeys and M.G's that were waiting to be raced in smaller classes that day.

Cutting through all this race pageantry, Elaine Jerome, one of the drivers' wives who'd been listening to the car radio in the Riviera, jumped out of the car and went running toward the pits.

"They shot him! Somebody just shot Lee Harvey Oswald! In Dallas some man shot him! Now we'll never know! Now we'll never know! Somebody killed him to shut him up!"

In a matter of a couple of minutes, the news rippled across the track. The white "Hold Your Position" flag was raised. The entire world felt locked in position - the planet was in a state of shock. Laura Lee sat in the front bucket seat of the Riviera. She smoked her cigarette -- devoid of emotion.

The Wilcox's sent their children off to finishing and boarding schools. This sending wasn't only to give their children a better education, but to allow Laura Lee to have the freedom she wanted without the children in the house. Mikie was sent to boarding school in Ojai, Calfornia, Thacher, which was established in 1889. Budd's best friend was gone in 1964. He went to school, but he only went through the motions. After dinner he would tell his parents he was going upstairs to study and then he'd locked himself in his upstairs bedroom after school and on week-ends to watch endless hours of television on his old Magnavox T.V., and listened to endless hours of jazz on his little, portable Zenith record player It became the only place he felt safe.

"Ladies and Gentlemen, The Beatles!" Ed Sullivan introduced the Fab Four to the States to a captive audience of 73 million people. The world roared with excitement. Budd was one of those 73 million. The Reverend Billy Graham, who never watched television on a Sunday watched the Beatles on the Sullivan show and said of them, "They're a passing phase. All are symptoms of the uncertainty of the times and the confusion about us."

Budd lay there alone on his bed, watching his television in his room with no one in his life and nothing to live for except the news on television. He watched an election year cycle and a war -- and Walter Cronkite was becoming the only person he did trust. Walter Cronkite became his only friend.

'Stand up, stand up for Lyndon, we must be firm and true.

Believe me, I admire him, the gossip's just not true.

`I'm nor for Gene McCarthy, or Fulbrig,ht's careless crew.

I will stand up for Lyndon, there's nothing else to do.'

—And that's the way it is, hot on the campaign trail in Abilene, Texas.. .

This is Walter Cronkite, CBS News."

Into Mikie's second semester at Thacher, Art was summoned. Mikie was in trouble. He had run away from school, and had thrown red paint on draft records at the draft board in Berkeley as a part of a protest. Boarding School was over for Mikie Art pleaded with the authorities. Because Mikie was a minor, they allowed Art to take him back to Texarkana under his legal supervision and under probation as his father. The two drove back from California to Texarkana.

Now, The House of Jonah was a sign of it's time. It was a coffee house that had just opened in Texarkana -- sponsored in part by the United Presbyterian Church and the Church of St. John. Rumor had it that it was a part of the Communist Party and a Socialist Front. Whatever it was, it provided a unique experience for Texarkana in the middle 1960's, a town whose politics were extremely conservative.

Budd had become such an introvert that he felt out of place in the established order at school and in the community -- even though he didn't look it. He'd received a phone call from Mikie He wanted them to meet at the House of Jonah. That Friday night, Budd went down to the coffee house without telling his parents where he was going. When he walked in he was surprised to see a totally different Mikie Wilcox than the one he had known. His auburn hair was now down below his shoulders, and he was wearing golden framed "granny glasses."

"What are you?" Budd asked.

"I'm a hippie. A counter-culture Marxist revolutionary. A proletariat disciple of Chairman Mao. Get with the times, Buddy. Get rid of your tortoise shell glasses and button-downed collar shirts. You're so 'status quo.' You don't care anything about the poor and down-trodden."

"That's not true. I care a lot about people, the poor. I'm just different from you, and I don't know what to do to show I care."

Claire Adelle, Flank Fitzhugh and Richard Harwood, fellow highschool students, were sitting near Mikie, sipping coffee and engaged in a heated conversation.

"And Gertrude Stein and DosPassos. Oh that was a writer, DosPassos. Someday I'll be another Gertrude Stein, critiquing young great writers like in Paris in the 1920s."

"How are you adjusting to Texarkana?" Budd asked Mikie

"Oh..." Mikie looked up, "fine, if one can. Texarkana, the eternal cesspool." Richard Harwood smiled, got up and walked away -- leaving two empty chairs at the table. Mikie turned back to Claire and sat down leaving one seat. "I've got the key to Dos Passos' writing," he exclaimed without further acknowledging Budd.

Budd stood there a minute, eyeing the other empty chair, then he asked the trio, "Do you mind if I join you?"

"Oh Budd, well... sit down." Mikie had acquired a certain snobbishness after going to boarding school in California. Coming back to Texarkana was a real defeat for him, and it increased his need to appear superior, while hiding his deep sense of inferiority underneath it all.. His one claim to fame at The House of Jonah was that he had thrown paint on draft records in Berkeley.

"I've read U.S.A. by DosPassos," Budd started. It was a true statement. Budd's father had suggested he read it, hoping to encourage something creative with Budd's time when he as locked in his room. He'd also suggested Budd read John Steinbeck, William Faulkner, W. Sommerset Maugham, Sinclair Lewis and F. Scott Fitzgerald. Budd did't tell Mikie his father's motivation for having him read these authors. It was an attempt by Budd's father to bring him out of his cocoon. At any rate, DosPassos's USA intrigued Mikie -- for as an intellectual, he held Budd's father in much higher esteem than Budd. After all, Mikie thought, Edgar Wilson was a graduate of New England Conservatory of Music in Boston. Budd was just his childhood friend.

"Ah! Hemingway! There was a man—a writer," began Claire.

"You see when I become the next Gertrude Stein, the critic, I'll encourage young writers. If only I could find another DosPassos or Hemingway in this pit of mediocrity."

"I like F. Scott Fitzgerald," Budd said. He had read Tender is the Night and The Great Gatsby when he was locked up in his room. Fitzgerald wrote about rich, young, beautiful Americans with many problems. His characters gave Budd a fantasy world to enter, and he set out then -- somehow, someday, to become Jay Gatsby in search of Daisy Buchanan, the love of his life, a fantasy he cherished whenever he was locked in his room.

"Yes Buddy-boy, you are Gatsby.. .or should I say Jimmy Gatz with your button-downed collars and blue blazer in search of Nicole." Claire was on the attack. "Fitzgerald was a weak man He had neither the strength nor talent of Hemingway. A Moveable Feast." Claire was a bitter phony. However, Budd had respect for her. She had her own battle to fight. She had polio and was in a wheel chair.

"You know this town is everything I tried to get away from in California.," Mikie said with disgust. "Let's talk about the Chamber of Commerce and my Dad," he said

sarcastically. "The Rotary Club. Damned fool as my mother plays around on him. Shipped me off to California, but here I am again, right here in Texarkana. All those middle class souls, like my Dad, who read their Wall Street Journals and go to their mundane jobs, fooling no one but themselves. At least your father reads The Atlantic Monthly."

"What's wrong with the Chamber of Commerce, and what does my father have to do with it?" Budd asked.

"You materialistic son of a bitch." Mikie spewed. He was bitter about his whole life.

"Oh, I see there's going to be a scene." Claire sighed .

"No there's not going to be a scene," said Budd, "because I'm leaving. You can have your little pseudo-intellectual discussion in private."

He got up and walked out. 'Damned snobs. Bet they haven't even read DosPassos or Hemingway.'

The sophomore high school year went on. Budd had no other place to go on Friday nights other than the House of Jonah. Bit by bit he was reaching out beyond his bedroom. So he went again and then again, trying to conquer his fears. He heard there was going to be a jam session at the coffee house -- spearheaded by Jimmy Aldon, the jazz saxophonist and jazz expert of Texarkana who played excellent old Charlie Parker be-bop lines. Budd knew all the piano chords to all these songs. After all, his father was a piano teacher, and his father liked jazz.

Other than the television shows blaring in his room, music was his only escape and it was the love of his life. It brought romance to his life.

"I'll show them," he said of Mikie and Claire. For once he saw this as his opportunity to come away from his T.V. For once he could come out of his cocoon and become popular.

Somehow, mentally, he viewed it as his debut. He flew home after school and began flipping through a stack of records. He ran over to the shelf and picked up his twenty dollar Melodica.. Later that week he went over to the Wilcox's home to show Mikie what he was trying to do on the Melodica.

"Wilson what are you doing?"

"Learning improvisations to blues progressions on the Melodica.".

"Wilson, you're weird."

"Yeah, I know," Budd replied. "Damnit, I haven't got enough keys or fingers." Budd laughed to himself "Gotta start it over. Gotta start it over."

"You're up to something." Mikie shrugged and walked away.

Budd practiced every spare moment at home, listening to old jazz records and playing with them on the Melodica.. Friday night at the House of Jonah finally came. The small stage was set, and the band was already playing when Budd walked in—Rick Rodkey on piano, Jimmy Aldon on sax,

Diddy Gerber on bass, and Dave Daley on drums They were playing their final number of a set. Claire and Mikie were sitting back in the heel of the place at one of the candle-lit tables made of old sewing machine bases with wooden table tops. Art and Laura Lee Wilcox inconspicuously walked in. They went anywhere there was jazz and being that there was very little of it in Texarkana, they frequented The House... Art was carrying a blue velvet sack under his arm, wrapped around a small bottle of Crown Royal. Only coffee was served at The House of Jonah, as fas as Budd knew.

"Hey. How are you doing?" Budd walked up to Alden.

"Hey man." He was glad to see him. "Gonna sit in tonight?"

"Yeah, I'd like to." Budd replied. "I've been working on a couple of things lately."

"Whada'ya got in that little case?" Alden asked, as he looked down at the Melodica.

"It's a three dollar harmonica, hooked up to a two octave keyboard, then you blow to make music."

"Oh, a toodlehorn." Alden laughed.

"Exactly!" Budd replied

"You gonna play it? What do you want to play?"

"Let's just start out with a little blues."

"Far out!" Aldon exclaimed.

"Rick, why don't you let Budd jam on some old blues riffs while I take a break?

Wilson's my friend. Gonna sit in with us."

"Oh. Yeah. Sure. What do you want to play, Budd?"

"'Just some blues on the toodlehorn."

"You going to play that?" Rodkey was somewhat taken back.

"Yeah, just some blues at a medium swing."

"Okay. . . ?" He addressed the audience. "We're going to do a little improvisation on some old blues riffs, and, uh, a newcomer, Budd Wilson, will be featured on the... on the, what's that thing called?"

"A Melodica. " Budd replied with a smile and a shrug.

Hank, Claire and Mikie looked up, aghast. Budd grinned.

"What key?" Rodkey asked.

"` B-flat,'" Budd replied, "and take it slow. I haven't got too many fingers."

He kind of mechanically breezed through the opening blues progression on the Melodica and all went well. Then he got a little raunchier, and took some risks.

Jimmy Aldon looked up with a faint, shocked smile on his face. "You're good!" he exclaimed "Let me get my horn." He picked his tenor up from the stand. The audience applauded. Aldon put the strap on his horn and licked the reed. Budd was bending notes all over the keyboard, blowing his head off.

"Damnit!" Budd exclaimed, "I haven't got enough keys. You take it, Jimmy! This is out of your generation. I haven't got enough keys or breath left." Aldon took the song out.

"A little blues!" Aldon was at the mike after the conclusion of the song. "A little blues," everybody...

The audience was roaring with applause, "And a very talented young man who walked up here with a Melodica tonight, Budd Wilson."

"Thank you," Budd said faintly as he looked at the audience in somewhat disbelief.

"Call the tunes, Budd." Alden said. "It's your set."

"Tramp?" he asked.

"Fine," Aldon replied.

They played "The Lady is a Tramp" and three other songs -- then he had to take a break.

He was out of breath, and the Melodica was leaking air.

"Budd Wilson!" Aldon announced to the audience. "Budd Wilson!" The people reached out and held his hand as he walked to the back of the room to get coffee.

"You're very talented." Laura Lee touched the side of his arm as he walked past her.

"Great!" "Tremendous!" "Fine Playing!"

He thanked them and walked to the back of the room.

Mikie and Claire were sitting at a back table. They tried to avoid making eye contact with Budd.

Undaunted, he made a point of going up to them.

"You see, art," he began, "is not only to be talked about. It's to be experienced. . . as a player, even if only on a Melodica. It takes an inborn talent -- but moreover -- self-discipline. Talent and discipline gives us the ability to create. Miss Stein, Mr. Hemingway, from Jay Gatsby or should I say Jimmy Gatz, adieu. Oh my goodness!"

"Where are you going?" Mikie asked.

"I've got to get home to my television upstairs. I'm missing Jack Parr."

"No. Stay."

Laura Lee sat at her table with her husband, smiling, purring.

The news of Budd's musical debut at The House of Jonah rippled throughout the high school. The doors of his bedroom flew open. He was at Fritz Cavanaugh's store buying Brooks style blue blazers and penny loafers. He was going to teen and adult parties and drinking Scotch. It was fashionable, even though he hated the taste of it. He found a young lady at The House of Jonah six years older than he with whom he learned about sex. He joined St. John's Episcopal Church. "It's the only sensible thing a young gentleman can do," Fritz Cavanaugh informed him. His parents bought him a new red Volkswagen. He enrolled in a highschool journalism class to learn to write. Again, Gatsby was in search of Daisy Buchanan.

Nickie White and Budd sat at the back of Mrs. Joy Arnold's journalism class. He was now a senior and she, a junior. She sat with her legs crossed in short mini-skirts showing a great part of her silk stocking clad thighs. She knew she was exciting Budd, and she knew he craved it. It was time for Gatsby to make his play for Daisy. Mrs. Arnold asked each class member what subject they would choose for their final exam as a comprehensive news story. Budd chose to write about a series of unsolved murders that occurred in Texarkana in 1946. The killer was labeled "The Phantom Killer." He interviewed the editor of the Texarkana Gazette. He went through old microfilm. He went out to the sights where the bodies had been found. Then he went back upstairs to room. He put it all together in his mind, and approached his old Underwood manual typewriter with confidence. When presented to the class, the story was the rave at Texas High School, and everybody wanted to read it. Mrs. Arnold read it aloud to the journalism class.

Later after the reading, Nickie White approached Budd, and it felt like she rubbed her breasts against his chest. "You'll be a great writer. You'll make a lot of money."

He was tremendously aroused; he knew he wanted her. At this point, the new Budd Wilson entered an unchartered phase in his development. New Year's Eve, 1967- 1968. Budd and his parents had gone to Dallas to see his sister and her husband. They had all gone to dinner and upon returning to the motel, later in the night, Budd started to have severe chest pains. He was rushed to the hospital. The doctors said he was having a heart attack. Later, the diagnosis changed: He had rheumatic fever. He was home tutored the rest of 1968, just in time to graduate with his class.

CHAPTER 1

As the 1980s came to a close, Budd Wilson was content without a partner. At this point in his life he enjoyed the company of his friends. He was trying to make peace with his parents. He adored his daughter, Jennifer As he approached forty, he had a simplistic view of his life. Even though he created that simplistic view himself, it served his purpose at the time. It was a credit to his intelligence that it did.

He had grown up a baby-boomer in Texarkana, Texas, a child of the television age. He was weaned on Captain Kangaroo and the Mickey Mouse Club. At age thirteen, he saw television news come of age with the coverage of the assassination of a president in Dallas, Texas. His politics, tastes and beliefs were shaped by Jack Parr and Walter Cronkite and the events of the day. He laughed at Jonathan Winters and Johnny Carson as they came into his life over an old Magnavox brown and white T.V. in his bedroom in the middle to late 1960s. Now the 1980s were here and Budd Wilson had no idea what the future would bring his way, but things were already in motion, things from the past that would reoccur and lead to things of the present and into the future.

He had hesitated for a week after the fire before he called on Fire Captain Jim Prichart. He didn't want to get involved in it. Yet he was involved. From the first night Steve Brantley had stepped upon his front porch that summer of 1988, it had a freakish, frightening quality.

In June of that year Budd Wilson had rented an old house down on the other end of the block from his parents' home. Although his daughter didn't like the place, he loved it. It had spacious rooms and a large front porch across it with old, white-washed wicker furniture. A swing hung from the ceiling and a ceiling fan kept him cool in the summer evenings as he sat on the porch at dusk waiting for the sun to set. The sensual droning of the locusts were as old and Southern as the Cape Jasmine and Crepe Myrtle that grew wild along the fence. He lovingly referred to it as "The Truman House". He envisioned himself giving fiery orations from his front porch in the style of Harry himself. Its was "his house". He kept the lawn and the shrubbery meticulously trimmed. It was his house, the first since his divorce four years earlier. It was his—Budd Wilson's and Harry Truman's.

One August night, as he was sitting on the porch, Steve Brantley stepped up out of the dark.

"Say!"

"Hello Steve. Have a seat."

"Don't mind if I do." Steve had been on what he would refer to as one of his nightly strolls.

"Say, you don't know a Nicole Smithson, do ya?"

"Nicole Smithson? Lord yes Stephen, I know Nicole. I've known her for twenty years, rather intimately at one time."

"You did?!?"

"I used to date Nicole Smithson. Only at that time her name was Nickie White."

"Did you, now?!?"

"She treated me about a year and a half ago on the fifth floor of

Municipal Hospital for a nervous breakdown after my divorce."

"She did!? Wea'll. . , what else do you know about her?"

"I used to love her," he softly said. "I used to love her."

"What did you say?"

"I said I used to love her! It was a long time ago."

Stephen had a way of irritating everybody in the neighborhood including Budd Wilson.

Budd remembered from the past when Stephen had returned from Vietnam. He could still hear that E-type Jaguar whine through its gears like a diving Stuka as it turned off Seventh Street, down Olive Street towards his mother's house. What got out of the car really wasn't Budd's conception of a hippie. Steve had a harsher look. He had a distinct motorcycle gang look, wearing mirrored sunshades, faded jeans, and an open leather vest and leather cap. His chest was covered with tattoos. His long hair and beard were dirty and unkept. With him was a blonde haired girl with long hair, and in tight jeans and a motorcycle jacket. It was quite a sight to greet Stephen's mother Margaret, and for that matter, the entire Piney Woods' town of Texarkana in the late 1960s. The world was changing. It had been since that fateful day in November, some five years earlier, some two hundred miles west of there in Dallas.

In 1968, Budd had rheumatic fever that spring semester and was tutored at home just in time to get back on his feet for commencement exercises. He knew he was in love. He had met her the fall before in a high school journalism class, and had remembered her throughout his illness in an almost metaphysical and animalistic way, and when he could get out, he went searching for her. She was already deep his system. Nickie White was his first love.

She was a year younger than Budd, and she was the most beautiful, remarkable, and provocative young woman he'd ever known. She was a natural blonde with a turned up nose and misty aqua eyes. Her voice had the resonance of honey and bourbon.

Nickie had controlled her world since she was a little girl, and everybody in it. She was adept at it, using a combination of beauty, charm and nerve. Budd and Nickie went steady for the latter part of 1968, all of 1969 and most of the time in college.

Budd had called them "The Best and the Brightest". They were beautiful snobs in 1968.

"Captain Prichart, I'm Budd Wilson. I live across the street from Steve Brantley. I saw it, every bit of it. I called in the alarm."

Prichart motioned politely for him to sit down. His assistant, Charles Bledsoe, joined the two. Prichart looked Budd straight in the eye but he did so in a kindly and gentle way as the discussion led on.

"Continue, please," said Prichart.

"I'd talked to Nicole Smithson and Steve Brantley the Saturday night before it happened."

"That would have been the night of April first?" Prichart had a quizzical look on his face.

"Go on."

"I'm sure it was Nicole's car. It was a small silver Mercedes, one like she drives, only I couldn't get a license number in the rain." He paused, then continued, "Nicole and Steve both had talked to me the Saturday night before it happened. He was screaming and shouting about Nicole. I didn't know what to do."

"How well do you know Steve?"

"I've known him all my life. I say I've known him. Truth is, no one really knows Steve. Anyway, I was just getting ready to go to the University when he was getting back from 'Nam. I guess it was late summer of 1968. I had just started dating Nickie at the time."

"Nickie White?" Prichart questioned.

"Nicole Smithson. White was her maiden name."

"You were dating Nicole when Steve Brantley came back from Vietnam?"

"Yeah. I had been ill the entire Spring semester, rheumatic fever, but after it was over I remembered her, and I wanted her, and I found her."

"Where were you?" Prichart brought the subject back to the present. "How did you see the fire? How involved were you with Brantley and Smithson in all of this?"

"I was inadvertently involved. I was caught in a crossfire, you might say. I'd talked to Steve. I didn't know what to do. I never really believed what he said until that Saturday night when the phone calls from Steve and Nicole started coming in. He had been talking to me since August about a Vietnam war counseling group that met at the Main Street Doctors' Plan. Nicole and a male counselor ran this group. There had been some falling out somehow between Nicole and Stephen. She called the police and had him ejected from the group. He accused her of falsely dipping into the till on insurance claims. Where he came up with that, I don't know. Anyway, it was enough to scare her, and she kicked him out of the group. After that, he had this ingenious way of keeping a record of who was there for every meeting and apparently it got under Nicole's skin."

"What was that?" Prichart inquired.

"Well, he took a picture of every license plate in the parking lot the night of every meeting for two years and he kept a record of it. Still does, as far as I know."

"He did what?"

"Yep. At least he says he did. According to him, after he was kicked out of the group, Nicole had him hospitalized in the psychiatric unit of the Municipal Hospital for a couple of weeks while she disappeared. I'm not sure that was quite right. Stephen's a pain in the ass, but he's harmless. I've confronted him to the limit and he's never harmed or threatened me, but then I'm not female and I'm not beautiful. I never really knew what happened that night in that meeting. He talked about everything but that night."

"And you knew all of this?" asked Prichart. "And Brantley called you the Saturday night before the fire yelling about Smithson?"

"That's right."

"What did you do?"

"Well, I didn't know what to do," Budd continued. "Dr. Dodd, my psychiatrist -- when I was in the hospital -- had died. I didn't know who to call or what to do."

The pastures were green that summer of 1968.

"Nickie, how come we're so beautiful, so proud?"

"Oh Budd, shut up, and come here. Kiss me. Love you, you idealistic idiot. . . and how many proud, vain children are we going to have, hmm Dr. Wilson?"

Her voice was a golden rasp. She stuck her hand down the waist of his bluejean shorts. "Why don't we start right now? Don't worry, I'm on the pill."

Budd slipped his hand underneath her short-sleeved, burnt orange University of Texas T-shirt.

She was petite. Her breasts were small but firm and fit the overall proportions of her body beautifully. It was a lazy, summer afternoon in East Texas in 1968. She began to peel her clothes off. It was a long, vigorous afternoon.

The blanket cooling, Nickie said abruptly, "I want you to pledge SAE when we go to the University, Budd."

"Sure, the future young doctor amidst the social whirl of sororities and fraternities in Austin.

Honey, I can't afford it and I won't have the time."

"Afford it? You can afford it. You're just cheap. Anyway, my mother, her sister and my cousins were Chi Omegas at the University of Arkansas. It's a family legacy. Some of the girls from Texas have been talking to me about it."

"Chi Omega? You're not going to do it, are you?"

She sat up abruptly.

"Of course I am. You've got to be an SAE. We've got to stick together in college. We've got to create ties if you're going to be a doctor."

"Nickie, I don't feel comfortable in all that mess."

"Budd! You crazy idealist! You and your books. Do you think they'll get you into medical school?"

"They should."

"Well they don't, not alone."

"Oh Honey, shut up. I came here to get laid, not talk politics."

"Not Republican politics? " she questioned in a rich purr and put her index finger to his nose, softly pushing him to the ground.

"Not even Harry Truman." His words were garbled as their mouths opened to each other.

"Not even J.F.K.?"

"Shut up, stupid shit."

Budd had just turned 39 years old. It was April of 1989. He was sitting in front of Captain Prichart and his assistant Charles Bledsoe.

"I thought about it. I knew I better call Nicole. At 9:30, Saturday night, April first, I left a message with Nickie's answering service. I was lying in bed listening to an old big band radio show on PBS-FM. I remember it was Benny Goodman's 'Don't Be That Way'. It had to have been around 11:15 when Nickie called. She seemed extremely eager to know what I knew. She was panicky but she seemed sort of normal. Now, Steve said that she could tell a straight-faced lie better than anyone he knew. I told her I didn't know whether Steve was delusional or WHAT. She said he was not delusional, but a psychopath. She seemed afraid, maybe paranoid. She thanked me several times for calling. She said that one of us would get in touch with the other Monday, April third.

She kept thanking me. I called her at the hospital Monday at noon. I couldn't reach her immediately so I left a message with the woman at the desk asking her to have Nicole call me. In about fifteen minutes she did."

"Budd, now listen to me, observe everything. I mean everything. He could kill me!

OBSERVE EVERYTHING!"

Then Budd Wilson looked at Captain Prichart and said, "I've avoided telling you this Captain Prichart. I was threatened several days after the fire. I was afraid." Charles Bledsoe, Prichart's assistant, picked up a pad when Budd said that he had been threatened.

"I didn't know what was going to happen. I was even afraid Nickie was going to kill me. At that point I thought I knew too much. I still may. I called an acquaintance of mine who worked for the public mental health facility. I'd hoped he'd be supportive."

"Was he?" asked Prichart.

"No..no, not at all. He told me that if I got into any kind of legal challenge on this thing they'd try to blame the fire on me -- which is impossible. I was on my front porch watching it all, and my parents were watching from my front livingroom window."

"Legal challenge?"

"Yes, I had a series of lawsuits after I got out of the hospital following my nervous breakdown. My insurance company wouldn't pay the hospital. I was having problems paying child support to my former wife, and the hospital was harassing the hell out of me to pay them.

One of my best friends was in the practice of law and was in business by himself. He helped me out when I needed it. Won two, busted even on the third. I never thought we'd win them. I assume the counselor thought after that I would bring charges on anybody for anything, including Nicole."

"Hum-p--ph." Prichart paused and spit. "What else did this public health counselor say to you?"

"He told me that I better keep my mouth shut about the fact that Nickie and I had been an item years ago, that I now considered her a role model -- well, always did."

"Who is this guy?"

"James Fromm at the public mental health center."

Both of the officers' pens hit the pads.

"Did he say anything else?" asked Prichart.

"He said they'd run me out of town if I talked about this."

"What did you say?"

"I told them I had a child here, that I soon would be forty, and that I was getting sick of this and that no one would run me out of my own home town."

It was late October, 1968 in Austin. It was the first cold week-end of Autumn. He had not seen Nickie since late August -- though he talked to her on the phone sometimes more than once a day. They had decided that he should go on to the University before her. As soon as she graduated from highschool, in May, she'd join him and they'd live together in Austin.

He missed her terribly. This would be the first week-end he'd come to Texarkana to see her. It would start a pattern. That Thursday night he called her at her parents' house.

"Baby, I'll pick you up at seven tomorrow night. Wear a cocktail dress. We're going to Shreveport and do a little dancing."

"But Budd, I've got an out-of-town football game. I can't miss it darling. And besides you can't get in from class by seven."

"Yes I can."

"Can you? Really?"

"Sure."

"Damn it, O.K. - I'll be ready. I don't know what you do to me but you do it. It's a damned good thing I'm not a virgin or you'd have lost me a long time ago."

"I did one night. Anyway that's the basic idea."

She took a glance around the room to see if her parents were within listening distance. "Screw you, Budd Wilson!"

"Again, that's the basic idea. I'll pick you up at seven, dressy. We ain't going to the Bossier strip."

Lacking discipline that day and having his mind on other matters, Budd skipped all of his classes on Friday and arrived in Texarkana around two.

Nickie was practicing her part for the senior play, George Orwell's *1984*. Budd snuck in the back of the highschool little theater. Only the stage lights were on. She happened to peer out and saw him. Putting her hand above her eyes and squinted a little.

"Budd? Budd?" she questioned softly.

"Hi, Baby."

"Budd, what are you doing here so soon?"

"I had good trade winds behind me, and I kept the accelerator to the floor all the way."

"I can't believe it. I'm so happy."

They both looked around to see that they had captured an audience made up of the cast and crew.

"Come on Baby. Let's go outside." He shut the door behind them.

"I missed you. Damn it, I missed you." She was exuberant.

He held her in his arms, picked her up and twirled her in an embrace. They moved like dancers on a revolving stage.

"I love you. God damn it, I love you."

"Yeah, me too," she said.

They kissed, and they kissed again.

"Budd, I've got to get back." She pulled away as they grasped each other's hands at arms length.

"It's good to see you." His face was beaming.

"I know. I know." She ran up, kissed him once quickly and then returned to the little theater.

"Wow!" He turned and walked away after the door shut behind her.

A part of how Budd judged every situation was how he dressed for it. He had been criticized as being shallow for this characteristic, and though at times he felt guilt for his vanity, he also felt pride at being a handsome young man. Tonight he was wearing a dark olive, three-piece wool suit, a starched, white oxford cloth shirt with a button-downed collar, a gold silk tie with matching pocket handkerchief, brown wing-tipped shoes, and a pocket watch held by chain that linked vest pocket to vest pocket. If Budd could look at himself in the mirror and feel vain before he went out, he liked it. He was vain. He liked vain people. He liked to surround himself with vain people.

He picked up his keys, tossed them up out of his hand, and caught them again with the other hand. He put on his trench coat and bid his parents goodnight. His mother told him to drive carefully and not to drink too much. There was a slight mist that night.

"How do I look?" she asked cautiously after she opened the front door to him.

"Nickie, you're beautiful. As always, you're beautiful, only more so."

She smiled. She stood proud.

They walked through the foyer into the den of Nicole's parents' house.

"Budd, Budd. Good to see you. How's the University? Mary, fix this boy a drink " Alex White was a retired World War II Navy pilot. He was hail-hearty with those he liked and openly disdainful of those he didn't.

Nickie stood in the den facing her parents, smiling and pleased at the camaraderie between her father and her lover.

"I'll get his drink Daddy. I know how he likes it."

"Now be careful, honey. You two are going out on the road tonight." Mary White was a good mother, one you could talk to about anything, one who was understanding.

"Here Darling, Scotch and water." Nickie placed the drink on the table, bending down with her knees together gracefully in her new mini-cocktail dress. Then she stood up, arching her back.

"There." She smiled.

"Look at you. God, you look beautiful!" Budd softly exclaimed.

"Thank you."

"Let me see you."

She looked around, smiled, rolled her eyes and curtsied.

Nickie looked beautiful that night. She was wearing a pale blue cocktail dress that made an an X across the bodice carefully showing the crease between her breasts. She wore a large, silver patent leather belt, with a large silver round wreath-like buckle in the middle that joined the top and the bottom of the dress. She had on light blue, short-heeled satin slippers, and light blue, lace designed panty hose. Her hair was coiffed in a bouffant style with a blue velvet hair band separating her blonde bangs from the small meticulously poofed body of her hair. She wore small, circular, wreath-like earrings, and a solitaire diamond pendant that hung down about six inches from her neck on a tiny silver chain. She had on dark eye shadow, dark eye liner and pale lipstick.

"While you're looking at me, let me share your cigarette and drink." She winked as she sat down next to him on the den couch.

"Only one if you're going out," Mary White said in friendly authority.

"I've always taken care of Nickie, Mrs. White."

"She's always taken care of you."

Nickie laughed, trying to control bits of ice and Scotch and water in her mouth, covering her mouth with the palm of her hand. She laid the glass down.

"Come on Budd, let's go. Let me get my cape." She walked to the foyer closet and pulled out a full, satin navy cape. He wrapped it around her. Then she turned to face him as he fastened the satin blue button at her neck.

"Good night, everybody." Nickie peered into the den and waved farewell for the evening.

"Goodnight, you two." Mary White smiled. "Be careful."

They headed out Highway 71, towards Shreveport.

"Well, we're alone on the road at last."

"Where are we going?"

"It's a surprise."

"I trust your tastes."

"How do you know that?"

"I know you Budd. After all, you've got me."

He laughed. "You're so sensible."

"That's what I mean. How much money have we got?"

"Not enough."

"Not enough for what?"

"Not enough for dinner, dancing and a motel too," he said.

"Okay, so we'll stay someplace sleazy. You know, second-floor walk-up."

"You going to turn enough tricks to pay for it?" He grinned.

"Shut up." She looked toward the road and was silent for a moment then she said. "Budd, do you realize it's almost 1970?" She turned and asked him seriously, "What'll we be doing in 1970?"

"I'll be a sophomore and you'll be a freshman and we'll be living together in Austin."

"I'll be so happy when we're always together. I hate being away from you Budd. I do."

"I do too."

"I miss you so badly."

"I do, too."

She stared out the window for a few more minutes.

"Wonder what we'll be doing in 1980?" she whimsically asked.

"Honey, in 1980 you'll be twenty-nine and I'll be thirty."

"Lord."

"We'll have three children, live in a split-level suburban house. You'll have an Oldsmobile station wagon while I work like a slave trying to figure out how to pay for it all. I'll be getting a bay-window and you'll be getting a little round at the ass. I'll be chasing my secretary and you'll be chasing the golf pro."

"People really do that. They do...God, I hope not. Can't we keep the excitement alive...forever?"

"We will," he said.

"We have to." She looked at him. "Isn't it thrilling, Budd? Isn't it all—life—thrilling?"

"Most of the time, Nickie."

U.S. Highway 71 and Louisiana Highway One merged north of town. The lights of the suburbs first appeared, then the mercury vapor street lamps, then the flow of the traffic of Shreveport.

"I kind of like a city, Budd. It's exciting. I mean maybe not Shreveport, but maybe Dallas?

Huh, Budd? Maybe we could live in Dallas someday. I'm afraid they roll up the sidewalks at sunset in Texarkana. It just won't do."

They drove down to the riverfront.

"Where are we going?"

"Henri's," he replied. "I've heard they have terrific food and a really good jazz band."

"I do love dancing close to you." She snuggled close to him in the front seat of his red Volkswagen beetle.

"I do too, Baby."

The valet came up to park the car.

"What style."

"Could we go to the bar first?" Budd asked the maitre d'. "Somewhere back in a dark corner."

The maitre d' showed them to a discreetly hidden table.

"Your waitress will be here in a moment."

"Thank you." She smiled at the maitre d'.

"Listen Baby, I want you to try a drink I got onto in Austin. It's called a Bacardi cocktail.

It's loaded with rum -- only it tastes like fruit punch."

"I'd like that."

The waitress arrived.

"Two Bacardi cocktails, please."

"Yes, sir." She laid down the cocktail napkins

"These are good, very good."

"You want another one?"

"Should I?" She laughed.

"Should you?" he asked.

"Of course."

A vocalist stepped up to the stand. The pianist did a slow, tinkling introduction. The vocalist approached the mike. She stood alone in the solitary blue spotlight.

'Embrace me, my sweet embraceable you.'

It was a torchy suggestion.

"Oh Budd, let's dance. She's such a beautiful singer and it's such an old romantic song"

They walked onto the dance floor. They held each other until they all but melted together.

She wrapped her left arm around his neck and openly French-kissed him.

"Come to daddy, come to daddy, do"

"You think we could find that sleazy walk-up motel now?" she whispered in his ear.

"You're the horniest woman."

"Hypocrite."

"Yeah I am, aren't I?" He kissed her again.

"My sweet embraceable you."

It was around 1:30 a.m. He headed onto the alternative highway from Shreveport back to Texarkana. She was kind of half purring, half snoring. He drove for about an hour listening to her purr and to his own thoughts. Out of nowhere he heard a strange voice from the right side of the car and an unusual rendition of a popular rock song of the day, unfamiliar to Budd at the time.

"You can get aieyn-thin' you want at Alice's Restaurant."

Then Nickie's head popped up from the reclining seat and she looked straight at Budd and wiped her snotty nose with the back of her hand. This time there was some semblance of a melody.

"Walk right in. Sit right down. . . Just about a mile from th' railroad track."

"Nickie, you a little loaded?" he questioned.

"You can get anything ya' want at Alice's Restaurant—excepting Alice."

Then she was quiet.

"Where did you get that song?"

"Such an ar-bi-trary subject," she said in mock British hauteur. "Show." She lay back in the reclining passenger seat. "Show."

And, with that, she was snoring.

"Crazy bitch." He looked at her and started laughing -- then he looked back at the road. About ten miles outside of Texarkana as they approached the town she quickly roused herself and blurted out,"Budd, Budd!"

"Who?"

"Budd, I'm going to be sick."

"Jesus Christ Nick, I'm on a bridge."

"Doesn't matter, I'm going to be sick."

"Where are you going to throw up?"

"In the God-damned river!"

And she spewed. Budd stopped the car four times along the ten miles into town.

"You all right?"

"I'm okay."

"If we can get you across town in one piece, let's get you to the Pitt Grill and get some coffee in you."

"All right. All right. I'm all right."

"You're sure?"

"Damn it, I'm all right."

They pulled into the parking lot of the almost empty Pitt Grill, and Budd maneuvered Nickie into the restaurant, then into a booth. It was late and the waitress was in no hurry to wait on them.

Just then, two chartered Trailways busses and one Texas High School bus pull into the Pitt Grill parking lot.

"Oh, my God!"

"Wha-is-it?"

"The pep-squad and the band. They're coming in from the out of town game."

"Jesus H. Christ," Nickie gasped, "Mrs. Miller, our sponsor, and the principal."

"If you think you can't talk, just smile "

"Gotcha."

"Shit you're still drunk."

Nickie smiled at him. The principal and the sponsor of the pep-squad came in. Nickie smiled at them. The room became full of people and Nickie worked her smile at all of them. Then,

In the assembly of oher peers at the Pitt Grill Nickie screeched, "Shit, I'm going to throw up!"

"Let's get out of here Nick. Let's go." He threw five dollars on the table. "I'll see ya'll later."

Nickie got sick all over the parking lot of the Pitt Grill in front of her captive audience.

"Get in the car!"

"I'm not through!"

"Yes you are. Get in the car and roll down the window and let's get out of here."

"I'm not through."

Budd got her into the car, window down, head hanging out. He pulled out of the parking lot and beat their way out State Line Avenue for the country. They drove up one country road and down another. Around four a.m., she stabilized. At five, Budd stuck her key in the lock of the front door of her parents' home.

"Jesus shit! It's dead-bolted. CAN we get in a window?"

"Uh uh. . . Better ring the doorbell. Wait a minute. Let me."

Nickie rang the bell. A few minutes later Mary White answered the door. She looked at the two with accusation and a somewhat comic empathy.

"Come in and go to bed, and don't say a word to your father about this. Thank God, for your sake, he slept through the bell."

"Good night." Budd tried to smile.

"I'll see ya' tomorrow." Nickie lay her cheek next to his - then she lurched into the house.

"Welcome home, Budd. We missed you," said Mary White.

"Yes, Ma'am. Yes, Ma'am. I'll see ya'll tomorrow. Yes, Ma'am." He couldn't look at her...

Budd ran to the car. Then he glanced back. Mary White was standing at the front door, arms folded, smiling.

"I missed ya'll too. . , very much, very much." He was passionate about his feelings for the White family. They were in tune with his own feelings, beliefs, and lifestyle. He started the car, looked back, and drove away.

Budd's phone rang at about 1:30, Saturday afternoon.

"Come pick me up in about an hour," said Nickie.

"How do ya' feel?"

"I'll live."

"You're sure?"

"Uh huh."

"What are we going to do?"

Nickie called Budd the next morning.

"I have a surprise for you."

"What is it?"

"It's a surprise. Now come pick me up in about an hour."

"Damn it, Nicole! I hate for you to start something and not finish it."

"Oh we'll finish it. Come pick me up in an hour. Okay?"

"Alright, Nicole."

An hour later Budd pulled up in front of Nickie parents' house. From within the house she saw him drive up and came out to meet him.

"Get in. Where we going?" he greeted her.

She reached into her right blue jean pocket and pulled out a key.

"To Hernando's Hideaway."

"Wha?" He turned to look at her with astonishment and amusement.

"Start the car."

"Yes, Ma'am."

"Yez-z, vee arhh goink to Hernando's Hideaway. Head out Richmond Road."

"I have a feeling I'm finally going to get laid this weed-end."

"Oh, you are. YOU ARE A perceptive young man, YOU ARE."

Budd smiled and drove the car out Richmond and turned into an apartment complex driveway. She put the key in the lock and opened the door.

"Not bad for Hernando's Hideaway," he said as he looked around.

"It's my boss's daughter's. She graduated from Baylor last year and is working for her dad.

Isn't it beautiful?"

"Yeah, no kidding. Must be nice to be the boss's daughter."

"Conveniently, oh so conveniently, she's out of town for the week-end and happened to lend it to me."

"Well." He smiled. "How convenient."

Nicole led Budd to the livingroom couch.

"Budd, sit down on the couch and close your eyes. Now keep them closed. I'll be right back. KEEP THEM CLOSED."

"All right, I'll play your game." He waited and listened as he heard zippers and clothing rustling. In about three minutes he heard her come into the living room.

"Okay, you may look."

"Nicole, you're stunning. God I've died and gone to heaven."

"Like it?" she coyly asked.

"Like it? I love it!"

She wore a silk, white laced teddy with white hose, white garter straps and the faintest, tiny little blue bow at her neck.

"Am I beautiful?"

"Oh, God yes. Yes you are."

"I mean, am I really pretty?"

"Yes! Yes!"

She led him to the bedroom.

"Take off your clothes," she purred as she pulled him to the bed.

"I am! I am, I am! Why don't you take that thing off?"

"Baby, I don't even have to. I've waited. I've wanted this so badly." She unfastened her lace-trimmed top -- let it fall off her shoulder.

They kissed. Their heat was heightened by the realization they'd not been together for nearly three months. She climbed upon him, straddling her legs around him.

"You can't get away from me!" she softly growled.

"Yes I can," he said as he pulled up from her hold on him. He pushed her back on the bed, lay down on top of her, pulled back a little, then he deliberately started embracing her body with his tongue. She was instantly aroused and participated in their ritual completely, for she knew he had created his style just for her and with her only -- to bring to her the greatest pleasure he could.

He explored every part of her body with his tongue, parts of her being she had shared with no one but him. In unhurried repetition, he moved up to her face, and began licking her cheeks, her eyelids and her neck. Then he let his tongue slide down her neck and tongued her.

"BUDD NOW, please!"

"Not quite yet, Baby." Again he licked and darted with his tongue.

"OH GOD, would you hurry up before it's too late!"

"Okay Baby," he responded. Her body pulsating under his. He entered her deeply.

He heard her scream and he tightened and then released in their clench as they came together, Nickie twice -- two lovers completing their dance of ecstasy, joy. And then they were very quiet, a penetrating stillness, a fearful pause, a cautious quietness; they were slumped in each others' arms, breathing deeply for what seemed like an eternity. He rolled over to his side of the bed.

"Hm-m-mph," he said. "I do love you so much. I do. I do, Nickie."

They lay there silently for minutes, then he said solemnly," I never had anyone like you. I never thought I could. I never dreamed in my wildest imaginings that someone like you would want me, would need me, would be faithful to me, would be mine alone."

She turned and looked at him. "I love you so much, too. I want to be such a good wife to you. I want to cook the right things. I want to say the right things. I want to be Mrs. Budd Wilson so bad, so soon. I want us to have so many children, little Budds and little

Nicoles, and cute Nicoles and handsome Budds. I want you to always desire me Budd, and I want to always make myself worthy of your desire. I was faithful to you, Budd. I didn't even flirt. I love you so much. I want you forever."

"I love you too, Darling." He held her as he lay draped over her. "That will happen. I've been faithful to you. All I did was go down to the Nighthawk and study."

"And flirt with the waitresses?"

"And smile at them occasionally?"

"You and your damned waitresses. Did you ever sleep with one?"

"No, never did."

CHAPTER 2

"Oh Budd, somehow we've got to keep this whole throughout our lives, throughout eternity, as two roses entwined lead up to heaven -- oblivious to the world and all its problems. Two roses, Budd. Two roses winding to God."

"We will Baby. We will. I promise you somehow we will." He kissed her, then again. His mind was confused with the promise of the future and frightened by the prospect of it. He got up and walked to the bathroom.

"Where's the liquor cabinet?"he asked as he came out of the bathroom.

"Fourth top cabinet on the right," she called out.

Budd fumbled around in the kitchen.

"Johnny Walker Black," he said in amusement. "How 'bout that? And the glasses?"

"Just below on the counter." There stood two etched crystal tumblers.

"W.G.W. William George Wilson. How beautiful!"

"I had a set of them made from Neiman's Every time we have a celebration we'll open a new bottle of Scotch and two more etched glasses." Niche was very proud of her man, and he in turn, adored her. Holding two cigarettes in his mouth and two crystal tumblers of Scotch and water, one in each hand, he crawled over her to get back in bed.

"Damn it, you're spilling it all over me." She started to laugh.

"Whatsa matter? `"

"It's cold, stupid shit! I'm going to get you for this."

She took the tumblers out of his hands and placed them on the bedside table and took the cigarettes out of his mouth and placed them in the bedside ashtray. She began to tickle him.

"Now Nickie! Nickie, don't do that!"

"Okay Buddy-boy. It's your turn this time."

"Nickie, I might spank you."

"Well!" She made a face. "I've never been into that but who knows? I might like it."

"God damn it Nickie, leave me alone."

By this time she was tickling him all over the bed. "You don't like to be tickled, do you?" she taunted.

"Nickie, let's call a truce. All's fair. King's-X."

She started to laugh that golden laugh. "And you didn't even spank me."

"Wanna bet?" He reached over and gave her a good swat on the rear.

They lay silently smoking cigarettes for what seemed an eternity. She turned sideways to face him.

"Budd, I adore you."

"I adore you too, my darling," he said quietly. "Come here. Turn over Baby."

"Why do all men love this?"

"How would you know?"

"So I've heard." She winked and smiled at him. She turned on her stomach. "Here honey, put a pillow under my tummy. Lower, a little lower."

"Get me in."

"Okay. Okay."

Again they began to make love. He heard her gasp. Whether it was real or to please him he did not know. He did not ask. He lay across her back.

"You proud of me?"

"Uh-huh. That's my Nickie." He rolled over to her side. She rolled over to face him placing her chin in her hands.

"Fred and Ginger." He started to laugh. "Screwing their way into America's hearts. A new release from RKO. Coming to a theater near you soon." He got tickled and couldn't stop.

"You're an idiot, you know that?" She reached over and hugged him and started laughing too. "My insane idiotic genius, whatever am I going to do with you?"

"Rent me out,"

He got up from the bed. She got up and started pulling at the sheets.

"What are you doing?" he questioned.

"Changing the sheets."

"Why?"

"'Cause they're wet."

"We're going to use them again tonight and tomorrow!"

"It's not my apartment. It's not my bed. We'll change them, use some more, change them again." She flashed a smile. "Then after you're gone Sunday night I'll do the laundry, and wash the whole bloody mess of them."

"Only they're not bloody."

"Astute observation sir. As I was saying, wash the whole mess of them Sunday night in your memory."

"Smart ass."

"Takes one to know one."

He walked into the living room.

"Let's watch a football game, damn it."

"Budd, what's the matter with you?" She walked across the room. There were tears streaming down his cheeks.

"Budd, you're crying! Oh my precious Budd."

"They give us thoughts," he started. "Moreover they give us feelings and desires and they don't tell us what to do with them. They don't tell us how to be adults. They don't tell us how to earn it. They just tell us to defer it all and go to some fucking college for four years or more, and we can come out and buy houses and raise babies and be married, and if we're lucky, maybe be happy."

"Budd! Darling, Darling! What's the matter? Please, what's the matter?"

"Nickie, I don't want to go back. I hate that place! I don't want to go back. I'd do anything, work in a filling station, if we could be together from this day on."

"I don't want you to go back either but you have to." She put his head to her breast and patted and rubbed him over and over on the back.

"I'm okay."

"I know you are. Sure you are,"

"No, I'm okay...God I'm a stupid shit." He started laughing. "God I'm a stupid shit."

"No, you're not."

"You're sure?"

"Yes...Come on, Mr. Buddkerson Stupid Shit Wilson...I'm going to fix you some dinner "

"Okay." He smiled, and wiped away the tears. "Can you cook?"

"Of sorts. Let's see what's in the fridge," she said as she pulled him into the kitchen. "Well, she doesn't cook as well as she lives."

"Maybe she doesn't have to," he wryly chuckled.

"Shut up."

She fiddled through the culinary junk in the cabinets. "Potato chips, kind of chewy. The bill d'fare for the evening is baloney sandwiches and potato chips. Mayonnaise or mustard?"

"Mayonnaise'll do."

"Good, I'm starved. I didn't have any supper last night or if I did I don't remember it."

"You did and for a fancy price."

"Listen Mister, I know your kind. Take advantage of a poor girl, promise her a night on the town, give her a couple of drinks and leave her at your mercy to throw up all over the Sulpher River."

"You had several more than two cocktails. And you continued throwing up after we passed the river and I vaguely remember a promise for a second-floor, walk-up motel in Shreveport only you were so loaded I WOULD have been taking advantage of you if we had."

"You're such a gentleman."

"I am, and it's a miracle I still am."

"Do you regret it? Ever?"

"No," he said softly. "I never have and never could." He looked up and smiled. "Oh Miss, bring my baloney and chips to the table over here. I want to watch the six o'clock news."

"I want to go to a movie, Budd."

"Okay. What time's it start?"

"I don't know. You see a paper?"

"No. Where's it playing?"

"The Paramount."

"Call them and find out what time it starts. What's it about? What's the name of it?"

"*The Fox*. I don't know what it's about, but it's the fox's eyes. I've seen them in the previews. They're so penetrating."

"You would go for something like that."

"Just because I'm with the times and you're not."

She found the phone book, looked up the number and dialed it. "What time does your next feature start? Thank you." She turned to Budd. "Seven-thirty, you want to go?"

"Sure, why not? How 'bout my baloney sandwich?"

"Listen Mac, I ain't no waitress."

"Yeah, you're not sexy enough."

"Fuck you."

"I'd like to, but honestly I'm all worn out."

"You ought to be." Her mind clicked in a different direction.

 "Aren't I domestic? Our first homemade meal."

"I"m so proud of you," he said sarcastically.

"You are." She smiled confidently as she slapped the sandwich together.

"Yes my dear, I am. I am. Thank you tonight for several reasons."

"You're welcome. One baloney sandwich and stale potato chips coming right up. I certainly hope you're a generous tipper."

"I'd have to be."

They settled on the couch and watched the news and a thirty minute sitcom. They freshened up and took off to the movies.

"I don't know what it's about," she said as they rode into town. "I think it's about these two women and a fox. It's his eyes."

They bought their tickets and walked into the darkness permeated by Tom and Jerry. After several coming attractions the feature began. *The Fox* was a typical late 1960's movie. It was a symbolic, depressing story of two lesbians, one of whom was haunted by a fox with piercing eyes. Suddenly a male (the fox) enters one of their lives. In the end, the jealous but forgotten female lover is killed by a falling tree that has been chopped down to fall on her by the male (the fox) thus leaving the two lovers without the third intruding partner. Then at the end you see the two eyes again.

"Jesus," he said as they walked to the car after the movie was over, "how depressing...that was disgusting."

"I thought it was sensual," she looked up at him and said.

"Did you really?"

"Yes, I did."

"What's so sensual about two lesbians and a fox?

"I don't know, but it was. Never mind, I'll take you any day." She linked her arm in his and looked up and beamed.

"I certainly hope so, my resident bohemian."

"I know." She smiled.

They walked away from the theater in silence. He unlocked the car and opened her door. She got in. Then he went around to his side and closed the door behind him. He reached out and put his arms around her. He kissed her, then he kissed her again. Then he pulled away.

"You hungry?"

"I thought you'd just eaten."

"Jesus Nickie, I didn't mean that. Are you HUNGRY?

"I'm famished."

"How about Spero's?"

"It'll do."

He put the car in gear and drove out to Spero's Restaurant. It was after ten p.m. They ate fish, french fries and plenty of onion. Later they smoked a cigarette, had a cup of coffee and sat there after their meal.

"Let's go home." He looked at her and smiled. "You game for another one?"

"A quickie." She smiled.

"Ah Nick, I was hoping we'd stay all night."

"It's late, darling and Mother's liberal, but not that liberal. A quickie. Don't worry my sweet, after Spring semester we'll be together forever."

"Oh well," he mumbled, "discretion is the better part of valor or something like that."

"Or something like that," she said.

They got up. He paid the check and they left.

All of their friends converged before the Sunday Eucharist at St. John's Episcopal Church on the sidewalk in front of the steps to the church. Some of them were still in high school. Some of them were now in college.

"How's Baylor, Johnny?" Budd called to his old friend, Johnny Hall.

"It's fine but they're not too liberal on the whiskey unless of course you're dating one of those Baptist girls. They have their own bootleggers."

"Nickie," asked one of her fellow cheerleaders with a look of devilment in her eye, "what happened to you Friday night at the Pitt Grill?"

"I was on an errand of mercy."

"Were you the one to be mercied or do you remember?"

"Unfortunately, I remember." The girls started laughing.

"Come on, you two. Sit with Niche and me," Budd said to Johnny Hall and his cheerleader friend as they entered the church. They found their way in and sat in a crowded pew. John and Nickie's friend sat at the end of a pew. Niche and Budd sat in front of them. During the Rector's sermon, one which Budd was listening to, concerning the role of the modern Episcopalian in the integration of the church and the social issues of the day, Nickie's friend leaned over and said, "You look radiant, Nickie. What's your secret?"

"You ought to know," Nickie said without moving a facial muscle, without turning her head.

The girl behind her laughed underneath her breath.

"I've never seen you two so happy."

Nickie turned around and faced her and said genuinely, "We never have been."

After church there were already five or six cars in front of Fritz's house. Budd and Nicole made their way to the front door. A crowd was beginning to gather and everyone was standing around the living room with drinks in hand and the room was full of cigarette smoke. This was one of Fritz and Meredith Cavanaugh's weekly, Sunday afternoon, after church get-togethers, and everybody who was anybody at St. John's Episcopal Church was there. Budd had been to the gatherings before. His parents were friends of the Cavanaugh's and with some members of St. John's Episcopal Church. This time Budd wanted to show his girl to some special friends.

"Hello everybody," Budd pleasantly spoke as they passed through the front door into the gathering of people. The room was bright. The brightness of the lamps in the living room made the room shine with warmth and joy. There was an expectation of something special, of some joy delectable as they entered the door of Fritz and Meredith Cavanaugh's home.

Liz and Bill Clark, Carol and John Harkness were there. Lena Conway and Mildred Patterson Stover were there. Hortense Willis Moncrief was there. The other young people from St. John's would soon arrive.

"Here we are, me and the most beautiful and smartest girl in Texarkana," Budd flaunted Nicole, "Nicole White."

"I'm so glad Buddy has found a girlfriend." Meredith was happy with Nicole. "We love ya."

Meredith quickly hugged them, then released them. They accepted her greeting and started making the rounds.

Meredith Cavanaugh was a tiny woman. She wore a plain black dress, very chic, very Chanel.

She had black, bobbed hair and bright red lipstick. She was around sixty years of age and had a definite aura of the 1920s about her. She held a cigarette in a black cigarette holder. Meredith was the hostess of some of the best people from St. John's who gathered to eat and drink in her home every Sunday afternoon.

"Hello, sweetheart," Fritz Cavanaugh came up and cordially addressed Nicole. He reached for Meredith's cigarette in holder and took a drag.

Fritz was a living image out of the roaring twenties; blue blazer, club tie, silver hip flask full of Kentucky Bourbon, and the Texas-Oklahoma football game. He was a buttondowned dresser right out of Brooks Brothers. Fritz and Meredith Cavanaugh looked like living characters from an F. Scott Fitzgerald novel as they had grown and matured, somewhat flamboyantly, through the stages of youth in the 1920s to the beginning of their later years in the 1960s.

"You are the cutest thing in Texarkana," Fritz continued. Nicole blushed.

"Well I always did have good tastes, Fritz." Budd walked towards the kitchen to fix a drink.

"Honey, do you want a drink?" Fritz asked her. "There's whiskey in the kitchen."

Nicole was still a bit uncomfortable, but thanked Fritz, accepted the offer and followed Budd into the kitchen.

"I better mix her's with coke," Budd called back to Fritz. "She's not an experienced drinker."

They both thought of the trip to Shreveport. She frowned.

"I'm glad your church has nothing against drinking," Nicole said. "At least I don't feel like a hypocrite." She looked at her drink and took a sip. Then they drifted back into the living room.

"Hello, Miss Hortense," Budd said rather cooly to Hortense

Moncrief. It was Nicole's first time to meet the formidable Hortense Willis Moncrief. The crowd varied each week, but there was always the usual clan and Hortense was always there.

Hortense, who was at least seventy-five, pulled an unfiltered Pall Mall out of a gold case in her purse, lit it, took a drag, and then said a very bland, "Hallo."

"I don't think Hortense liked me," Nicole softly spoke as they circulated throughout the room.

"That's okay. Hortense doesn't like anyone but Mike O'Connor and she's old enough to be his grandmother." He looked at Nicole and smiled. "It's okay. I don't give a damn who likes you or doesn't. That's just Hortense. She's an old bitch."

"Hi there, honey," came the slow Louisiana drawl of one of the most beautiful, middle-aged women Budd had ever known, Liz Clark. She had the masculine beauty of a Joan Crawford but not the harshness. "Buddy, I'm glad you brought your girlfriend, huh?"

"Yeah, Mizz Clark, sure did."

"Well dear, if you can get used to this menagerie, you've got it made." She smiled at Nicole.

Nicole smiled back. Nicole liked Liz Clark. Although they had just met, Nicole felt a bond with her.

"She's certainly a beautiful woman, isn't she?" Nicole whispered to Budd as they walked back to the den.

"She was Miss L.S.U., 1941."

"Really?" Nicole's face beamed. "Neat! I like your friends."

"I do too. Come on, let's 'circulate'."

The den was a cozy room, and Dixieland jazz was playing on a small, Magnavox cabinet model record player.

"I love that music," she continued the conversation. "Daddy always liked 'Muskrat Ramble'.

I wonder if Fritz has a record of that?"

"I'm sure he does, but I'd rather hear him play it," Budd arrogantly replied.

About that time Fritz walked into the den. This time he had a cigarette in holder.

"Fritz, can you play 'Muskrat Ramble'?" Nicole enthusiastically questioned.

"Sweetheart, that's God's music, and yes I can play it."

Cavanaugh had learned to play Dixieland piano as a young, white man in the brothels of New Orleans after he dropped out of the University of Arkansas in the early 1920s. He worked his way up the Mississippi River to Memphis and then later to Chicago where he came in contact with "The Austin High Gang". There he met Benny Goodman long before Goodman became the popular big-band leader of the thirties and forties, and there he also made the lifelong friendship of guitarist, Eddie Condon. In the late 1920s, Fritz formed his own band. It was a white, collegiate band and by the time they reached New York they were playing the posh speakeasies of Manhattan. The depression would dash his chances of being a professional musician and send him home to Texarkana to work in the men's clothing business selling "Brooks" style suits, marry and raise a family, and never be in the music business again in New York.

Fritz took the cigarette out of it's holder and let it hang down from the side of his mouth.

He lay his drink down on a coaster and began playing the Dixieland standard. His demeanor was somewhat like that of Hoagy Carmichael as he slouched over the keyboard. Meredith walked into the den while Fritz was playing and she smiled at Nicole. "That's God's music,"

Meredith concurred.

"Fritz, play 'Can't Get Started'," Liz Clark requested as she entered the den.

"'I Can't Get Started'? Buddy, you want to play that one?" Fritz asked.

Budd started picking out "I Can't Get Started" on the piano in the key of "C".

Liz Clark draped herself over the piano and began singing with Budd's playing.

"'I've been around the world on a plane. I've settled revolutions in Spain'. Lord, I can't sing."

She laughed. "Bill and I used to dance to that. . . Bunny Berrigan. . . Long time ago.

Come on Honey, let's dance." She pulled the hulking Bill Clark to his feet.

"I want to dance, too," Budd said as he ended the ballad. "Fritz put something real on the record player."

"Oh Buddy, don't stop playing now," Liz Clark softly demanded.

"I never could play the piano, Mizz Clark. Let's dance to some real music."

Fritz put on a ten-inch L.P. of Jack Teagarten's rendition of 'When

It's Sleepy Time Down

South.' Although it was not the original recording of the song, it was spellbinding and lovely to dance to.

"Come on, Babe," Budd softly said to Nicole and looked her straight in the eye. She smiled, and they began slowly dancing. He held her tightly in his arms.

"You happy?" he asked.

"Yes, are you?"

"Oh yes I am." He laughed softly to himself.

"There you go laughing." She looked at him. Then they both began laughing.

Suddenly Jack Harkness, Pat and Mike O'Connor and Christy Trice came in with a case of beer. They were peers of Budd's and young friends from St. John's.

"Mike!" It was almost the only thing that Hortense Moncrief said all day.

"Hello, dear." Mike O'Connor went over and kissed her on the cheek.

"Where'd you get the beer?" Carol Harkness asked her stepson, Jack.

"Daddy said we could take it to the trailer." The Harkness family had a trailer on Lake Texarkana.

"Hell Carol, leave him alone," John Harkness replied. "I bought it for them."

"Alright John. I merely wanted to know where he was getting it.

They are under-age. Is that too much to ask?" Carol and John Harkness had not been getting along well for some time. It was their politics. He was a Republican and she was the director of the new "War on Poverty" program in Texarkana and a decided Democrat. The issue of step children also presented a problem.

"Hello, Nickie," Jack said rather cooly as he walked into the kitchen with the beer.

"Hello, Jack." She had an excellent poker face. Neither one of them cared for each other.

"Come on, Nickie. Let's talk. Don't you just love Fritz and Meredith?" Christy Trice led

Nicole back into the living room full of people.

"Yes, they're lovely people," Nicole replied as she followed.

"Isn't she great? Nicole, I mean," Budd questioned Jack after he pulled him back into the den.

"Well, we'll see," Jack replied.

Budd looked at the two girls. Both of them were beautiful. One of them was his. One of them was another's. He was proud of Nickie. In his eyes she measured up the best.

"I've got the Queen, Jack." The two young men continued their conversation in the den.

"We'll see. That's all. We'll see."

"Oh Jack!"

Budd went back into the living room and joined the two girls. Jack followed. Father Thomas, the Rector of St. John's and his wife Grace walked in.

"What are all you young people doing drinking?" Father Thomas scowled, then laughed and smiled a broad, jovial smile. "No, I'm just kidding. Going to have one myself."

"Hello," Grace said with almost no emotion. She was a quiet person, a person who had kept her husband's pastoral confidences as he ministered to the high and low brow of Texarkana, as they often mingled. Grace Thomas was discreet.

Nicole took Budd's flattery with her usual accepting boredom but she was also a little self-conscious of his making a fool of himself over her. She realized she was in a different element of Texarkana society than she had known before and she liked it.

"We're going to the lake, to the trailer. Ya'll coming?" Jack Harkness called to Nicole and Budd -- who were now in the kitchen sharing their drinks.

"Oh come on Babe, let's go for just a little while?" Budd turned to Nicole.

"No! You've got to get back to Austin and I've got to study. We've both got to go,"

Nicole gracefully slid out of the possibility of spending the afternoon in the company of Jack Harkness at the lake.

"Jack, let them go. They both have other places to go. We'll catch them next time," said Christy Trice.

Christy, Jack, Pat and Mike O'Connor left for the lake. Most of the adults were leaving, too.

All that were left were Hortense, who nursed her Scotch and water as she prepared for the effort to get up from her seat on the couch and toddle across the street home, Fritz and Meredith, John and Carol Harkness, and Father Thomas and Grace, who were engrossed in a discussion about the necessity of the civil rights movement and the integration of the church. Such were the people and the times of St. John's Episcopal in the late 1960s.

"It was so nice to be here." Nicole began her farewells.

"Oh darling, you're always welcome," Meredith replied. "We're glad to have you."

"Thank you."

"The girl wonder has to go home and study and I've got to get back to Austin," said Budd.

"I'm sure that a little of that studying wouldn't hurt you either," Meredith said to Budd.

"Come back, Nicole." Meredith held her hand in hers.

They left the weekly Cavanaugh ritual and walked to Budd's car. He was a little tipsy by this time.

"Oh me," he said as he sat at the wheel.

"Are you all right?" Nicole asked.

"If there is anything I can do, it is to hold my liquor," Budd replied.

"All right." She smiled.

"Come on. Let's get out of here."

They drove out north Richmond Road, parked in front of the apartment, put the key in the door and went in. He held her.

"I love you. I've got to go back to Austin. I don't want to. I've got something to tell you.

Austin's so weird. The people are so damned weird. They're dirty. Women don't shave their legs."

"How decadent." She smiled and winked at him. "Maybe I shouldn't shave under my arms."

"They don't Nick, really."

"They don't in France either."

"Well, anyway," he was flustered, "if you believe in anything conventional you're an outcast. It's the only place I've ever been where it seems you have to defend traditional values. Hell, they're all into drugs. Not only do the students attack everything you believe in so do the faculty and the thing is that those bastards are getting paid for it. Nickie, you and I've talked for over a year about my going to medical school after I graduate. There's a war going on down there in Southeast Asia." He looked at her softly. "I want to go do Officers's Candidacy School— The United States Air Force."

"I see." There was silence. "Come here. Kiss me." They held each other, then she turned her back to him. "Undo my dress."

It was seven p.m., as Budd in his Volkswagen passed through Mt. Pleasant, Texas. He tuned in WFAA-Fort Worth and Dallas, on his car radio. It was nine p.m., as he passed through the mixmaster in Dallas that merged Interstate 30 East into Interstate 35 South towards Austin. He stopped for gas. The sounds of KRLD-Dallas were playing on the car radio. He felt so alone that Sunday night. Then he was somewhere between Waxahatchie and Waco. For some reason, unbeknownst to him, he was listening to Garner Ted Armstrong. He fiddled with the dial. Wolf Man Jack from Del Rio, Texas invaded his solitude. The sordid radio personality's voice was irritating to Budd and he turned the radio off. Between Temple and Georgetown he turned the radio on again to the clear channel voice of WOAI- San Antonio. Then there it was, the tower,The University of Texas at Austin.

"Hook 'm Horns," he said softly to himself. "502 Elmwood, Apartment 101, Austin, Texas.

It's a dump, but soon it will be ours." He exited off Interregional at Nineteenth Street.. .

"Off we go into the wild blue yonder..."

It was the night of April 3rd, 1989. Budd was at the Truman house. His father, mother and daughter Jennifer had joined him earlier for dinner. It had started raining, and the wind was blowing. His parents and daughter were still waiting for the rain to subside before they walked home.

"It's blowing in something horrible," said Budd's mother.

Budd turned around and looked out the shades. "Gee, it's blowin' rain in sheets. Looks like you're stuck here for a while." He looked out the shade again. "I'm going to step out on the porch for a minute,"

Mr. and Mrs. Wilson looked at each other and then back to Budd. "Are you expecting something'?" They were aware of the telephone conversations between Budd and Nicole and some of what Budd had told them about his conversations with Steve Brantley.

"I don't know. I don't know," he mused.

The sky was lit up by a spiderweb network of lightening. It

illuminated the entire surrounding neighborhood. The lightening flashed and bounced all over the sky. The rain continued wave after wave. The mercury vapor street light shook from side to side in the wind. Then it's power was gone. Suddenly a transformer popped and all the electricity went out. The rain was blowing all over the porch. The Main Street Doctors' Plaza was three blocks due south on Olive Street, then two blocks west to Main Street.

"I don't even know if they are having a meeting tonight," Budd thought to himself. He had learned that Stephen had spied on these meetings for quite some time, and that he, Stephen, had kept up with all of Nicole's activities. The information had been both frightening and fascinating to Budd.

He looked at Stephen's front porch, then south down Olive, then Stephen's front porch again, then south down Olive. Thirty-five minutes had passed and the storm had not let up yet. He looked to the south again. A solitary automobile, three blocks south, turned left and headed north.

"Oh my God! It's Nicole's!" Through the illuminated sky he could see the Mercedes grill as the car deliberately but slowly bore its way through the intersection of Seventeenth and Olive Street and headed north churning up waves as it went.

The car passed right in front of Budd, went up a half block, made a U-turn and came back south. It was going very slowly as if it was looking for the right house. Then it turned north again. At Olive and Nineteenth Streets the car turned left and went around the block. It came back again to Eighteenth and Olive and turned right in front of Budd's house going south on Olive. Budd had been outside for about forty minutes.

Budd's parents were looking out the front windows of the house. With the electricity out the whole block was dark except for the tremendous lightening. Budd's mother opened the screen door.

"What is it, Budd?"

"It's Nickie Smithson's car."

"It can't be."

"It is."

"Get in the house, Budd."

"No, I want to see it. I want to see what happens." Again the car passed and slowed. Budd ran out toward it.

"Go home, Nicole! Go home! Go home!"

The car stopped directly in front of Budd. He backed up on the porch. The rain and lightening were ferocious. What appeared to be a long haired white man in jeans, bluejean jacket and a cap jumped out of the car and poured something on Stephen's yard, criss -crossing it. The Mercedes was idling. The driver's door was open. The man struck a match and it went out. Then he struck another criss-cross after the pattern lit up. There were twelve to fifteen foot flames. The entire yard went "WOOSH" as it ignited. Budd was backed up against his front door on the porch. The man ran to the Mercedes, jumped in, gunned it and took off.

"Oh my God!" Budd screamed. "Oh my God! Oh my God!"

His mother was at the front door. "Get in, Budd! Get in!"

He flew through the living room to the bedroom phone. He remembered that Stephen had told him that he had a stockpile of weapons from the Vietnam war in his house and that he had a firearms dealer's license and kept quite a collection of firearms and explosives in his home. That was enough for Budd.

"Get Jennifer to the back. Get Grandad and Jennifer to the back!" he yelled to his mother. He hit 911 on the bedroom phone.

"Fire! Seventeen-hundred block of Olive! Fire! Get everything you've got out here! Whole yard on fire!"

"What's that address?"

"1716. 1718. I don't know."

"And your name?"

"Budd Wilson."

"Your address and phone number?"

"Budd Wilson, 1719 Olive, 797-7221."

He ran to the living room. Then he stopped on his feet, u-turned and ran back to the phone and frantically dialed the Municipal Hospital switchboard.

"Fifth floor psychiatry. Move it!"

"Fifth floor psychiatry," the nurse's voice answered.

"Find Nicole Smithson! Find Nicole Smithson!"

"What?"

"There's been a fire in the seventeen-hundred block of Olive Street. It was her car. The whole yard's on fire. Find Nicole Smithson!"

"And how can she reach you?"

"Budd Wilson. 797-7221."

From two directions he heard the sirens. Fire trucks came from two directions as did police cars. By now neighbors were out in the street. Budd Wilson was in a daze. He walked along the line of fire trucks closest to the yard. "It was Nicole Smithson's car," he said softly. "It was Nicole Smithson's car."

He thought he heard his mother's voice yelling from the porch. "Budd! Budd! You've got a phone call!"

He ran across the street and back to his house. He jumped upon the porch from the bottom step to the top step clearing the two middle steps in the process and flew into the living room.

"Who is it?"

"It's Nicole."

"Nickie! Nickie, are you all right!? Are you all right!"

"What's going on, Budd?"

"You don't know?"

"No I'm sitting here at home reading and the hospital calls and says they have some insane call from you. What is going on?"

"I thought maybe he'd killed you and taken your car and was going to burn up his mother."

"What are you talking , Budd?"

"Somebody just drove up, poured gasoline all over Steve Brantley's yard and lit a match. Nickie, it was a small silver Mercedes."

"Budd. Listen I have been here all night reading a book."

"Nickie, it was a small silver Mercedes."

"Budd there are a lot of small silver Mercedes in this town."

"Yeah, but Nickie, all the events leading up to this. The phone calls from Stephen and you, `OBSERVE EVERYTHING!'"

"Budd, I was here reading a book. Look Budd, I swear I'm going to sell that car. It's caused me nothing but trouble."

"Jesus shit Nicole, why don't you get a Ford or a Buick or something less obvious."

"I've thought of getting a Volkswagen."

There was a silence for a moment.

"Nicole, how come when you try to help someone out you always get it in the ass?"

"I don't know," she said softly. "I don't know."

"Nicole, may I express my feelings?"

"Sure, go for it."

"I never loved anyone but you. I never loved Sissy. She's a good woman, the mother of my child, but I never loved her. I never loved anyone but you. What's that old song, If you can't have the one you love, love the one you're with.'"

"Yeah I know...,"she said. "Sometimes we fulfill a conflict with someone other than the one we mean to be with."

"Nicole, as far as I am concerned there never was a conflict Well, I have as funny feeling tomorrow's going to be a long day."

"Yep."

CHAPTER 3

"HAS ANYBODY HERE SEEN MY OLD FRIEND BOBBY?"

ROBERT F. KENNEDY | NOVEMBER 20, 1925—JUNE 6, 1968

"WITH ABRAHAM, MARTIN AND JOHN"

"GOD IS DEAD"

THE STUDENTS OF A DEMOCRATIC SOCIETY

THE WEATHERMEN

THE 1968 DEMOCRATIC CONVENTION—CHICAGO

"All week, Chicago was badly divided, and nowhere were the divisions more visible than in the blood-spattered streets near the convention amphitheater. Tens of thousands of young people came to Chicago to protest the war, but flower power was no match for police force. `Kill 'em! Kill `ern!' the police shouted as they charged. `Pigs, pigs, oink, oink!' the demonstrators screamed back. One witness heard an officer yell, `We'll kill all you bastards!' as he clubbed a protester. And as news cameras rolled, and clubs flew, the protesters chanted, `The whole world's watching! The whole world's watching!'

- Chronicle of America - Chronicle Publications -

"At this point, Election night, 1968, it looks as though Richard Milhouse Nixon, the Republican candidate for president is taking a lead over Hubert Horatio Humphrey, his Democratic contender.

with third party candidate George Corley Wallace, trailing a distant third. But it's early in the night and anything can still happen. Stay with us. This is Walter Cronkite, CBS News. With this, we pause for these commercial messages."

"NO ASS!

NO GRASS!

lxxix

ROBERT WALTERS

NO FREE RIDES!"

WOODSTOCK

"BLOW-UP"

"THE GRADUATE"

"ALICE'S RESTAURANT"

"That's one small leap for man, one giant leap for mankind."

-Astronaut Neil A. Armstrong-

Live from the moon, 10:56:20 P.M., E.D.T., July 21, 1969

"The first big blow-out came on October 15, the day of a nationwide demonstration calling for a moratorium on the war. On October, 15, 1969, came their supreme moment, the Moratorium, a day on which millions decided not to do business-as-usual, but took part in a cascade of local demonstrations, vigils, church services, petition drives replete with respectable speech makers and sympathetic media fanfare. On November 15, 1969, (the second moratorium) perhaps three quarters of a million people, the largest single protest in American history, a veritable mainstream, flowed through the streets to the Washington Monument. Senators George McGovern and Charles Goodell gave speeches. John Denver, Mitch Miller, Arlo Guthrie and the touring cast of *Hair* sang. Pete Seeger led the throng in choruses of 'Give Peace a Chance'."

U69

THE YEAR EVERYTHING CHANGED

-Rob Kirkpatrick-

(and)

The Sixties

Years of Hope, Days of Rage

-Todd Gitlin-

"The answer my friend is blowin' in the wind.

The answer. . . is blowin' in the wind."

-Bob Dylan-

502 Elmwood Street, Apartment 101, Austin Texas, had been shared by Nickie and Budd since June of 1969. Budd's Volkswagen and Nickie's yellow GTO with a black vinyl top were parked in front of the apartment. They liked living together. They liked their intimacy. It gave each of them more time to explore their love for each other, their thoughts, feelings, sexuality, responsibilities. Many a Saturday night rather than go out, they'd stay at home, lie in bed and study or watch T.V. Budd was cramming for his mid-term exams. Nickie had just finished the supper dishes. She climbed into bed next to Budd and began reading. Budd's feelings for the war were shifting, and he had decided to concentrate on psychology in hopes of becoming a therapist rather than go for Air Force O.C.S. Somehow the thought of war was becoming very distant to him. There was a three year doctoral program in clinical psychology at Southwestern Medical School in Dallas, and the thought of studying at a medical school was exciting to Budd.

"Whatcha reading?" he asked Nicole after she curled up next to him in bed.

"The Lively Art of Writing, by some lady named Lucille Payne. Goes with freshman comp. Going to write my memiors some day."

"You probably will. They'd certainly be lively."

"I will. You wait and see. Hey. What are you reading?"

"Oh, I'm sorry. It's a book."

"I gathered."

"Just a textbook for abnormal psychology."

"Sounds so terribly interesting "

"It is, really. The theories of various neuroses and psychoses."

"Let me see...." She thumbed through the book. "Neurotic disorders, psychotic disorders, schizophrenia, manic depression. You ought to be right at home, Budd. Post traumatic stress disorder. I guess we can all go over the brink every now and then. Well, not me! I'm invincible."

"Can I have my book back?" he asked.

"Kind of interesting. I guess." She tossed the book back to Budd.

The phone on the bedside table rang. Nicole answered it.

"It's that nutty friend of yours, Richard Harwood," she said as she held her hand over the receiver. Budd grabbed the phone from Nicole.

"Richard. Hey!"

She rolled over away from Budd and continued reading her book.

"Why I got involved with you and your stupid cronies," she muttered.

"Shut up Nickie, let me talk, and besides you aren't involved with Richard....No Richard, Nicole hasn't changed a bit."

"Have you heard about the Vietnam War Moratorium on Wednesday, October 15' 17' Richard excitedly asked.

"Yeah, I've heard about it. Supposed to be some real blow-out down here, a march from the campus to the Capitol."

"I bet. But I want you to speak at Texarkana College."

"On Moratorium Day?" Budd asked. "At Texarkana College?"

"We're going to have a symposium not a demonstration. The

administration would go wild if we said demonstration," Richard continued.

"I don't know, Richard. I make a lousy outside agitator. Besides, Nick and I kind of want to stay in Austin and get some pictures of what's happening here with her new Nikon. Well, I do have a test Friday but I don 't have another one `til next Friday. I might be able t—"

"What is it?" What does he want?" Nickie crowded up to the phone.

"He wants me to participate in the Vietnam War Moratorium, next Wednesday, at Texarkana College as a speaker."

"Do it!" she snapped.

"What?"

"Do it! I think it's a neat idea. Do it."

"Okay Richard." Budd was a little startled at Niche's response. "I'll do it. I'll call you Tuesday evening when we get in town."

"I knew you wouldn't let me down, Buddy," concluded Richard; knew you wouldn't."

"See ya' Tuesday." Budd finished the conversation and turned to Niche. "Nickie, why do you want me to do that?"

"How do you feel about the war?"

"A year ago it was a war I would have fought in. Now I'm against it."

"That's reason enough, isn't it?"

"But, why should anyone give a damn about my opinion?"

"Richard Harwood, rising left-wing politico. Look Budd, you're articulate. You can get your point over. Richard knows that. You're well known. Harwood knows that, but most of all, you represent the emerging status quo who are against the war and Richard knows that."

"I'm not even a student at Texarkana College. . . Well. . ," Budd knew he was licked, " I guess I could live without behavioral statistics for a couple of days now that you're so enthralled with the idea of me becoming a campus radical."

"Astute observation, Dr. Freud." She winked at him and smiled.

"Oh. . . okay. Let's go." He smiled.

"You're on, Senator."

"Senator?"

She smiled at him with a smirk on her face.

"Blow it out your ass, Nicole. . . . Jesus, I've got to think about what I'm going to say."

It was Tuesday morning. Budd had already packed Nickie's GTO for the trip the night before. They drove down to the Nighthawk and ate breakfast. Budd ordered homemade chili and eggs. Nickie, a mushroom omelette. They had homemade biscuits, butter and strawberry jam. Both had coffee and orange juice, and of course, they browsed the headlines of the Austin American. Then they got in the car, turned left on Nineteenth Street and left again onto Interstate 35 towards Dallas. From Dallas they took Interstate 30 to Mt. Pleasant, Texas, to Simms and to New Boston they took highways 67 and 98, and then back onto the unfinished Interstate 30 to Texarkana. They drove straight in, stopping only for coffee and gas. Around a quarter of four, they pulled up in front of Budd's parents' home in the 1700 block of Olive Street. His parents' white

Chrysler Newport four door sedan with blackwall tires sat outside the house.

They all sat in the living room. At first there was no sound at all. Then Mrs. Wilson began making small talk. The conversation was forced. No one mentioned that Budd and Nicole were living together, even though Budd's parents knew they were.

"Read any good books lately?" Edgar Wilson began. There had always been distance between Budd and his father. They both found it difficult to communicate.

"Depends on whether you call abnormal psychology and behavioral statistics interesting."

Budd called Harwood. Richard informed him that an organizational meeting of the Texarkana Moratorium Committee was being held at St. Paul's A.M.E. Church at seven-thirty that night. They left Budd's parents' and went to Nickie's parents' home around five. They were finally home.

"Well, how are you two?" asked Alex White. "Your mother and I want to take you two out to dinner tonight. Of course, if you don't have anything else planned."

"Daddy, we kind of do have plans...around seven-fifteen."

"Ya'll hungry? Let's just go the way we are right now."

"You've got a point," said Budd. "We haven't eaten since breakfast."

"Well, let's go." Alex White was in a jovial mood and glad to see them.

"Let me freshen up a minute," said Mary White.

"Me, too," echoed Nicole.

"These women," the elder White said after mother and daughter had gone down the hall. "Come on, let's fix a drink while they're fixing their face. Course, I guess you know all about that now."

Budd was silent.

"When are you and Nicole getting married, Budd?"

"When we can afford it," replied Budd.

"Hell, if you didn't live so high and mighty you could afford it now. I remember when me and Mary got married. It was 1948. We were broke. I was stationed in Honolulu. Now you might not know it now, but Miss Mary was a good lookin' girl in 1948."

"I bet she was," Budd smiled and answered. "She still is."

Budd and Mr. White gulped down a quick Scotch and water. The younger couple followed the senior couple in their red Cadillac Eldorado to the Cattleman's Steakhouse.

Mr. and Mrs. White had steaks for dinner. Budd and Nicole split a dozen raw oysters with cocktail sauce, and a dozen boiled shrimp in the husk with hot lemon and butter sauce. They had salad, garlic toast and a couple of beers -- all compliments of Nickie's parents. Later, they left for Richard's meeting.

They were twenty minutes late getting to the church. As they walked in, a young black man around forty was giving instructions, "If the pigs go for you, roll over in a ball like this. If they carry you away, go limp."

The couple stood in the corner and continued to listen.

"My God, Budd. Could this happen?"

"Yes. Sure. Anything could happen. Don't know what's going to happen."

"But violence?"

"Possibly. Perhaps left wing students, communist infiltrated radicals, or extreme right wing neo-Nazi reactionaries. Even local good ole' boys. Any side could start it."

"Well, whadya think of it?" Richard Harwood walked over to Budd and Nicole after the

Meeting. "It's-uh-it's unique."

"Nickie, you gonna be there tomorrow? We might be on national news."

"I'll be with Budd. I'll be there."

"Ata girl!"

She looked at Budd. Her eyes were wide with apprehension.

It was 1 p.m., Moratorium Day, Wednesday. October 15, 1969. The Texarkana College Auditorium was electrified with youthful excitement. Rumors were spread that the FBI, major daily papers, the Associated Press and every kind of law enforcement agency were there. All kinds of people were in the College Auditorium on that day. Richard, Budd and the other participants sat on the stage. Nickle sat off stage in the wings in sight of Budd and in partial sight of the audience.

In Austin, between 4000 and 6000 students were gathering on the Main Mall of the University of Texas. On the morning of November 15, 1969, the second moratorium, there were massive rallies in New York. At the Washington Monument, Caretta Scott King, widow of the assassinated civil rights leader spoke. Martin Luther King, Jr., had been a strong advocate of a Vietnam pullout.

On Boston Commons, police estimated there were between 75,000 and 100,000 people at a rally. Forty members of the British Parliament signed a letter demanding withdrawal of American forces from Vietnam. On October 15, in Austin again, the continuous line of protestors moved from Twenty-first Street on the south edge of the campus towards the Capitol for the three o'clock protest.

In Texarkana, the moratorium symposium was in progress. Two speakers were left, Harwood and Budd. Richard began, "Our movement has been gaining strength for over five years. The fruit of our efforts have culminated across the world today, October, 15, 1969, Moratorium Day. It is sad to say that our president, Richard Nixon, came into power with a promise to end this war. Most Americans believed he would end it, but the war did not end and and today it is bloodier than ever. What was Johnson's war is now Nixon's war. A bit of history—On August 7, 1964, with the Gulf of Tonkin Resolution, President Lyndon Baines Johnson unequivocally declared war on North Vietnam. Why? Because he was incensed by an attack on an American destroyer by the North Vietnamese. Our destroyers were in North Vietnamese water. The North Vietnamese patrol boats were no battle for American destroyers. So why did we escalate a war. Lyndon needed an excuse to start one. That was good enough.

"January 31, 1968, the North Vietnamese launched the Tet Offensive. They took parts of Saigon and Hue in a major coup. The American government was shocked that their impenetrable embassy in Saigon could be violated, but it was. They attacked Westmoreland's headquarters, General Fred Weyand's corp command, and blocked the roads to prevent American and South Vietnamese reinforcements from entering Saigon. The Vietcong attempted to take the presidential palace. American forces turned back the onslaught and recaptured most areas. Even though it was a defeat for the Vietcong, it was a tremendous political and psychological victory for the North Vietnamese. The U.S. military assessment of the war was questioned. We had no business there then; no business there, now. Through their execution of the Tet Offensive, they have shown the world that fact. We are murdering innocent men, women and children for the cause of imperialistic expansion by the United States. It began with Eisenhower and Kennedy. Then Johnson made an overt full scale war out of it, and now Nixon continues that tradition by campaigning with a promise to end the war 'with honor.' Honor? I wouldn't buy a used car from the man."

Someone snickered, then someone yelled, "Sit down, commie. Sit down."

'Freedom of speech. Freedom to assemble,' Budd said silently to himself as he waited in his chair. Nickie looked out from the wings. A police officer moved in and stood by the heckler. Harwood continued, "Now we hear also about a place called My Lai, March 16, 1968, a massacre of innocent people killed by men of the Charlie Company, llth Brigade when they entered the town of My Lai. 'This is what you've ben waiting for—search and destroy—and you've got it,' said their superior officer. A short time later the killing began. The number has been reported to be from anywhere of at least 175 to possibly 400 innocent men, women and children being annihilated. Murder, acts of rape, sodomy, maiming and assault against innocent individuals have been reported to have occurred at My Lai. When news of the atrocities surfaced, it sent shockwaves through the U.S. political establishment, the military's chain of command, and the already divided American public. The United States government concluded that no civilians were gathered together and shot by U.S. soldiers. This is a falsehood. This is murder - on Nixon's watch. Is a small piece of ground in Southeast Asia worth the commitment of cold blooded murder?"

Richard concluded and stepped back from the podium and walked over to Budd.

"NO! NO! NO! NO!" came from the crowd. The sound became almost deafening.

"Hit 'em kind of hard, didn't you?" Budd yelled above the roar.

The crowd was in high gear and was on a roll.

"STOP THE WAR!" "STOP THE WAR! "STOP THE WAR!"

"STOP THE WAR!" "STOP THE WAR! "STOP THE WAR!"

"STOP THE WAR! "NO MORE WAR! "END THE WAR!"

"Somebody says Dallas News and Associated Press are out there," yelled Richard.

The crowd was still roaring. "Well, I just laid my balls on the line. It's your turn."

"Thanks a lot Nicole." Budd looked at her. He walked up to the podium. Again he looked at Nicole. She was nervous.

"Let 'em calm down," yelled Richard above the roar.

"Knock it off! Let the man speak!" came a voice from the crowd. That young man had been Budd's neighbor since the early sixties. He was a member of the VVAW, Vietnam Veterans Against the War. His name was Stephen Brantley.

"Thank you. Thank you. I'm Budd Wilson." He looked at the crowd in the Texarkana College Auditorium on that October day in 1969. "I'm a graduate of Texas High School, 1968.

Some of you may remember me. I was asked to speak here today by my friend, Richard Harwood. I am not an intellectual or an authority on the war in Vietnam. I can only say what I feel as a citizen of Texarkana and of this country.

"The world today is full of strange and evil people. On August ninth of this year, actress Sharon Tate and a group of her close Beverly Hills' friends were murdered by cult followers under the direction of Charles Manson. Manson is an evil and inhumane monster with an uncanny ability to control and manipulate those with lesser strength of mind than his. From October eighth of this month, for four days, a group of extreme radicals, the Weathermen, a faction of the Students for a Democratic Society, the SDS, trashed and destroyed property on Chicago's Gold Coast in protest against the war in Vietnam. From my understanding, Manson and his followers and the Weatherman are revolutionaries who are determined to destroy our American system as we know it. Many of us are confused by these left wing revolutionaries, and yet also by the extreme right—the American hawks—the military and political establishment that is running our country daily, deeper into a war that many of us in the middle are turning against. All of this is being depicted on our television screens nightly. As a result, many of us, WE THE ORDINARY PEOPLE, are turning against the war, not knowing what to go by, except by what our hearts, minds and the national news tell us. Perhaps Walter Cronkite IS the only person whom we can really trust.

"As a middle class citizen of a middle American city, again, I can only say what I feel. To deal with our present day political and military situation we must look to the past, to the documents that set the foundation for our country. Our American experience, in part, has been based on the freedoms our forefathers fought for. Paramount among these are the United States Constitution and the Bill of Rights. If it were not for these two documents, I doubt that any of us would be here today enjoying the freedoms that we do have. Never-the-less, these rights are being tread upon by an insensitive government—The United States of America—and trashed by a new order of revolutionary youth that I can't begin to understand."

Budd paused... "I had always wanted to be an Air Force pilot. A year ago, I convinced myself that I just might make it. Perhaps God blessed me or cursed me one with a rheumatic heart condition. I realized then as I watched the news that I'd never fly for my country for several reasons. My future father-in-law was one of the finest Navy pilots of World War II. I admire him very deeply. But Vietnam is not World War II."

There were tears streaming down Niche's cheeks.

`'Our American heritage is based on these freedoms, fought for and won by men like my future father-in-law. Our forefathers gave us these rights and today the politicians and military of the United States government, and the revolutionaries on the other side, are abusing and destroying them. These atrocities that have occurred at home and in Southeast Asia are crimes against man, nature and God."

"Sit down, pretty boy!" a heckler yelled. "Draft dodger, sit down!"

"Let the man speak!" yelled Stephen from the crowd. "Let the man speak!"

Budd quickly glanced at Nickie. Her eyes were right on his. She was scared. He was becoming confused. He decided to wing it.

"Look," he started again. "Let me speak, please. I don't believe in killing anybody. What's happening in Vietnam is horrible. It really doesn't make any sense."

Someone from the audience voiced something. Budd didn't catch it.

"Let me continue. When a war is fought we know we are going to lose some of the 'best and brightest'. In the past, America has sacrificed men and women for the cause of freedom. Now we are sacrificing our 'best and brightest' for nothing." He regained his composure. "This useless killing must stop before we, perhaps rightfully, lose America to a radical order that goes against every thing good I was taught about our country. Why? Because we are engaged in a fruitless war being waged by crooked politicians and an inept military who are abusing and manipulating the very principles our country was founded on. I don't want our country to flounder and fail, and I don't want my brothers and sisters to die in vain. Well, I guess that's all I need to say."

For a couple of seconds there was absolute silence.

"Thank you, and have a good day." Budd stepped away from the podium. The applause started slowly, then grew and grew.

"Mr. President!" Nickie bit her lip. "Mr. President! Damn you were good!"

The symposium was over.

"Thank you. Thank you." Again Harwood was at the podium.

"May I have your attention. May I have your attention, please. There will be a round table discussion among members of the media, the clergy and local civic leaders back here in the auditorium at three-thirty. Thank you. Thank you."

Ronnie Dugger, former editor of the University of Texas' Daily Texan and editor-at- large of the Texas Observer began parallel demonstration speeches on the Capitol grounds in Austin at three p.m. "We are a people of love and peace. We come together today in mourning, in shame and in resolve that the United States shall withdraw from Vietnam."

The lowering of the American and Texas flags to half-mast brought a standing ovation from the crowd in Austin. In counter demonstrations supporters of the Nixon administration's Vietnam policy hoisted flags to full staff and turned on automobile headlights.

Sherrill Jeter, an ex-Marine sergeant and 1969 University of Texas government student closed the rally in Austin by discussing his experience in Vietnam. "To me, the whole country of Vietnam is not worth the loss of one American life. It is time to get up and stop the killing. Think about yourself. You could be next."

The only battlefield protest reported that day was the wearing of black armbands by members of a platoon of U.S. infantrymen on patrol near Chu Lai, 360 miles northeast of Saigon.

Associated Press photographer Charles Ryan said more than half of the 30 men in one American division platoon wore the antiwar armbands and the platoon leader, First Lt. Jesse Rosen told him that it was just his way of silently protesting.

"Personally, I think the demonstrating should go on until President Nixon gets the idea that every American should be pulled out of here now."

Earlier in the day, Rosen's men had killed two Vietcong, one a woman armed with a Chinese-made rifle.

Senator Barry Goldwater, R-Ariz., declared in California that demonstrators were "playing in the hands of the people whose business it is to kill American fighting men."

Budd stood there. People started coming up on the stage. Nickie walked over to him as he stood in the crowd.

"Mr. Wilson, Larry Powell, Dallas Morning News."

Mr. Wilson, Steve Huddleston, Associated Press."

"My goodness, you WERE here," Budd exclaimed. Nickie put her arm around Budd's waist.

"Why are you speaking here at the Moratorium in Texarkana?" asked the reporter.

"As I said, Texarkana is my home. Richard Harwood over there," Budd pointed towards Richard, "is my lifelong friend. He's the coordinator of the Texarkana Moratorium. He asked me to speak here today to represent the mainstream of middle Americans who are turning against the war."

"What is your political persuasion, Mr. Wilson?"

"Somewhere between Democrat and Republican. I'm a moderate, an establishment liberal."

"And what are you, today?"

"Today, I'm Budd Wilson."

"Do you feel that demonstrations across the country like this one on National Moratorium Day will help end the war in Vietnam?"

"Yes, I do."

The reporter turned to Nickie.

"Your father must have been the World War II fighter pilot he spoke of... How do you think he'd feel about your being here today, Miss....?"

"Nicole White. My father has always been proud of me. He taught me a long time ago to think for myself. He's proud of me, today."

"Well, very good," said the reporter. "And, you two plan to marry soon?"

"I certainly hope so," Budd said with a big smile. "Richard Harwood over there, he's the coordinator of the Moratorium in Texarkana. He's the one you need to talk to," concluded Budd.

"Mr. Harwood, Larry Powell, Dallas Morning News."

"Mr. Harwood, Steve Huddleston, Associated Press."

Budd and Nicole walked down from the stage into the almost empty college auditorium toward the side exit.

"Honey, you're shaking," Nicole exclaimed. "I'm so proud of you. Here, let me hold you."

She wrapped her arm around him and flashed that royal Nickie smile. "Come on, let's go get something to eat. I'm famished."

"I'm sorry, Nicole. Right now, I'm just not very hungry."

Despite differences on either side, incidents of violence throughout the world on Moratorium Day, October 15, 1969 were few. Americans would peacefully express themselves again, one month later, November 15, 1969 with the second Vietnam Moratorium. Winter turned to summer at 502 Elmwood. The window was open. It was hot, late and drizzling outside. The study lamp was shining in Nickie's eyes. She was trying unsuccessfully to sleep. Budd was staring at his book and rubbing his eyes. His concentration was gone.

"Whats'a matter?" She turned to him.

"I don't know. I don't know." He pulled off his glasses. "I guess I'm worn out."

"Budd, it's two-thirty in the morning. Can't you stop? You're obsessed. What good is it doing you?"

"We gotta eat. Neither one of us comes cheap."

"Budd look, let's blow it off. Let's do something "

"At two-thirty in the morning? What? Screw? I'm too tired."

"Let's go for a walk in the rain," she coaxed.

"A walk in the rain?" he questioned. "It's too hot."

"It'll get your juices flowing again."

"All right, Baby." He smiled. He pulled on a pair of jeans, a t-shirt, and his plain rubber flip-flops. He instinctively grabbed his keys and wallet. "Okay, let's go. I'm ready."

"Wait a minute," she said. "Let me finish getting dressed."

In a minute they stepped out into the dark. The drizzle had stopped, but it was still thick. The streets were steaming.

"Hot," he said as they walked down to the triangular intersection of Elmwood, Duval and San Jacinto Streets.

"Isn't it? I'm so sticky," she said to him. "Kiss me, you idiot. You haven't had time for anything but those books. Kiss me! See?" She grabbed him by the shoulder and turned him around. "It's very simple. You place one lip on the other and open your mouth like this."

"It's nice," he said after and smiled.

"Shut-up and kiss me again"

"Woah, Baby. Watch out," he said as she bit his neck.

"I'm horny. Can't I be horny? I need my time too. You stick your nose in those damned books all the time while I'm your dutiful .. ?"

"Lover."

"I'm beginning to wonder."

"You wanna go back to the apartment?"

"Let's walk a little bit more then I want you to take me home and have your way with me."

"Yes ma'am." He smiled. It turned into a broad grin. "You're so subtle."

"Aren't I?" She kissed him again. They walked in the heat down San Jacinto. The walk seemed interminable. They arrived at the tower and stared.

"Do you realize what this place means to me?" he began.

"Yes I do, Budd. Yes I do."

"I mean when I was growing up in East Texas, there was only 'The University'." Budd continued. "Baylor was for Baptists, and SMU was only for rich kids. It was 'The University'"

They approached War Memorial Stadium. Construction on the new upper tier of the stadium was under way. It was a mammoth undertaking. They turned right off of San Jacinto onto 21' Street and walked up the hill.

They passed the University Christian Church. Then they approached the massive fountains at the end of the South Mall on the right and paused a moment to reflect on the tower as the symbol itself of the University of Texas at Austin. The almost completed Dobie Center stood on the left, on the corner of 21' and Guadalupe Streets.

"It's swank," she said.

"J. Frank Dobie would have hated it."

"Why?"

"Because he was a true Texas naturalist. Anyway, I'm sure it has a 'swank' price tag."

"You, Budd Wilson, are so cheap it's disgusting. You're cheap. That's a good word for you Budd, cheap."

"Practical, please. Like J. Frank Dobie. Practical."

He paused for a moment. "You hungry?"

"Yeah, but I look horrible."

"So does everyone else in Austin this time of night."

"Probably."

"Let's walk over to the Plantation. It's so sleazy. They've got such good, greasy chicken fried steaks. We'll feel right at home."

They walked down Guadalupe to 19 th Street and jockeyed down across to the end of the eighteen hundred block of San Antonio and to the Plantation Restaurant, a 24-hour greasy spoon, a University student tradition. They ate their meal and finished with coffee. It had stopped raining and the heat had dried up some of the steam.

"We gonna walk home?" he asked.

"Let's take a cab." She smiled her devil impish smile. "It's too hot out there."

He paid the bill and went to a pay phone to call a cab. They waited outside until the cab arrived. They sat in each other's arms in the back seat. The air-conditioning in the cab felt cold against their damp shirts.

"I'm going to have you!" She turned to him. She attacked his lips.

They were entwined in each other's arms for several minutes, then he came up for air. He pulled his lips away from hers. *"The Sun Also Rises,* Ava Gardner and Tyrone Power or Rock Hudson? Who was it?"

"It was Hemingway." She put her lips disdainfully to his again.

"Not the book, the movie. Tyrone Power or Rock Hudson?"

"I have no earthly idea. You have such an aptitude for trivial detail."

"Isn't it a pretty idea to think so," he said as he thought of the Hemingway ending.

"502 Elmwood," said the cab driver after waiting several minutes.

"Oh, yeah, sure," Budd said. "Here." He pulled a twenty from his pocket. "Keep the change."

"A twenty! You're getting better."

"Well, you have to blow it every now and then."

"I certainly hope so," she said as she pulled her way out of the back seat of the cab. They walked up to the apartment.

"Take me," she half purred and half growled. "Pick me up and carry me in."

"Hell, you weigh too much. I haven't got the muscles."

"Lazy son-of-a-bitch."

"Okay, unlock the door. Damn, you're heavy!"

"You're so chivalrous."

"Yeah aren't I? Turn on the light so I can see."

"I like the dark. Don't drop me, damn it."

"Right on the bed." He let go of her.

"Take me." She looked up.

He tore off his clothes. He was all over her.

CHAPTER 4

Budd sat in the chair at the ophthalmologist's office. Please read aloud from the top, the front page story of the Austin American. It was an article about the Vietnam war.

"What did you read?" the doctor asked him.

"I don't know."

"Mr. Wilson, I'm going to prescribe reading glasses with a prism in each lens for you. Could be strain. Probably burn-out. Possibility exists that you've got a learning disability."

"Learning disability?"

"A dyslexic condition. If so, perhaps the University isn't the place for you at this time.

You said you have a 3.3 G.P.A. It's a miracle."

"I've had to work for it."

"I believe that."

"What will I do? I mean, for a living?"

"Mr. Wilson, all of us have to adjust to our limitations, no matter how large they may be.

That's one of the ways in life we can deal with success and failure."

"But I've fought to be a doctor and I'm not giving it up. Not for you or anybody else.

What will I tell my fiancee?"

"Again, in my opinion, the mark of maturity is adjustment. If we don't adjust, we become stagnant and growth stops; we turn inwards or backwards. Successful living is a constant series of corrections. That's how we continue to grow, yes?"

"But I'm not giving up! I'm not giving up."

"Mr. Wilson, I want to set up some time to run an E.E.G. Can you make the time?"

"I don't know. I guess I must. We'll work it out some way."

"I'm going to refer you to a doctor here in Austin. I want to put you through an extensive series of tests, first."

Three weeks later, Budd picked up his half glasses. He walked into the apartment. Nickie was cleaning the stove.

"What do you think'?" He put the glasses on.

"Why Darling." She began to laugh. "You look so..so.. middle aged... for a young man. I bet you can give one Hell of an evil-eye over the top of those things."

"Seriously Nicole. I have to wear them."

"I know," she softly said. "Well, anyway, they make you look distinguished. My older man."

"Shut up," he said. Then his thoughts turned.

"Take off your gloves and powder your nose.

Let's go look for a new place to live."

"What did the doctor say?"

"I'm just tired. Just tired. He's going to run some tests. Come on, let's find another place to live. Something swanky where you don't have to clean the oven. This place is turning into an eternal dump."

"I tend to agree." She frowned, holding down her gloved hands as oven cleaner dripped to the floor.

Dobie Center, 2021 Guadalupe, was a newly completed complex of private suites and dorm rooms across the street from the University. The tower was the newest and the finest private student living building of its day. It stood as a monolithic symbol in the Austin skyline. Budd and Nicole walked together up the powerful, dynamic tier of steps to the promenade deck.

"Gee, I feel just like Gatsby and Daisy Buchanan."

"No kidding. Budd, we can never afford this place."

"Well, let's check it out and see. You never know `til you ask."

"I'm climbing each step, step by step," she said softly to herself.

Budd looked at her questioningly, then decided to drop the subject. They sat in front of the leasing agent in her office.

"Are you interested in a suite or a room?" The woman was poised . She made the couple feel at home.

"Well, I don't know. I suppose a suite." Budd was a bit uncomfortable.

"Let me take you upstairs and show you one." The leasing agent grabbed her keys and the three headed towards the elevators. The elevator zoomed to the sixteenth floor. The agent took the master key and placed it in the lock of suite 1604. They entered through a galley. There were two bedrooms, one on each side of a small living room. The walls were a pale yellow and the carpet was a dark brown pile. Suite 1604 was tasteful, but muted and conservative.

'This could be our bedroom,' Budd mused as he crossed through the living room from bedroom to bedroom. "This could be a study and den," he said, as he looked at the second bedroom, "with a hideaway for out-of-town guests." Each bedroom had its separate bathroom facilities. The living room had a bay window that overlooked the city. It jutted out from the building itself. There was a couch in the window, and from there one had an excellent view of the city.

Nickie sat down on the couch. She just sat there looking out the window.

"It's so beautiful," she whispered. "We really can't explain this to our parents as a measure to save money Budd. . . but I do like it."

"Would you like to go back to my office and discuss prices and fill out some paper work?" The leasing agent asked.

"We'll take it" Budd softly stated.

"But you haven't seen the rest of the facilities. You don't know what payment options are available to you."

"Budd! Budd! I don't believe it! I don't believe it!"

"We do have some paper work to do. You should see all of the facilities available to you"

"I don't have to," whispered Nickie. "Do you have maid service?"

"Please, let's go downstairs," the leasing agent coaxed.

"Come on, let's satisfy the lady and take the grand tour," Budd said.

They followed the leasing agent through the shopping center underneath Dobie. There was a movie theater, restaurant and a bar below. There was also a bakery where one could get excellent kolaches, and there were various other retail outlets underneath the student tower.

They looked at the outdoor pool, the dual saunas, the student cafeteria and the study room on the main deck.

"I love it!" exclaimed Nicole.

"I'm sure you two will be very happy here," said the leasing agent." Budd and Nicole followed her to the lobby and into the office. "We need to sign some contracts," she reiterated.

A suite in Dobie Center was considerably more expensive than their apartment on Elmwood Street had been. After going over the paperwork Budd said, "I need to go across the street to the Texas Bank and have some funds transferred. Hold the contract and I'll be back in thirty minutes."

They crossed Guadalupe Street to the bank. Budd was smiling. Nickie was waving her arms and talking rapidly. She was in a state of rapture.

"Is there anything wrong?" asked the teller after the couple hurriedly approached her.

"No...I have a trust fund for college. I want some funds transferred from my bank in Texarkana to my account in your bank here."

"I see." She punched a button on the phone. "Mr. Wright, there's someone here who better see you. Something about a trust fund. Thank you."

A middle-aged, well-dressed gentleman stood up from his desk across the lobby and motioned to Budd and Nickie. He greeted them and they sat down.

" My name is William George Wilson. I have a trust fund for college set up in the name of Devereaux in the trust department of the Bi-City National Bank in Texarkana, Texas. My college education is to be provided for by the Devereaux estate. Right now, I have three hundred dollars a month transferred from the Bi-City trust department in Texarkana to my checking account here in your bank. I'd like to increase that."

"To how much, Mr. Wilson?"

"Unlimited checking privileges."

"I see. Who is the trust officer at your bank in Texarkana?"

"Mr. George McDonald, Bi-City National Bank Trust Department."

"Unlimited check writing privileges?"

"Yes. I want my girl friend and me to move into Dobie Center and buy some new clothes."

"New clothes?"

"Yes."

"Miss Perkins," the bank officer said after he picked up the phone. "Get me in touch with Mr. George McDonald at the Bi-City National Bank in Texarkana, Texas, the trust department."

He turned to Budd and Nicole. "I hope you don't mind me calling your bank officer in Texarkana. Your request is somewhat unusual." The bank officer was a responsible executive, but never-the-less was polite to the young couple.

"Mr McDonald, this is Henry Wright with the Texas State Bank in Austin. There's a Mr. William George Wilson in my office. Says he has drawing privileges on an estate for college— the name is Devereaux. Says he wants a suite in Dobie Center for his girlfriend and him and some new clothes. Must be nice clothes. Says he wants unlimited check writing privileges.

What? Give it to him? If he doesn't beat town. I see. Okay. Yes sir."

"He doesn't really mean if I beat town. Let me talk to him," Budd demanded of the bank officer as he grabbed the phone out of his hand. "Listen George, I've lived cheap in college for roughly a year and I'm tired of it. I'm going to live rich for a while. How's Nickie?" He beamed over the phone. "She's fine. Yeah, she's sitting right here. I'm fine. Yes, I'm okay. I want to thank you now for the additional money." He turned to Nickie and the trust officer. "I guess he didn't mind "

After conferring a few minutes more with Budd's trust officer, Mr. Wright concluded, "The fund is for your higher education, Mr. Wilson. You have some discretion as to how it is spent along with your trust officer at your bank in Texarkana."

"I'm not going to spend a whole lot of money."

"It's yours to decide. Welcome to the Texas Bank, Mr. Wilson. If there is any way I can help you."

It was later on that night, an early autumn dusk. Budd and Nicole just sat there on the couch in the bay window of Suite 1604 of Dobie Center. Henry Mancini and his orchestra were playing his own song, "Dreamsville" in an anthology of Mancini hits on a new portable machine, an audio cassette tape player, that they had recently purchased and brought over from the apartment on Elmwood. The music was soft, sophisticated and romantic They could see the tiny little cars light up below on Guadalupe Street. They watched the lights come on all over Austin from that bay window. On the left was the Capital. Directly below them was The Nighthawk restaurant.

The Texas Bank was just right of center on Guadalupe Street. They watched the night approach from the window of the sixteenth floor of Dobie Center, 2021 Guadalupe St, Austin Texas. Budd avoided having the EEG run as the ophthalmologist had prescribed. He never admitted to a weakness, the possibility of a flaw, not even to Nicole. It showed, but he did everything in his power not to admit to it. After seeing the ophthalmologist, rather than following his advice, Budd went to the University Health Center. He went alone.

"Sometimes I can't see anything," Budd said to the doctor. "And, sometimes I see bright colors. I feel like I'm going to pass out all the time."

"Mr. Wilson, I want to put you on vitamin B-12 and Dramamine to start with. You seem very weak. Do you do anything but study?"

"I have a girlfriend."

"Sexually active?"

"Not as much as we used to. School's the most important thing to me now."

"The way you're going, you're going to lose both if you don't watch out."

Mrs. Helene Wolfe was a landmark in Austin. She was a patron of the arts and a liberal political force in the city. She was a graduate of the New England Conservatory of Music. For forty years she had run the most successful music store in Austin. It was the Steinway affiliate. When forced to retire by her sons and grandsons, Mrs. Wolfe bought an old auto repair garage two blocks from Dobie and there she rebuilt and sold quality used pianos. From many vantage points, Helene Wolfe knew more about the guts of a piano than anyone in the Hill Country.

On Saturdays, Nickie always slept 'til noon. Budd was habitually up by eight. Because of their different hours, he'd tiptoe out of the suite, walk down to the Nighthawk and eat breakfast alone. This would give him some time for private exploration of the city without Nickie. It was on one such trip that he had discovered Mrs. Helene Wolfe. He had heard piano music, followed his ear, and stuck his head in the door of the barn. Following the music again this Saturday, he came back to the barn and Mrs. Wolfe. This time he had left a note for Niche saying where he might be.

"What is that? My dad plays that."

"Rachmaninoff s *Predule in D. Minor.*" The large, old woman turned to Budd. "Your father must be a classically trained pianist."

"He is. I suppose. I never really thought much about it."

"Rachmaninoff s *Prelude in D Minor* has some difficult passages. Do you play?"

"Only second rate jazz and stuff like that in smoke-filled rooms."

"Jazz is a legitimate art form. Go ahead. There' s an assortment of pianos. That Chickory over there is a pretty good piano."

"Okay," he said and approached the piano, "Billy Strayhorn's 'Take the A Train'. One, two, on two three four . . ."

She listened. She patted her foot. "You're very gifted."

"Thank you very much." He continued to play.

"You should be playing in some exclusive club. You're very talented."

"Thank you."

"What does your father do, the one who plays Rachmaninoff s *Prelude in D Minor?"*

"He's a piano teacher. He was a graduate of New England Conservatory of Music in Boston."

"I've heard of it," she said in tongue in cheek fashion. "Do you play professionally?"

"Only for my own amusement."

"You're wasting your talent. Perhaps you feel like you've failed to live up to a musical legacy that you can't equal in your own mind."

"Perhaps." He brought the song to a conclusion. "Maybe I'm just more materialistic than my father is."

"Ever feel guilty for that?"

"Somewhat."

"Jazz, again, like your father and Rachmaninoff, is a legitimate art form," she said.

"Take, for instance, Ellington's 'Satin Doll'."

"You play jazz?" he asked.

"Only as an avocation, but I accept it as a serious art form just like Rachmaninoff. I'm afraid I'm getting too old to play anything seriously anymore."

"Let's do a duo on 'Satin Doll'."

"Young man, I'll set the tempo."

They were off to a medium swing on the Ellington classic.

"You take the bridge. I'll follow on a walking stride. Gee, this is neat!" He started to sing:

"She's nobody's fool --so, she's playin' it cool as can be."

"You play better than you sing," she said.

"So I've been told." He laughed. "So I've been told."

A small crowd had gathered at the door of the piano barn.

"Don't stop! Keep going!" yelled someone. Then Nickie appeared. She pushed through the crowd. She was smiling radiantly.

"Look at us, the Ferrante and Tiecher of 52n d Street." He turned to Mrs. Wolfe. "Let's take this thing home. Last chorus?"

She nodded back. The duo ended their exercise for that day.

"Look at all these pianos, Nick."

"That's a nice miniature baby grand over there," said Mrs. Wolfe. "She has a good sound for a little piano."

Budd walked over to the tiny baby grand. "Yeah it does, doesn't it?" he said as he fingered the keys of the piano. "How much do you want for it?"

"Well, it's been sitting there for a while. Nobody wants a baby grand that small. For you, six hundred dollars."

"Oh Budd," Niche gasped.

"Do you think we could get it in on the ground floor elevator up to the sixteenth floor of Dobie Center?"

"Well, it's just a block and a half. We can try," said Mrs. Wolfe. "Let's go measure. Also depends on the weight We'll try. We'll try."

"God, Budd, a piano in our own suite. You'll have to play. We'll have to have a party."

"Let's see if we can get it up there first," said Mrs. Wolfe.

"It is a miniature baby grand," he replied.

"I think it'll fit," said Nickie.

"It's the weight also," said Mrs. Wolfe. "It's the weight on the elevator also."

They pushed the piano on a dolly into Suite 1604 of Dobie Center. Budd wrote Mrs. Helene Wolfe a check.

"I'll take Manhattan, the Bronx and Staten Island, too."

Budd sat at his own piano in his own suite, wearing a tuxedo, playing and singing cocktail jazz. Somehow a remnant of a major Chi Omega party had ended up on the sixteenth floor of Dobie. Nickie was wearing a formal, emerald sequined dress. It was tight and low-cut with chiffon sleeves and a slit up each side of the skirt of the gown.

"Budd, this is Bunny Belowe. She's a Chi-O, and this is Charley Smithson from Houston. He's a professional golfer." She put her arms around the golfer. "Aren't you?"

"Well, yes. Hi, Budd."

Budd stopped playing the piano. He yawned. "I'm sorry. Can't talk and play at the same time. I'm tired."

"Let me get you a drink since Nickie has you tied to the piano. What's your drink?"

"Scotch and water." He yawned again and started playing the piano. "Where's Nicole?" he found himself saying. "I thought the son-of-a-bitch was getting me a drink." He glued his hands to the piano.

The ophthalmologist that Budd had first seen and the University Health Center had told him he probably had a dyslectic condition among other things. The ophthalmologist suggested an E.E.G. The health center suggested the University Learning Disabilities Lab. Budd walked into the disabilities lab and talked to the receptionist. He could deal with that.

"I'm trying to make it through school but I need some help because I'm flunking out of my courses and all I do is study. I've got to make it through school. I guess I'm going to have to see somebody. You've been recommended."

"What seems to be your immediate problem?" the receptionist asked.

"I don't know. I keep working and studying, and somehow I keep flunking -- and I know I'm smart."

"Could we set you up for a program run by one of our psychologists for text anxiety? It sounds like you're putting a lot of personal pressure on yourself. Perhaps your family. College is tough. Families have expectations that are sometimes difficult to live up to."

"On the contrary, for some reason my making it is a family quagmire. My name is William George Wilson. I live in Suite 1604, Dobie Center. My phone number is 474-2991."

"We meet here every Wednesday at four p.m. with Jim Carson."

"Yes, I'll be here."

Budd enrolled in the University's remedial reading program. As he sat there reading fourth grade material he thought of his cousin, Jim Beutner. Jim had always thought he never had the right opportunities. His parents had wanted him to go to work as soon as he had graduated from highschool. He had always wanted to go the University of Texas. Now here was Budd at that same University of Texas reading fourth grade material in a remedial reading program.

One afternoon shortly after lunch Budd received a call from his mother. Fritz Cavanaugh had suffered a heart attack and was in critical condition back in Texarkana. Budd rushed home alone. Nicole chose to stay in Austin. When he arrived at the hospital it was early evening. Meredith and a number of Fritz's friends were in the waiting room. She greeted Budd with an embrace. Meredith was strong and not outwardly emotional. She had always been the strong one of the family.

"How is he?" Budd asked.

"Pretty bad, Buddy," she replied. "He's asked for you."

In the early part of the evening Budd was allowed to see him. He was an old man dying. Budd thought about all of the spare time he had spent with Fritz listening to Dixieland music on that old Magnavox record player and drinking cheap Kentucky Bourbon. It seemed only like yesterday that it was the first Sunday afternoon that he had gone to Fritz's home. With Nicole in Austin and him in Texarkana with a dying man, Budd ruminated about the life of this mentor, musician and friend, about his own life with Nicole, and about his own mortality. Fritz died later on that night. Roy Riley, Fritz's first drummer was at the hospital when Fritz died. He got on the phone and called some of the musicians that Fritz had played with in the early years. If Fritz was going out, he was going out the right way. Later the next day the musicians began to gather at Fritz and Meredith's home. They were sad about the loss of a close friend. On the day of the funeral they took their instruments. As the casket was being carried in, the aging musicians followed directly behind the pallbearers and sat in the choir loft of the Episcopal Church.

When the service was nearly over Josh Jaquet began the music. He was an old black man of Cajun descent. Fritz had known him as a respected musician from the early days of New Orleans, but moreover as a friend for all of his life. In many ways the color barrier never existed among jazz musicians. They spoke a common language and that language was music. Standing up, Josh wiped his forehead and began to sing, "Just a Closer Walk With Three". After he had finished, the pallbearers began to carry the casket out. The clarinet, the trumpet, the trombone, the bass horn and the bass drum followed the casket. The funeral attendant walked up and asked the band if they would like to get into one of the funeral cars that had been arranged for them.

"We gonna walk this man home," Josh told the funeral director. "Yes sir. . .We gonna walk Mr. Fritz Cavanaugh home."

The band gathered out in front of the hearse and began to play the funeral dirge. With a police officer directing the procession they wound their way to the cemetery. After the casket had been lowered into the ground, the band struck up "The South Rampart Street Parade" -- a spirited, jubilant celebration of the life, death, and resurrection of a close friend. Budd walked away from the music. It drifted into memory as it wafted from the past, to the present, and into the future for eternity . He thought to himself, Nicole is in Austin and he's alone in Texarkana. Innocence was so close in the past, and yet so lost and far gone away. He made the long drive back to Austin.

It was a two story, stucco edifice at 2405 Neuces, just a dog-leg from the Castillian private dormitory and behind Les Amis sidewalk café on San Antonio. The afternoon was cool. It was an Autumn afternoon, yet Budd sat outside at the cafe drinking wine and reading the papers. The building behind Les Amis had always intrigued him but not enough to check it out. Nickie was in a late class and he now had the time to go investigate. He picked up his papers and walked back to the structure.

"Seamstress—Original Creations" said the sign on the door of the stucco building. He walked in. There were beautiful gowns, dresses and frocks.

"You design all of these and make them?"

"Yes," said the young French woman.

"They're beautiful. Is business good?"

"It's a little slow."

"Look, I want to give my girlfriend a Christmas present. Could you make her something in time for Christmas?"

"I'm sure I can. What do you want?"

"Now, here's the idea. I want a pants suit in white silk. I want a very flowing, bell-bottomed leg. Can you do that?"

"I must have her measurements."

"Oh I'm sure Nicole wouldn't mind. She's petite."

"I still must have her measurements. I must have her in for fittings."

"Yes. I'm sure I can get her here. . . And I want white ostrich feathers bordering at the bottom of the leg. Then I want flowing, white silk sleeves covered with the same white ostrich feathers. Kind of a modern day, Age of Aquarius-Ginger Rogers outfit, you get it? Oh, and I want the neckline high in the back, very low in the front. I want it to form a 'V' from the shoulders coming to a point at the waist." The concept for the pants suit poured out of his mind as fast as he could get the words out as though he had been meticulously planning the outfit for months rather than off the top of his head, as it was.

She smiled. "That's some outfit."

"For some price. How much would it cost?"

"I'll tell you what. If she will tell everybody where she got it and that it was designed and custom made by me when she wears it, I'll charge you five hundred dollars."

"I don't know about Nicole, but I'm a bargain hunter. You've got it. Are you sure you can get it before Christmas for all of the parties?"

"It will be ready. It will be ready. But I must have her in for measurements and fittings."

"You're on."

The Glenn Miller Orchestra under the direction of Buddy
DeFranco was coming to the Austin Convention Center for New
Year's Eve. Some of Budd's friends from Dobie suggested that they
pool their resources, share the cost and buy tickets for the sixteenth
floor. It was going to be dressy and Nickie would be there in white
silk and ostrich feathers.

"Happy New Year's Eve, 1972, Ladies and Gentlemen. The City of
Austin and the Austin Convention Center are proud to present the
Glenn Miller Orchestra under the direction of Mr. Buddy
DeFranco."

The band began to play the soft, reedy sound of Miller's theme,
"Moonlight Serenade".

During the opening applause, couples drifted onto the dance floor
en masse. Budd and Nicole were among hundreds of other dancers
that night. They stood on the dance floor and applauded after the
introductory ballad had finished.

"And now Mr. DeFranco and the Glenn Miller Orchestra will put
you in the mood with, you guessed it, 'In the Mood'."

The crowd roared.

"Can you jitterbug?" Nickie shouted above the din of the crowd
and the music.

"I think so. Can you?"

"Start rocking to the beat."

After an ungainly attempt by the two at jitterbugging, "Serenade in
Blue" began. It had always been one of Miller's haunting ballads.
They decided to sit out Pennsylvania 6-500 and have a drink. They

walked towards the cash bar.

"Hi everybody," Charley Smithson said after he walked up. "Hi Sugar." He winked at Nickie.

"I didn't know your were here."

"How could you miss her with all those plumes. I had that pant suit designed--- "

"Yes Charley," Nicole said somewhat sarcastically, "he had this seamstress girl make the outfit for a special price only if I'd tell everyone her name, and that she'd cut a deal with Budd to make it. Budd," she laughed, "you are SO cheap."

"Well, you look great to me, no matter what it costs, and you don't have to teach me how to jitterbug." Charley flashed his toothy smile. "I already know how to dance."

"Well, you make the right moves," mumbled Budd. "Gotta hand it to you."

"Come on Nickie, let's dance. May I, Budd?"

"Most certainly. I'd never be one to stand in the way of true love."

"Budd, don't be a jerk," chastised Nicole. "I'll be right back."

One dance for Charley Smithson and Nicole led to another. One drink for Budd led to another. "Somewhere relatively between the oral and anal stage, it all sucks." Budd looked around. He was talking to himself. He walked up to a table of friends and plopped in a chair.

"Slow down, Budd," said one of his friends from the sixteenth floor. "It's no big deal."

"I'm too tired to be angry. Reckon he wears dentures? Ceasar

Romero out there? Maybe it was the guy who created the Henry J who said it."

"Said what, Budd?"

"That life sucks. It does. Anybody got any Scotch or bourbon or beer -- or ethyl alcohol?"

The couple continued to dance and Budd continued to drink. Finally, Nickie and Smithson walked up to him.

"Budd," she asked. "Do you mind if we dance some more? Charley's such a marvelous dancer."

Budd looked up at her and furrowed his eyebrows and forehead. "Did you ever drive a Hudson? Did you?" He directed his question to Nickie.

"Budd, you're a little loaded." She grinned.

"Let me ask you something, Charley. Did you ever drive a Kaiser or a Henry J?"

"No, I drive a Porsche." He chuckled.

"Figures. Never touch the stuff."

"We'll be back, pardner," said Charley.

"Happy trails. . . Or was it a Studebaker. . . ? Damned good car, the Studebaker. . . I'm going to get on my Studebaker and fly home. Happy New Year everybody. I'm intensely bored."

"Budd," pleaded one of his friends, "don't drive. You've had too much to drink Take a cab, and besides, aren't you going to see the New Year in?"

"Oh, you mean a yellow Studebaker. Gotcha! I'll take a yellow

Studebaker home. Tell her and Ceasar Romero to catch a broom if she needs one. . . . On second thought, she won't . He's got a Porsche. I'm going home and going to bed.. You may use that for reference. On second thought, you probably won't have to."

He weaved up to the girl at the coat check counter. He handed her his ticket.

"Like to dance?" he asked the young lady.

"I'm sorry, I can't. I'd like to, but I have to work right now."

"Doesn't matter. I'd step on your toes right in the middle of the 'Anvil Chorus'."

"Pardon?"

"Or was it Jimmy Dorsey and 'Tangerine', or perhaps it was Benny Goodman's 'Let's Dance'? I did ask you to dance, didn't I? Of course I did. . . Oh well. . . . doesn't matter.

Miss, would you call me a yellow Studebaker?"

"Beg your pardon?"

"A yellow cab, the first available yellow Chevy."

He looked toward Nickie and Charley Smithson, out on the dance floor. "Or maybe it was Tommy Dorsey's 'Getting Sentimental Over You'. I always was sentimental over her. Probably was a mistake. Oh well, Happy New Year," he said to the coat check girl. "Adios."

He walked outside and waited for his cab. It was late afternoon, dusk, January 22, 1973. People were scurrying across the campus who'd just heard the news. The word floated across the nation, the

Capitol and the city of Austin, the thirty-sixth President of the United States, Lyndon Baines Johnson was dead. In front of the student union people were saying "President Johnson is dead." On the shuttlebus students who had just heard the news on their way home were already talking about the life and career of the first and somewhat controversial Texas president, a man who was deeply tied to The University of Texas. Budd walked into the suite he and Nicole shared after the 5:30 national news had ended. Nicole was on the couch locked in Charley Smithson's arms. Budd stood there, silent...

"Excuse me," said Charley, out of embarrassment as he turned around to face Budd.

He had heard the lock of the front door of the suite click open then shut. The three of them were there, together in the living room of Budd and Nicole's suite.

"No, excuse me," Budd softly said.

"Lyndon Johnson died of a heart attack," Smithson said. His face was red. He flipped the remote control switch for the television to off. "Damned Nigger lover," he said. Nicole looked to and from each man. She was silent. Charley got up and switched the T.V. on again.

"President Johnson's casket has been flown from Brooks General Hospital in San Antonio to Bergstrom Air Force Base here in Austin. The President's body will remain at the Weed-Corley Funeral Home overnight, then his casket will be transported tomorrow to the LBJ Library for public viewing. It was his wish to be with the people of Austin and his beloved Hill Country at his departing." The news was all over the Austin television and radio stations. Budd turned around and started for the door.

"Budd, please! Budd where are you going?" cried Nicole.

"I don't know. Can't you see, Nickie? I don't know. . . To pay my last respects, I guess."

He walked out of Dobie Center. The neon lights flashed in unusual patterns, crisp and bright. The globes that surrounded the street lamps angrily glared at him. He was aware that something was wrong but he didn't know what it was. If something had happened to him, he didn't know what it was or could be. For hours he walked through the streets of Austin. The darkness led into the light but he could not tell the difference. He found himself waking from his sleep, on his own bed, in his full clothes in the suite that he and Nicole lived in, only he was alone. It was dark and 24 hours had passed since he had seen her.

"Where are you Nicole?" he asked. "Where are you?" He waited. Nicole did not come. He got scared, then he remembered that the Johnson casket would still be at the LBJ Library for public viewing early that night and that he had promised to pay his last respects. He grabbed a jacket and flew out the door. The mourners were asked to form two rows, side by side. The lines ran for miles, up one street, down another, side by side. Over thirty-two thousand people were waiting and walking in rows of two to see the casket that day and evening. Helicopters were landing and taking off from the top of the L.B.J. Library. Signal lights flashed in one direction than another. The cameras of NBC, CBS and ABC panned the people walking two by two. Budd had been walking all the previous night and part of the day. A President of the United States was dead. He had to make one more walk. The line crept up the multitude of steps leading to the entrance of the library. Then, Budd was inside. He turned up the steps inside the Great Hall and approached the library mezzanine where the casket was lying in state.

"President Johnson did more for the poor man than any president in history."

An old black man stood next to Budd and held his hat over his heart. Budd walked down the steps of the Presidential Library. He started to run.

'Ticket to ride. I've got a ticket to ride.' He kept repeating. 'I've got a ticket to ride.'

He started running across the campus. The city lights hid the stars. However in the darkness from within his mind were paisley designs of and on hallucinatory fish in colors like yellow, red and chartreuse, squiggling and pulsating at him through a sky that seemed like a giant tent made up of royal blue canvas with bright, tiny crystal lights, like piercing little white Christmas lights that shot painful, judgmental rays through and against Budd himself. He had never taken hallucinogenic drugs. Whatever designs his mind was playing in front of and through him were caused by the bio-chemistry of his own brain and not that of an induced external drug. The next thing he knew he was standing in front of the tower staring at it.

"Ye shall know the Truth and the Truth shall make you free." "The truth shall make me free. Finally the truth will set me free." Then he was running down the South Mall back to Dobie, bouncing off each building in his mind whatever it was. If he could only get back to Dobie. He was scared, but he knew he would have to endure it all. This is what God had given him for better or for worse. He threw open the door to their suite. He rapidly walked into the bedroom. On their bed was a note.

My beloved Budd, Somehow to me, our life has been a lovely but chaotic roller-coaster ride since the day we began. For some time now, I've known you and I cannot be forever. For us, forever has passed into history. I truly believe we both need a new and individual start for our own personal stability and happiness. I'll be getting my things later on this week. In my own way, I will love you forever,   Nicole.

He went flying through the suite, slamming one door, opening another. "Goddamnit, Nicole! You're fucking around on me and I know it. I know it!"

He sat down on the bed.

"Have a drink, a little drink. Well, maybe I need some sleeping pills." He went to the bathroom cabinet. "I haven't slept in three months. Maybe longer than that." He reached for the pill bottle. "Maybe I need some sleeping pills." He went to the kitchen and poured a tall, eight ounce glass full of straight bourbon. Then he went into the livingroom. Budd turned on the stereo. He flipped on the record and swallowed the pills and whiskey.

'And to fight for a cause they've long ago forgotten, then she'll be a true love of mine. '

He lay on the emergency room table at Brackenridge Hospital.

"How many pills did you take?" the emergency room doctor asked.

"Twenty, maybe more."

"You sure?"

"Yes."

"Who's Nicole?"

"My fiancee."

The doctor looked at the crumpled note. "She's not anymore."

"Damn! Nicole! Da—"

"Hold him down. Better get the pump on him," the doctor said to the nurse. The pump went down his throat into his stomach.

CHAPTER 5

America had recently suffered the disgrace of the resignation of a president. The country was brought back to equilibrium by Gerald R. Ford. It had been three years since Budd had seen Nicole. He walked into the street level of the recently opened Brooks Brothers store in Dallas, Texas, located on the first floor and in the basement of the newest and tallest building in Dallas at that time, Interfirst Tower, all fifty-six floors of it, located at 1201 Elm Street. Brooks Brothers' entrance was located on the side street of the structure at 201 Field Street. Due to the nature of the building, the times, and that it was the first Brooks Brothers store in Dallas, it created somewhat of a small sensation when it opened.

'It looks just like I thought Brooks Brothers would look,' he said to himself as he looked around the store after walking in. There were three button, blue blazers and dark solid and pinstriped suits displayed on mannequins. There were button-downed full cut oxford cloth dress shirts. There were Izod-Lacoste golf shirts and those of the Brooks Brothers' own label,"Golden Fleece." There were Church and Alden shoes and Bass penny loafers. Budd crossed over the blue carpet to the stone floor. He admired the vast array of silk ties, reps, clubs and foulards, and silk handkerchiefs, solids and paisleys. He dabbed a bit of the Brooks Brothers' own Spice and Bay Rum on his wrists. The store had the aroma of fabric and a well-to-do-bank, the aroma of money.

"May I help you?" asked an attractive middle-aged woman.

"Yes, I'm looking for Mr. Miller, the manager. He ran an ad in the Dallas Morning News. I have an appointment."

"Oh Mr. Miller's office is downstairs. Just take the stairs to the left or the elevator. The lady noticed the resume in Budd's hand. "You look the part," she said and smile

"It's a Cricketeer from Dillards," Budd said of his suit.

"It'll do." She smiled again.

Budd walked down into the lower level of Brooks Brothers. The very expensive suits were sold on the lower level. Men worked mostly their own customers on straight commission and made a decent living.

"May I help you?" asked one.

"May I help you?" another immediately echoed.

"I'm looking for Mr. Miller's office."

"New blood for Brooksgate," grumbled another salesman about the prospective employee for the college shop on the ground level where all new young sales representatives began their careers with Brooks Brothers. "Miller runs too many ads."

"He'll be weeded out before he even gets down here," said the other salesman, referring to their fine suit department in the basement level. "He's too young. Probably has no clientele."

Budd passed the young lady sitting at the main office desk. Then he turned around. The desk plaque read: "Cecelia McGill Office Manager"

She was sensuous in a plain kind of way. Her hair was light auburn and cut short. She was wearing tortoise shell glasses. She had on a black and white dress, black beads and small round black earbobs.

"Pretty dress," he started.

"Why thank you." He embarrassed her. She put her left fingers to her lip.

"I'm looking for Mr. Miller's office. I have an appointment at two. I'm Budd Wilson."

"Have a seat Mr. Wilson. I'll ring Mr. Miller."

Mr. Miller's office was paneled in dark mahogany. The carpet was royal blue. On the wall was the Brooks Brothers' "Golden Fleece" logo. Underneath it was written "Established 1818".

Mr. Miller was a short, nervous, wiry little man who sat at a mahogany desk reading the Wall Street Journal. He had on a pair of black rimmed half glasses and wore a Brooks Brothers' "Maker" suit.

"Your experience is horrible! You have no real upscale retail work experience at all. Still," he looked up over his half glasses, "you have a certain look, more than a Brooks Brothers look.

I'll start you in Brooksgate at $185.00 a week plus three percent commission. No benefits for the trial period. We'll see if you make it or weed yourself out."

"Yes sir!" Budd was elated.

"When can you start?"

"How about next Monday?" asked Budd. "I've got to move my stuff here from Texarkana."

"All right, you can start in Brooksgate next Monday. We open at ten. I expect my employees to be in our second floor employees' lounge by nine-thirty. Our man will let you in our south door."

"Thank you, sir. Very much."

"I hear a lot of thank yous. They don't mean much until you're producing sales."

"Yes sir."

Budd walked out of the executive office. Cecelia McGill looked up from her work.

"I'm in! He hired me!"

"Good!" She beamed. "When do you start?"

"Next Monday."

"I'll *see* you then. I'm pleased. That's good."

Cecelia McGill was a soft and gentle young woman with a somewhat inquisitive mind and a restless air. She was different from Nicole. Nicole had the world at her command.

Budd spent the next week moving in with his sister in Dallas. If all went well he'd find an apartment.

The first hour at Brooks Brothers was spent with Larry Constant looking at rows of suits and sports coats, and stacks and stacks of shirts.

"It's a little before eleven," said Constant. "Why don't you go to lunch now? Mr. Miller likes us all on the floor at noon. We have a lot of lawyers and professional people browse during the lunch hour. They make good sales."

"Thank you. I'll see you in an hour." Budd hurried downstairs.

"Hi!"

"Hi, Budd," said Cecelia.

"What time do you go to lunch?"

"I should go now. Mr. Miller likes a full staff at noon."

"I know. Let's go."

"Oh." She looked around. "Oh, okay."

She clocked out.

"Where can we eat around here?" he asked.

"I usually eat at Sanger's lunch counter or bring my lunch."

"Let's go to Sanger's"

They walked out of the store and up to the street level and then crossed over to Sanger Harris.

They waited to be seated. They were shown to their table, ordered breakfast and began to talk.

"Tell me about yourself," he started.

"I grew up with three brothers and a sister. There wasn't much room to talk but I didn't miss much. I'm a good observer."

"Did you go to college?"

"No, I didn't. I made straight A's in highschool. We were poor. I liked to sew. I was good in English but my mother was practical. I studied home economics. I wanted to be a fashion designer. When I got out of highschool there weren't many opportunities open to me in fashion design, so I got a job as a secretary. I succeeded, and then I got another, a better one. Now here I am, a combination of the two. Brooks Brothers is fashionable enough in a conservative kind of way. Did you go to college? You must have."

"The University of Texas. I had good grades too, but I didn't finish."

"How come?"

"It's a long story."

"Forgive me."

"That's all right." He smiled. "You're forgiven."

"Were you ever in love?" she asked.

"Yes, once."

"Was she beautiful?"

"Yes, she was."

"What was her name?"

"Nickie White -- Nicole White."

"What happened?"

"It was just one of those things. It didn't work out."

She put her hand to her lip, then withdrew it. "I'm sorry. It really isn't any of my business."

"I like you," Budd said. "You're different from anyone I've ever known. It's as though you don't play chess, but you watch everyone's moves and win in your own mind." Cecelia did watch her world and made her decisions based upon those observations.

"Why, thank you, I guess. My name is Cecelia but everyone calls me Sissy."

"So it's my turn to ask the questions. Where do you live Sissy, and what do you do when you're not at Brooks Brothers?"

"I'm alone a lot. I like to be alone. I rent a trailer on four acres outside of Arlington."

"You rent a trailer... on four acres.. . outside of Arlington?"

"Yes. I drive to work everyday on the turnpike in my little green Datsun."

Sissy had purchased a new, green Datsun 1200 coupe upon getting her first job after graduating from highschool. She was very proud of the car and serviced it and changed the oil herself.

"Aren't you afraid to be out there by yourself?" he asked.

"No. I like being out in the country with the trees, the flowers and the birds.

"Not another flower child?"

"Excuse me?"

"Sorry... doesn't matter."

"Do you go to church?" she asked Budd.

"Oh, I'm a nominal Episcopalian."

"My sister and I go to a little Christian Church in Ft. Worth, Disciples of Christ. I spend lots of week-ends with my sister. People say we're two peas in a pod, my sister and I. I'm boring you."

"No, not at all," said Budd. "I find you refreshingly different."

"What was she like," she cautiously questioned, "your girlfriend?"

"We met in highschool. Went to the University together. I guess Nicole had a sort of electric-kinetic personality. She was a snow queen in a kinky kind of way."

There was a silence.

"How old are you?" she asked.

"Twenty-seven."

She looked at him and smiled. "Is Texarkana your home?"

"Yes it is."

"I've never been there."

"I'll take you some time." He looked at his watch. "We've got to get back. It's twenty 'til noon." He picked up the check.

"No," she said. "I'll pay for breakfast. You haven't had a paycheck yet. You'll need to save your money `til you get paid."

"That's one thing Nicole would have never done." He laughed. They walked out of Sanger Harris amidst tall buildings and a blue sky.

"It's a beautiful day, isn't it?" He looked up.

"Yes it is," she said softly and smiled.

"We'll have to do this again. I've enjoyed your company, very much."

"Why, thank you."

They left on a Sunday morning and went to Texarkana together for the first time. Budd had a prior engagement to play piano at the country club that particular Sunday. It was a good chance to introduce Sissy to his family and home. They took Sissy's car. Budd's red Volkswagen was now a faded rose color. The engine clattered and the mileage was high. They felt safer on the road in her car.

"I've never lived in a small town," she said as they approached Texarkana.

"Texarkana is around 50,000."

They exited off of Interstate 30, drove down Summerhill Road, crossed College Drive and turned south on Olive Street.

"Oh Budd, this is just like my Aunt Rose's neighborhood in Houston, old houses, lots of trees."

He stopped the car.

"Is this your home?"

"Yep, this is it. 1723 Olive Street, Middletown, U.S.A."

"I like it." She sighed a sigh of pleasure. "It looks homey."

They walked up the front porch steps. Mildred and Edgar Wilson met them at the front door.

"Mother, Dad, this is Cecelia McGill. We work together at Brooks Brothers."

"Hello, I'm Mildred Wilson." She extended her hand warmly,

gently to the young woman.

"This is my husband, Edgar."

"Mother we need a place to change. I"ve got to play at the country club, at noon."

"Well, you know where your room is. Cecelia, let me show you to my room"

"You can call me Sissy. All my friends call me Sissy."

They turned through the two columns. The narrow road wound its way past the condominiums on the left and the golf course on the right. They crossed the tree-lined wooden bridge and into the parking lot.

"It's beautiful," Sissy whispered as they passed through the double doors, the foyer and into the main ballroom. Women who worked in dining were putting the finishing touches on the dinner tables for the Sunday crowd. Texarkana Country Club had that certain rich, mellow, Southern ambiance.

Budd and Sissy walked across the hardwood floor of the ballroom. An old Knabe baby grand piano stood in the corner. He opened the lid.

"Still the best piano in town. I can make this thing sing soft -- just light as a feather. You can do that on an old Knabe. Oh well, we've got over a half hour to kill Let me show you around."

He opened the window-paned double doors at the back of the ballroom and they walked out onto the veranda. It was a comfortable place with old, white wooden wicker cushioned chairs. It was a bright, sunny Indian summer Sunday.

"Oh Budd, this is so beautiful." Sissy looked across the flow of the golf course at the green grass and trees. "It's like a picture book."

"It's a facade," he wryly said.

"What?" She looked at him with astonishment.

"Believe me, I know. It's a facade. I've been here enough. After all, I may be the best dressed man here today, but I'm still hired help."

"Budd, Budd Wilson!" His old friend John Hall walked up.

"Hello, Johnny," Budd replied and smiled warmly.

"Well Budd, I'll be! What are you doing now and who is this young lady with you?"

"Oh, excuse me. This is Cecelia McGill, my . . .my fiancee."

She looked up at him with astonishment. He pressed her hand in his, signaling for her to go along with what he had said in front of his friend.

"Well I'll swan! Come on. Let's go back to the grill and have a drink and celebrate this,

Cecelia." John took her hand and led them to the bar and grill "What are you doing now, Budd?

The last time I saw you, you were flyin' all over Austin, Texas, with Nickie White."

"I work for Brooks Brothers, in Dallas."

"Brooks Brothers! Well that's fine. You certainly look the part. Old Fritz Cavanaugh would have been proud of you. He would," John reflected. "Would have had a drink with us."

Johnny Hall played each scenario for what it was worth, but did so with genuine warmth.

"How 'bout you Johnny?"

"Oh, I'm a lawyer here. Divorces, bankruptcies. You name it. Anything to pay the bills and keep the lights on."

"I'll bet you're good at it. You always were a good debater and you could always think on your feet."

"We're not lettin' this young lady get in a word edgewise."

"Don't worry. I'm a good listener." Cecelia beamed. John laughed that robust, hearty laugh of his.

"Well, Cecelia, where do you work and what do you do?"

"I work at Brooks Brothers, too."

"I thought Brooks Brothers was a men's store. What do you do there?"

"Oh, we have a lovely women's section, but me, I'm a secretary." She smiled hesitantly.

"Is that pretty frock you're wearin' from Brooks Brothers?"

"This?" She smiled again. She was blushing. Her right hand started to go to her mouth to cover her insecurity -- then she purposely pulled it down. "No, I made this. I have some Brooks Brothers things, but I made this. I sew."

"Well I'll be. It's beautiful. Listen, you can make good money in a city sellin' for one of those fancy clothing places."

"Well, not as good as a home grown attorney, Johnny," said Budd somewhat patronizingly.

He was uncomfortable and felt a certain sense of inferiority in the presence of his old friend -- a professional.

"Shoot! Just keep the lights on. Just keep the lights on. Just a country lawyer, that's all."

Budd realized his feelings were unfounded.

"Johnny, we've got to go." Budd gulped down his drink. "Believe it or not I'm playing piano out here today. Some people are having a special dinner party and they asked me months ago to play."

"Are you really? Well I'll be." He turned around. "Koki," he turned to the hostess, "see that the future Mr. and Mrs. Wilson get anything they want today and set up a table for the three of us when they finish. We've got to talk about old times and future times."

"Why, thank you." Cecelia smiled. "Thank you very much. I appreciate your kindness."

Budd grabbed John around the shoulder. "Good to see ya, Johnny We'll see ya in a little bit."

Sissy and Budd walked out of the grill and into the ballroom towards the Knabe grand. The members and their families were coming in from the churches through the front double doors of the country club.

"For hired help, you certainly get along well with the members," Sissy said solemnly.

"Johnny? Yeah, he's my friend." Budd smiled. "Some of them I do." He pointed towards the people coming in the door. "Some of them I don't."

"That's life, Budd. There are all levels of people in the world, shades of gray in-between the black and white. I'll go sit down"

He started off with "A Foggy Day in London Town"

They drove down the brick street, Beech Street. He stopped in front of the decaying wall in front of the large, old two story house.

"This was my family home," he started. "My great-uncle built this place a little after the turn of the century. He was in the creosote business, the tie, timber and telephone pole business. Had a large plant south of town. It's all gone now kind of like this old house. I don't remember him very well, but I know I loved him. There are those who have been critical of him, but to me he was a kind man. I guess he was self-made if there is such a thing, a real Herbert Hoover. Made a fortune out of both world wars. Knew every pine forest in East Texas. He was the first to start refurbishing the forests when he harvested trees. I loved him. I always remember him as being kind."

"It's all impressive," she said. "They had money."

"They were comfortable."

"What was your great-aunt like?"

"Marguerite Devereaux was spoiled and tempestuous. Yes, Mizz Devereaux. No, Mizz Devereaux. She enjoyed ordering people around and always got her way."

"Sounds like a Nicole."

"Yes I guess it does. In search of Nicole. Let's get out of here."

"Mr. and Mrs. Devereaux were your family role models, weren't they?"

"Yes, they were."

"Why are you not close to your own parents, Budd? I sense you're not."

"My father and I have nothing in common. My mother will never mind her own business.

Each of them tried to choose roles for me without ever consulting me."

"Budd!"

"It's true."

"Don't ever say that about your parents. You don't entirely know what they've been through, or lived."

"My great-uncle always wanted me to be a doctor or a lawyer. I wonder what he'd think of me working at Brooks Brothers."

"Do you feel you let him down?"

"In a way."

"Brooks Brothers is one of the most prestigious clothing stores in the world. There's nothing wrong with being hired help. I've been hired help all my life. I'm very proud to work there.

Would your great-uncle have worn a Brooks Brothers suit?"

"Probably did. And if he were out inspecting a work site and something went wrong, he'd throw his coat over the fender of his company Ford, unfasten his collar, roll up his sleeves and get it dirty."

"A real hands-on man, huh?"

"Yeah he sure was."

They drove three or four more blocks up the brick street. He stopped in front of a two story Spanish stucco with an Imperial tile roof built in the 1920's

"Isn't it beautiful, Sissy? I always wanted this place to be our home."

"Our--?"

"Ours. I've always fantasized this home for my family, whomever I would be with. Come on.

It's for sale. Let's look around." They walked onto the veranda and peered through the glass into the spacious living room.

"Sissy, would you marry me?"

"I thought you'd already established that at the country club." She grinned. "I like Texarkana. I could sew with your mother. I've saved some money."

"Sissy, I'm not asking you how much money you have or how well you can sew. I'm asking you to marry me."

She watched the slightly turning trees sway in the early autumn breeze on Beech Street. He kissed her.

"This is crazy. I don't even really know you," she said. "Oh, who am I kidding? You're everything I ever wanted. I don't want to pass you by. You might never happen again." They embraced.

"I don't know what I'll do for a ring right now. I'd like for you to wear my great-aunt's.

How about me taking you to dinner to celebrate our engagement when we get back to Dallas?"

He put his arm around her waist. "Some of the guys at work have been talking about this fantastic singer at The Seasons restaurant in Energy Plaza."

"The Seasons. Of course I want to go. I don't have anything to wear."

"How about that pretty black and white dress you were wearing the first time we met?"

"No, not to The Seasons."

They took the elevator to the tenth floor. The elevator door opened and they walked into the posh lobby of The Seasons. The restaurant was on one side of the lobby and the lounge was on the other. Their reservations were confirmed and they were shown to a table overlooking North

Dallas. Not really knowing what to order, they left it to the waiter's discretion. He brought cocktails, a Scotch and water for Budd and a white wine for Sissy, a pate do foie gras for Budd and a green salad for Sissy. Then the waiter served Chateaubriand for two, and as suggested, a bottle of vintage St. Emilion. They finished with a blueberry sorbet for Budd and a creme brulee for Sissy, then a demitasse café followed by cognac.

Budd had cashed the biggest part of his two weeks' paycheck to pay for the meal. After dinner, the bill came. For a moment his heart palpitated. Then he looked down at the bill.

He had enough money for the dinner and enough left for the music to come. He was elated! It would be a good night! He could tell.

'If we thought of it,' --- She casually slung the microphone cord over her shoulder. 'bout the end of it, when we started painting the town, we'd've been aware—that our love affair was too hot not to cool down.

'So good-bye, so long and amen, here's hoping we meet now and then.

It was great fun, but it was just one of those... Doodle-le,doodle-le, doodle-le, doodle-le, doodle-le, doodle-le DO-THINGS.'

"Jane Mitchell. The Dallas Jazz Quartet. We'll return in a minute. Thank you."

She went and sat at the bar. Her dark hair was pulled back in a bun. Her long evening gown was sheer black. She had on black slippers and seamed black hose. Jane Mitchell was chic.

"I'm going to ask her to join us for a drink." Budd grinned. "Engagement and all that."

"Oh Budd, don't make a fool of yourself."

"Well." Jane looked up from her seat at the bar. "Sure. Why not?" She was not only the singer at The Seasons, but a veritable public relations person. Jane could spot someone new to the club, and she and the bartender had a ploy with house champagne to induce her new prey and make them feel welcome to come back.

"Hi. I'm Jane Mitchell." She extended her hand to Sissy. Her voice was husky. She was in command of her own territory.

"I'm Sissy McGill." She stood and introduced herself

"Sit down, please," said Jane. Both women sat down in the lounge seat next to Budd.

"I hear you're going to be married," said Jane. Budd had told her of their engagement plans at the bar.

"Yes we are," replied Sissy.

"May we buy you a drink?" asked Budd.

"No. This is your celebration. Michael!" She called the bartender.

"A bottle of champagne on the house." The bartender pulled a bottle of Pol Roger, a good house champagne, helping lay the web to impress the new customer to The Seasons, but moreover, to Jane Mitchell, the singer, the chanteuse, the seductress.

"Thank you..very much," said Sissy. She was impressed.

They had several rounds and several toasts. Jane looked at her watch. "I've got to get back."

"Before you do, do you know an old song entitled 'Embraceable You'?" questioned Budd.

"Sure."

"Would you sing it?"

"For you two?" She winked. "Sure."

From the stand she said, "I have a request from a young couple. I can only wish the best for them." She peered beyond the lights. "What are your names again?"

"Budd and Sissy," he yelled.

Jane Mitchell smiled. She set the slow beat.

'Embrace me..my sweet embraceable you.

Em-bra-ce me..you irreplaceable you.

Just one look, and BABY, my heart goes tipsy.

You and you alone, bring out the gypsy in me.

I love, I love the many charms about you.

Above all, I want my arms about you...'

HEY BUDD!!

Don't be a naughty baby...,

come to Mamma, come to Mamma, do.

MY SWEET EMBRACEABLE YOU."

The piano started to take a chorus.

"She's kind of suggestive," swallowed Sissy.

"No kidding," said Budd.

The night continued.

'I've got the world on a string,

sittin' on a rainbow.

Got the string around my finger

What a world, what a life,

I'm in love.'

***

'Spring this year has got me feeling,

like a horse that never left the post.

I lie in my room, staring up at the ceiling.

SPRING CAN REALLY HANG YOU UP THE MOST.'

***

'Where has the time all gone to?

Haven't done half the things we want to.

OH WELL,

we'll catch up some other time.'

***

'There will be many other nights like this,

and I'll be standing here with someone new.

There will be other songs to sing,

Another fall, another spring,

but there will never be another you.'

***

'There may be trouble ahead,

but while there's moonlight and music,

and love and romance,

let's face the music and dance.'

"Thank you. A song from the new show *A Little Night Music* by Stephen Sondheim."

She stood in the solitary blue spotlight.

'Isn't it rich? Are we a pair?

You here at last on the ground,

me in mid-air.

Send in the clowns.

There ought to be clowns.

Don't bother, they're here.'

"Jane Mitchell. Thank you. The Dallas Jazz Quartet. Join us at nine Tuesday night in the lounge of the beautiful Seasons restaurant in Energy Plaza Thank -you."

"You were very good!" said Budd as he walked up to the stand. Jane Mitchell was packing her music.

"Are you two still here? It's one a.m." She started to laugh.

"Devoted listeners. I need more of you."

"You really are very good," Sissy echoed. "I've never heard live music like this. You were very good."

The three stood there for a minute staring at each other, smiling.

"Would you like to join us for breakfast?" Budd blurted out.

Jane Mitchell looked around. "Why not? Just a minute, let me make a phone call." She carried on a short, private conversation then she returned to the couple. "Where to?"

"How about JoJo's up on North Central?" Budd asked.

"Okay. I've got a silver Buick convertible down in front of the first floor entrance. Follow me."

"All right."

JoJo's was crowded on a Sunday morning at 1:30 a.m.

"You don't know how many a singing job I've finished off at JoJo's or Denny's waiting for a table at one-thirty in the morning," said Jane as they waited.

"Oh I'm sorry," Budd said.

"Don't take me seriously. I'm very plain spoken."

"Table for three. Right this way."

Jane lit a cigarette and took a deep drag, exhaling through her nose.

"What do you do besides sing?" started Budd.

"I live on Bryn Mawr in University Park. I walk every day. I exercise. I paint and study languages at Richland College."

"Married?" he asked.

"Separated. Three children, a fourteen year old daughter."

"You have a fourteen year old daughter?" asked Budd. "I'm twenty-seven. You don't look any older than me."

"Budd!" Sissy exclaimed.

Jane smiled a wise, warm smile. "I'm thirty-five." She smiled again. She knew how to handle people.

Strangely enough it was a delightful evening for all of them. Budd was very knowledgeable about jazz and expressed his knowledge eloquently much to Jane's amazement. He wasn't the novice she figured him to be. They ate, talked jazz, drank coffee and talked more jazz.

"Oh." She looked at her watch. "It's nearly four. I've got to go. I've had a good time. I hope you two will be regulars at The Seasons."

"If we can afford it," said Budd. "Speaking of that, you bought the champagne. We're buying breakfast."

"Don't be silly." Jane Mitchell grabbed the check out of his hand. "I've got more money than you do, Sport."

She went fumbling through her large bag. She pulled out several cards. Finally she pulled out an American Express card. "Ah hah!" She handed it to the cashier.

"Good night," said Sissy. "Thank you for a lovely engagement evening."

"Good night, you two." Jane Mitchell flashed that smile. "We'll see you again."

Budd and Sissy walked out of the restaurant.

"Well," said Sissy, "you've graduated to Mrs. Robinson."

`It doesn't mean anything. This is our engagement celebration."

"Yes, I guess it is." She looked up at him, smiled - her fears temporarily subsided.

CHAPTER 6

Sissy gave up her trailer outside of Arlington. Budd moved out of his sister's townhouse. The two set up housekeeping in an old apartment in the 4300 block of Lomo Alto, thirty feet inside of Highland Park. Autumn led to Winter. Winter led to Spring, and Spring to Summer. It was hot and each day they would ride the Lemmon Avenue bus home from work and take the Lomo Alto stop. They'd cross the street to the bar at Strictly Tabu on the corner of Lomo Alto and Lemmon and have a cool drink, then they'd walk the two-and-a-half blocks home to the apartment. The apartment was spacious and a murphy bed folded out of the wall. A large, old, Philco window air-conditioner cooled the entire apartment. Sissy would begin dinner, but before the dishes were done the murphy bed had been pulled down and the lights were turned off. You could hear the cool air purring out of the Philco. It was summer and it was hot. It was a year of good times with old friends from Texarkana spent at The Seasons and at happy hour dinners at The Filling Station and Annie Santa Fe's. The juke box at The Knox Street Pub played "I Can't Get Started With You" by Bunny Berrigan and "Gloomy Sunday" by Billie Holiday. Jane Mitchell sang "What's Your Story, Morning Glory?" and a catchy tune called "I'm Hip" by Dave Frishberg and Bob Dorough. The trio, Jane, Sissy and Budd took in the Dallas Symphony open air concerts at Lee Park, sitting on blankets in front of Turtle Creek across from the park. They caught the Marshall Ivory Quartet at the Recovery Room, and Fred Crane and sometimes Red Garland at the 6051 Club. Jane Mitchell was married by name only. Sissy and Budd talked of moving to Texarkana.

They left Brooks Brothers one day at lunch. They walked to Thanksgiving Square. The conversation about leaving the city began.

"I don't know what we'd do, but let's go home before the whole thing falls apart," she started.

"Why should it?" he asked.

"Jane. I mean I like Jane. I like her very much, and I know you haven't done anything. It's just.. .let's go home...before you do." She turned and looked at the traffic then she turned back to Budd. "I love you and I don't want to lose you to anybody. I used to love this city. Well I'm tired of it. I love Texarkana now. Let's go home." She paused. "What would we do?" She changed the subject to practicalities.

"I don't know. You're a good secretary. You could always get a job. The new mall's open. A recommendation from Brooks Brothers swings weight anywhere. I'm sure it would in Texarkana. We'll turn in our resignations today. Can we live off of some of your savings until we get a paycheck?"

"Yes, of course. Are you sure this is what you want?" she asked.

"Yes, I am. I'm positive."

After their resignations were accepted, Budd rented a U-haul truck. He called an old friend of his who was a student at El Centro Community College. His friend offered to help them pack.

They worked throughout the afternoon and early evening. They loaded the van and attached one vehicle to it. Later that night, Budd and Sissy got into the other car and went to tell Jane the news.

It was quiet at The Seasons.

'We may never ever meet again, on the bumpy road to love. Yet I'll always, always keep the memory of..., the way you hold your knife, the way we danced 'til three, the way you've changed my life, no no, they can't take that away from me. No, they can't take that away. No, they can't take that away. No, they can't take that away from me.'

"Thank you. Thank you very much."

It was a Tuesday night. Jane Mitchell took a break. She walked over to Budd and Sissy, who'd just come in.

"What's cooking, gang?" She sat down at the table with the two.

"We quit Brooks Brothers today," started Budd. "We negotiated, and they let us leave."

"I'm sure they appreciated that." Jane was instantly impatient with the couple.

"We rented a U-Haul after lunch," Sissy explained. "An old friend of Budd's helped us pack everything. We're going back to Texarkana -- tonight."

"I see," Jane said. "Well you always wanted to. So be it."

"We love you Jane."

"Back at you honey. Back at you. I am overwhelmed." She sighed and laughed at the same time. "My goodness, I suppose I should sing." She approached the stand then conferred with her pianist. She sat on the stool and deliberately thought how she'd address the song and her feelings. The pianist did a slow introduction. The blue spot shown on her.

Slowly she looked up:

'Maybe I should have saved those leftover dreams,

FUNNY, but here's that rainy day.

Here's that day that they all warned me about,

and I laughed at the thought that it might turn out this way.

Where is that worn out wish that I threw aside,

after it brought my lover near?

Funny how love becomes a cold rainy day.. .

Funny. . . oh so funny. . . that rainy day is here.'

She looked up and they were gone.

It was two a.m. The battered U-Haul was somewhere between Greenville and Sulpher Springs, Texas, on the way to Texarkana. At best, it would make forty miles per hour. Budd towed one car. Sissy drove the other car. The sky was full of stars. If one looked carefully, one could see the big dipper. At 6:15 a.m., they pulled in front of the Wilson home, 1723 Olive Street.

To Budd's surprise, Brooks Brothers only swung weight in Texarkana with a privileged few in the retail clothing crowd. To the average departmental head the question was "Brooks who?" Doubleknits were popular and everyone wore jeans in Texarkana.

A man in a three-piece, worsted wool suit was kind of an anachronism. Once again, Budd Wilson was "hired help".

Sissy immediately landed a job as a secretary with one of the biggest law firms in town. Budd had a harder time finding work. He began to get melancholy. To him it seemed his entire life had taken a tailspin and a great part of him lingered in Dallas. Finally he got a job with a department store in the recently opened mall. Sissy found an apartment in a suburb of Texarkana. They moved out of his parents' home. It took nearly all of her savings to make the transaction.

Budd and Sissy were wed in a small Christian ceremony.

They kept their ties with Jane. The next April, she spent a weekend in Texarkana with them. Although she was their guest, the apartment was only one bedroom and it was overflowing at the seams. Jane would sleep alone in Budd's bed in his parents' home.

Count Basie and his orchestra were coming to Texarkana for a concert. Jane would be Budd and Sissy's guest for the event. Count Basie was known even in Texarkana and those people there who enjoyed big bands were excited. The jazz community of the town was small but fiercely loyal. It was headed by a man named Jimmy Aldon, a Texarkana businessman and the host of a Saturday afternoon jazz show on the local PBS radio station. He was a good saxophonist and an expert on modern jazz. What Budd knew of progressive jazz he had learned from Jimmy, as opposed to Dixieland, which he had learned from Fritz Cavanaugh.

Jimmy Aldon was of the "Cool School" from BeBop to West Coast on to modern jazz. Unbeknownst to Budd, Aldon and his wife Betty were having an early cocktail party for Jane that night in their home before the concert. Budd heard Aldon on the phone. "Budd Wilson, we're having a party for Jane Mitchell NOW. Come on over."

"Did you tell him I was coming?" she asked.

"I may have mentioned it. Yes."

"Oh well, I guess we should go." Jane knew that her talent alone had not made her a success, but that it equally depended on how she worked her fans. She bordered on being ruthless in her pursuit to keep them happy. It all went together to create Jane Mitchell, the jazz icon of Dallas in the late 1970s, early 1980s.

"I'll stay here." Sissy grew pensive. "I've got some things to do."

Jane and Budd did a double take.

"Sissy are you sure?"

"Yes. You two go ahead."

"Okay. . . ?"

Budd and Jane both knew something was wrong with Sissy. Not being able to pry anything out of her, they reluctantly went on.

Jimmy greeted Budd and Jane at the door of his home. The living room and den were full of people, and the bar was going strong. They made the necessary rounds meeting everyone, then Aldon brought up a small audio cassette recorder.

"Jane, as you know, I host a jazz show on the local PBS radio station. We'd like to tape a little of this for our listeners who aren't here tonight. Do you mind?"

"Oh no. Certainly not." She smiled.

"How did you get your start in music?" He adjusted the dials on the machine.

"I originally sang folk music in coffee houses in the middle sixties."

"And from there?" Aldon asked.

"I heard Anita O'Day and Chris Connor, and I knew I wanted to sing jazz. One thing led to another -- I developed my own style, and here I am."

"Could you sing a little something tonight for our listeners, while I've got the recorder on?"

"Well, yeah -- sure." She looked at the piano, then at Budd. " Could you help me?"

"Jane, I've never backed you before," Budd replied.

"You can do it." She flashed that big smile. "'Spring Can Really Hang You Up the Most' in the key of 'C'."

"I don't know the intro."

"It doesn't matter, we'll start with the chorus. You can do it ... You can do it."

And so they began. . . . . . and later, they joined the Aldon party to hear Count Basie at the Perot Theater.

"One More Time!

April in Paris.

Whom Can I Turn to?

April in Paris.

"Just One More Once!

April in Paris.

Whom Can I Turn to?

APRIL IN PARIS.

"Jingle Bells, Jingle Bells,

JINGLE ALL THE WAY."

"Thank you. Thank you! Count Basie and his Orchestra. The Count Basie Orchestra."

The Basie bus had stopped in Texarkana that night for a needed rest. The band's next concert was Tuesday in Baton, Rouge, Louisiana, so they took a breather and some of the members were to come over to the Aldons' after the show to have a few drinks, to listen to some recordings and to share their love of music. It was a public relations affair in part sponsored by the college radio station and Aldon himself. As people dispersed from the the theater, Budd and Jane got in the car to head back.

"I'm worried about Sissy," Budd said as they drove away from the theater.

"I am too," Jane replied. "Do you think we should go to the Aldons'?"

"I'll take you out there," he said. "You go ahead. Someone will give you a ride back. I think I'm going to go home."

"No. No, let's both go home. That's that." Jane readjusted her priorities.

They pulled into the driveway and walked into the apartment.

"Sissy, what on earth is the matter with you?" Jane asked.

She looked at them both and smiled.

"I found out Friday, I'm pregnant."

"That's wonderful!" said Budd. "That's truly wonderful."

Jane's eyes darted from side to side. She looked out into space, then her eyes seemed to come back into herself as she regained her composure hiding the pain. She flashed that smile— the smile she smiled every night from the stand as she faced her listeners, a smile she owed to her public, for they wanted her happy whether she was sick or well, elated or depressed, that smile that no matter what, defined the strength of Jane Mitchell and she said, "Well, little momma's going to be a mother. That's fantastic. Let's pop a bottle of Perrier or Canada Dry ginger ale. No more drinking for nine months."

Budd wanted to be alone with Sissy. He wanted to share some intimate, private time with his wife but he didn't possess the tact to know how to get rid of Jane. They sat way into the night trying to think of names. It narrowed down to William Devereaux Wilson if it was a boy, and Jennifer Lee Wilson if it was a girl. Later on that night, after he had taken Jane to his parents' house, he was finally alone with his wife and the mother of his child to be.

She started timing the beats around seven p.m. Budd got her in the car and raced to his parents' house which was closer to Municipal Hospital. Around ten-thirty, Sissy went into the hospital. She had been pre-admitted. All she had to do was give her name.

The anxious father and grandparents waited. It had been a rough night. Neither Sissy nor the baby had made any significant move. A spinal bloc had to be administered. By nine in the morning the doctor had decided on a C-section.

Mother and child were wheeled through the hall so family and guests could have their first glimpse of the newest Wilson – Jennifer Lee.

"She has red hair! Look Budd, she has red hair. I can't believe it!" Sissy said with astonishment.

"She's an active baby," said the doctor. "She'll be an active child."

"And what is the name of this child?" asked Father Thomas.

"Jennifer Lee," said the mother and father. "Jennifer Lee."

A pink, floral wreath was placed on the door by Budd's father. It said, "It's a girl."

Later, after all the commotion had died down and mother and daughter were sleeping, Budd went back to his parents' home and picked out a tune on his father's piano—Thad Jones' "A Child is Born".

There was no room for the expanded Wilson family in the apartment. Budd heard of a good deal on a small, white World War II bungalow in Wake Village. Wake Village was a community outside of Texarkana that had been built during the Second World War. Budd had changed jobs twice now. He had always thought of himself as a salesman. However his ability to sell seemed to diminish each day. All he yearned for were the trips to Dallas to listen to jazz and see Jane.

Once every two or three months Budd and Sissy would take off for a week-end to visit her. They'd be guests at her home on Bryn Mawr. Once every few months, Jane would reciprocate and come to Texarkana to see Budd, Sissy and her God-daughter, Jennifer Lee.

Budd was doing heavy labor for a chemical company. He was doing work that a man ten years younger should do. He couldn't keep up with it. Budd's employer found it convenient to dismiss him. The couple needed Budd's insurance . Sissy tried frantically to convert the company's hospitalization policy to an individual policy. The conversion could be made, but at a great loss of benefits and at a higher price.

He and Sissy began fighting. The baby would cry hearing them argue. Budd was getting severe migraines. He would try to pick up Sissy from work. She would drive home, because a combination of migraines and car sickness would make him violently ill. He threw up each time he was a passenger in the car.

Jane kept calling. Why didn't the two of them and the baby come to Dallas and live with her until they could find a job? She could afford it. By this time, even Sissy was desperate. They took her up on it.

As soon as they got to Dallas, his migraines disappeared. Sissy's boss in Texarkana had taken an interest in her as an employee and a person. Although he didn't completely understand the situation, he tried to set Sissy up with interviews in Dallas with some attorneys he knew there. Sissy's first interview was with a law firm on the thirty-sixth floor of a major downtown building. Jane drove them down there. After Sissy had gone in for her interview, Budd and Jane took the elevator to the first floor. In jeans, T-shirts and sneakers, they walked out into the bright sunlight.

"Sing us a tune, Jane, my dear."

They looked up at the tall buildings and walked down the sidewalk. She began singing,

"I'll take Manhattan, the Bronx and Staten Island, too. . ."

"How 'bout 'A Foggy Day In London Town?'" he interrupted.

"...had me blue,"

She took off at a terrific pace.

" had me down.

Then suddenly, I saw you there,

and through foggy London town

the sun was shining everywhere."

"I like it slower," he said.

"I don't. I like to really swing it," she replied. They kept walking.

"Ah hah!" she said and looked back, "the Oyster Bar. Perhaps we should have a tiny drink, only one, while we wait for Sissy. Dutch treat, of course. Dutch treat."

They walked into the cool bar.

"Hello, Johnny "

"Hi Jane. What'll be?"

"Oh, a spritzer."

"And for the gentleman?"

"A gin and tonic, thank you," said Budd.

"This one's on me." She reached in her purse and handed the bartender a twenty dollar bill.

"You always were generous."

"Only with those I love." She looked down. Then she looked up, straight into his eyes.

"God I missed you, Jane." He sighed both in sorrow and relief.

"I know. Me, too. I know. Well, drink up. The next one's on you."

They walked around the long block and stopped at a couple of bars along the way. It was a good thing the lawyers' office where Sissy was interviewing was well insulated for when she came out of her interview, Budd and Jane were sitting on the floor of the hallway by the elevator singing, "If you don't happen to like me, deal me out, thank you kindly, pass me by."

"Hi," said Budd. He was having too good of a time to be embarrassed.

"Look at you two, Spike and Spud. Never a sorrier sight."

"Didn't bother you, did we?" asked Jane.

"No," she said softly, "not having shorthand is what is bothering me."

"Let's go have some coffee," suggested Jane.

"Let's do." Sissy began to laugh. "Looks like you two could use some. Where on earth have you been?"

"We stumbled across a bar and kept stumbling thereafter," said Budd.

"Well, stumble into the elevator. I heard that the vending machines are on the tenth floor."

"Shit, I can't get up," struggled Jane.

"My dear, may I be ever so humble as to assist you?"

"You never were humble," Jane gracefully asserted.

"You two." Sissy rolled her eyes and punched the elevator button. "Whatever am I going to do with you?"

The elevator door opened on the tenth floor. They sipped coffee. Jane took a drag off of a cigarette.

"They require shorthand. I never had it. They say all the law firms in Dallas require shorthand. I never had it."

"Well, why don't you two get a job at a Steak 'N Ale or someplace as one of those husband and wife duos waiting tables? I could check at The Seasons."

"You mean we'd have to answer to you?" asked Budd.

"Certainly." She took another drag off her cigarette.

"What if I played somewhere?" Budd had never really played piano anywhere other than at the country club and for some private parties in Texarkana. To play piano in a large, musically competitive city like Dallas was a little bit frightening to him. Dallas had it's share of good musicians. He saw himself as a limited pianist, at best.

"You know, play the piano," he continued.

The two women looked at him.

"It might be our inside card," said Jane.

"You may be right," said Sissy.

Budd went from place to place with little more than some promises from people. He sat in here and there. He got some compliments. The Wilsons had been in Dallas two weeks with no jobs. They missed Jennifer who had been staying with Budd's parents. Sissy helped Jane get ready for work one Friday night.

"We're going on in later tonight and get Jenny," said Sissy as she worked with Jane's hair.

"Bring her here?"

"Yes."

"Oh I'd like that very much." Jane looked at herself in the mirror and smiled. "I'd like that very much."

"I guess we'll be back sometime Monday or Tuesday," Sissy continued.

"It'll be nice to have a baby in the house." Jane softly giggled. "It's been a while."

"Don't tell anyone Jane and they will never know the difference."

"Hah! That's a laugh!"

The Wilson family, Budd, Sissy and Jennifer arrived in Dallas on Tuesday evening. Jane had already gone to the club. The three Wilsons lay in bed in the master bedroom and watched T.V.

"Daughter dear and I are going to sleep," Sissy said to Budd over the ten o'clock news. "It's after ten o'clock and tomorrow's going to be a long day. After all we've got to find a job, two jobs. You going to sleep?"

"No, I guess not. I'll go in the living room and wait for Jane to come in."

"Good night Darling."

"Good night," he said.

He turned out the light, closed the bedroom door and walked into the living room. He fell asleep on the living room floor. The opening of the front door woke him. He stood up. And just like that, they were in each other's arms.

"God I missed you," she said.

"I'm not supposed to miss you, but I did too." He pulled her to the floor. Around four a.m., he went back to bed with his family. Sissy was asleep. He thought for the remainder of the night.

He had a child, now. There was a child involved. Things were different. He was married and had a child. They weren't making progress in Dallas. He could not stand riding the fence. It made him dead anxious. He wanted to solidify his relationships one way or the other. Siding with his family was the least complicated and most sensible choice to make. At the time he felt such a decision would be the least painful for all concerned.

"Honey, would you and Jennifer like to go home for good? No more Dallas?" he asked Sissy at the breakfast table. Jane was still asleep.

"Yes," she said with a combination of joy and sadness, "let's go home." Later that day they told Jane.

"But you mustn't! You've just barely tried Dallas. Budd, you're a good piano player.

Because you don't know shorthand?" She bit her lip. She looked at the two of them. "When are you leaving?"

"Tonight," said Budd.

"You always leave me in the middle of the night. You always have. You always leave me in the middle of the night. Well, at least come down to The Seasons for a drink and dinner before you go . . . on me."

"We'd love to," said Sissy.

They left the baby with Janel's daughter for the evening. They walked into the bar of The Seasons. Jane was on the stand. She turned to face him. It was obvious to whom she was singing. He was both proud and embarrassed. They pushed through the crowd and found a table halfway back through the room, across from the bar.

'I want a Sunday kind of love, a love to last past Saturday night.'

His heart ached. What if he never saw her again?

'I'd like to know it's more than love at first sight., I want a Sunday kind of love.'

"Who's that guy with his wife Jane's singing to?" asked one man at the bar.

"I don't know, but he must have something," said the other.

'I do my Sunday dreaming, and all my Sunday scheming

every minute, every hour, every day.'

"Jane's got a lot of nerve. I feel sorry for his wife, poor lady," said a middle-aged female patron.

'Will I ever see her again? Will I ever see her again?'

'I''m hoping to discover a certain kind of lover who'll show me the way. My arms need someone to enfold to keep me warm when Mondays grow colder'

"Come on, Sis. Let's get the hell out of here. Everyone's looking at me. Let's get Jennifer and go home."\

'A love for all my life to have and to hold... I want a Sunday kind of love.'

"But Budd, aren't you having a good time?" asked Sissy.

'I want a Sunday kind of love. . . .'

Jane watched them walk out the door.

'I want a Sunday kind of love.'

When Budd and Sissy left for Dallas, Budd's parents maintained the lease on their house for two more months. This would give them ample time to move their furniture and belongings should they find jobs in Dallas, and a home to go to if they had to return to Texarkana. When they came back to Texarkana, Sissy was fortunate to get her old job back with the law firm.

"What's wrong with me? Why can't I inspire you like Jane or Nicole?" Sissy asked as they sat in their living room one evening soon after they returned from Dallas.

"You just can't."

"Am I no good in bed?"

"Sissy you know that's not true."

"Well what have I got to do to get you up and do something, or is it your privilege to sit around and feel sorry for yourself because you married the wrong woman? What makes you think it would be any better or easier with the right one?"

"Sissy, don't say that!"

They watched T.V. The Glenn Miller Story was playing that night on the Saturday night movie. As Miller lost his life over the English Channel during World War II, Sissy began to cry.

"I love you," she said.

He turned to her.

"I love you," she said again. "Doesn't that mean anything to you? Doesn't it?"

She was hurt, frustrated.

"I was talking to Jane today," he said.

"You CALLED Jane Mitchell? Here we are with one income and you're sitting at home calling Jane Mitchell - long distance!!? How often do you call Jane Mitchell?"

"Almost every day for the last two or three weeks unless she calls me."

"That does it!" She turned to face him. Jennifer was in tears. "First Nicole, then Jane. I want a divorce."

"Sissy, let's get in the car and ride around and talk about it," said Budd.

They got in Sissy's car. Jennifer was crying harder.

"There's nothing to talk about!" Sissy continued.

They started the drive up one street and down another.

"Can't you change your mind?" asked Budd.

"No!"

"What about the future?" he asked.

"It's too late for a future with me. Live for yourself or for Jenny who is sitting in the back seat crying. I'm sorry this had to happen, Budd, but it's over."

"You won't change your mind?" he asked again as they stopped in front of Budd's parents' home.

"No."

"Then leave me. Just go and leave me."

He would go by the house every morning at seven to see Jennifer and her mother before she went to work. Then, it had to stop.

"Budd, please don't come by here anymore in the mornings."

"Is there another man?"

"That's my business, Budd."

He walked down the sidewalk to his car. Jennifer was hiding behind her mother's housecoat.

"Bye, Jenny," he cried. "Bye-bye, Sissy."

He started the motor.

"Bye, Jenny. Bye, Sis."

He pulled onto the access road of Interstate 30 at Mt. Vernon, Texas, around 8:15 Monday morning He hadn't eaten breakfast and he was hungry. Down the road was a little café. On the sign it said, "Breakfast, Lunch and Dinner." People were inside but the doors were locked. He rapped on the window and caught the waitress's eye.

"Are you open?"

She read his lips, came to the door and unlocked it.

"Just some ole' timers. Come on in. We're opening later, now. Just don't get the business anymore."

"Think you can stir up a couple of doughnuts and a cup coffee?"

"Sure."

"Say, you know where the Chamber of Commerce is?"

"Just up the access road, take a left over the interstate, and that'll lead you right into town. You can't miss it."

"Thanks." Budd smiled. He finished his doughnuts and coffee.

"More coffee?"

"No thanks. I got a full day in front of me." He picked up his insurance referral slips and his briefcase. He got into the small Toyota and backed out of the parking lot, then headed up the access road toward the bridge over Interstate 30.

"Now, I've got to stop at that Exxon and get some gas."

Suddenly two slips fell from his hand and dropped to the car floor. He reached down to pick them up.

There was a crash. The Exxon was in front of him—then it was behind him—then everything was whirling at breathtaking speed with tremendous centrifugal force—then THUD, the car stopped.

"I can't get this car to start." Blood was all over him and the inside of the car. "I can't get this damned thing to start. I'll just have to walk over to that Exxon."

People were running up from every direction.

"What' sa matter? I'm okay."

"We can't get the door open."

"I'm okay. I can walk."

"No you can't. Just sit still."

A paramedic who had just gotten off duty and was on her way home had seen the wreck and stopped. She radioed for the ambulances to come and rushed to render help.

"I'm okay. I can walk."

"You're injured. You may be bleeding internally. You've been in a bad wreck. Sit there quietly. Don't move."

"I'm okay. I can walk. I can walk to that Exxon."

"Be quiet. Just sit there and be quiet." She ran to her truck and brought a bandage to put on Budd's bleeding forehead. The ambulances arrived.

"What are all the ambulances doing here? I'm okay. Really, I'm okay."

"The door's jammed," said one of the EMTs to the other. "It's flimsy. We'll have to pry it off. Push the seat back, completely down."

"It won't move."

"Break it."

"I'm okay."

"We're going to have to lift him out of the seat onto the stretcher." They pried the door open.

"I can walk."

"Be quiet!"

They lifted the stretcher next to the horizontal bucket seat and gently slid Budd from one to the other. He looked back to what was left of the Toyota. It was only then that he realized he had been in a wreck. The EMTS were loading Budd and the other people into the ambulances.

"Are you okay?" Budd asked one of the other people from the other car. "Are you okay?

"Be quiet!" The heavy doors of the ambulance shut behind him.

The intense surgical lamp was shining in his face, blinding him to where he was.

"Please don't cut that off. It's a Pendleton."

"Be quiet. We're going to give you a little shot to make you calmer and ease the pain."

He didn't know when he woke up. He didn't know where he was. He didn't even know what room he was in. Instinctively, it started coming back to him. He reached for the phone by his bed.

"Operator." He gave the hospital operator the number and asked her to charge the call to his room.

"Sissy, I've been in a wreck. It was a bad one. I don't know where I am."

"Your mother called me. How are you feeling?"

"Fine. Okay."

"You need to get some rest, Budd. I'm busy right now, besides you need to get some rest. Do you want me to tell Jennifer anything for you?"

"Yeah." He thought for a minute. "Ma, Pa, it was a tough fight, but I won."

"Budd. You've been in a very bad wreck. I'm -- very busy. I'll have to go. I'll see you later."

"Bye."

Sissy got up from her desk at the law office and stared out of the eighth-floor window. She tapped her red fingernails nervously over and over on the counter. "He wasn't wearing a seatbelt." She shook her head at the information Budd's mother had given her. "He wasn't even wearing a seatbelt. I'll be."

For a week Budd sat in the hospital alone. His parents had rented a car to take care of their needs. It was their car he'd wrecked. On the day of his dismissal they drove to Mt. Vernon to pick him up. He was instructed by the doctors to lie down on the back seat for the trip home. He had a concussion. The three of them drove by the salvage yard behind the Chevrolet dealership. There sat the mangled Toyota. Only then did they realize the severity of the accident.

That night he and his parents sat around the kitchen table. His parents were setting rules. They loved to set rules when Budd was vulnerable.

"Since this was your fault, I guess you know our insurance rates are going to go way up?"

"Daddy, it was an accident. Is this really the time to talk about it?"

"It certainly is." His mother jumped into the conversation. "You listen to your father." By and large, she fought his father's battles for him. "You've caused us a lot of trouble and expense. Let me tell you something. I will never let you use a car of ours again, young man! You don't need to be working. You need to be on disability."

"Mother, I'm thirty-six years old. I need to have SOME life of my own."

"Well you don't behave like you're thirty-six years old. You don't act like an adult. You don't act like you want a life of your own. You act like some adolescent tearing around in that car and tearing it up."

"Mother, it was an accident."

"I think you were trying to attract attention, sympathy from Sissy now that you don't have her."

"I was not."

"You are not to leave this house under any circumstances. When we buy a new car, you are not to use it for anything. Do you understand me?"

"But I make my living in a car."

"Not anymore. Nor will you use it for dating. If you want a date, you'll have to have her come pick you up. They do that these days, as we well know. And don't expect a penny from your father and Ito pay for it either. Besides, you should be doing everything you can to make amends with Sissy, involved with that trashy singer friend of yours in Dallas."

"Mother!"

"When I think of all the money your father and I put out on you for you to go to the University of Texas only for you to come home because you were having problems with that little tramp, Nicole White. You couldn't cope! You couldn't cope! It's disgusting."

"To my knowledge, the Devereaux estate paid for most of my college. You don't care about me. All you want me to do is to wait on you hand and foot in your old age."

"I think you should have realized a long time ago you won't have any choice. You know you're mentally ill. I want to take you immediately to apply for social security disability."

"Let me tell you something," the anger had been building up in Budd, "I may be disabled, but I'm strong enough to beat the shit out of you!" He addressed his father rather than his mother. "Go on, get out of here!

Go on! Go on!"

"You are being abusive to a poor old couple." His father made his first real defense for the evening.

"We're going to notify the appropriate authorities. We are not going to let you get away with this."

"Daddy, you're always wanting some peace and quiet. Well, get the hell out of here, I want some for a change!"

"Alright, we're leaving," said his mother. "It's obvious you're dangerous right now."

"I'm not dangerous. I'm just sick of you. I want to be alone."

They left. He heard them get into the car. He sat at the kitchen table for a long, long while. Then he got up and walked to the grand piano in the living room. He tinkled on the keys for a few minutes and then began to softly sing:

'Won't you tell her please to put on some speed, follow my lead.. .oh, how I need.. .. . . Someone to watch over me.'

CHAPTER 7

The doorbell rang.

"Mr. Wilson, you'll have to come with us." They put the handcuffs on his wrists and the shackles around his ankles. "You have been reported to be violent. We have a warrant for your commitment."

"I'm not going to hurt anybody."

"Come on!" They lifted him across the street and into the waiting patrol car.

He sat in the lock-up ward of the psychiatric unit on the fifth floor of Municipal Hospital. He kept looking at the young blonde in her early thirties through the wire meshed glass window. She looked so very much like someone he'd known in the past. On the second day she took her key, unlocked the door and sat down by him.

"Nickie!" he exclaimed.

"Hello, Budd."

"What are you doing here?" Was he having a vision? Was it a delusion?

"I work here. I'm a psychiatric social worker."

"You mean you're a shrink?"

"Of sorts," she said. "I'll be working with Dr. Dodd in your cases. We've talked about this quite a bit. We feel that I might serve a more useful role in communicating with you than anyone else. Again, this was discussed. It's an experiment. Budd, I'm not going to spoil you -- no matter what happened in the past. Do you understand that?"

"Yes."

"I see that your parents haven't changed much. So be it." The precocious wit of Nickie White -- teenager and college student, had matured into the frank cynic, Nicole Smithson, a professional woman in her early thirties.

"My parents can fool everybody with all their sanctimonious bit."

"You did run them out of their own house."

"So what? I wanted to be alone."

"I think it's accurate to say your parents have put out so many mixed signals to you throughout the years that it's no wonder that you're 'crazy.' I hope you don't mind me using that word. And, it seems to me that you've developed a very complex and manipulative coping system to deal with your inability to function in this world. It's a complement to your intelligence, but emotionally, right now, it's not working too well for you."

"I'm okay."

"No, you're not. I see you're living life as a hermit on a tightrope. You're not functioning very well." She looked up. "Budd, do you still smoke?"

"Yes."

"Yeah, me too." She smiled. "I shouldn't do this. I'm breaking every ethics rule in the book. Nurse, bring Mr. Wilson a cigarette. Budd, you're not totally crazy. You understand, you're here on a thirty day restraining order."

"Yes. All things considered, I'd rather be."

"Why?"

"You're... fair. It's good to see you."

"Budd, I'm not going to indulge you. I'm not going to let that manipulative system of yours control me. What happened with your parents the other night?"

"I needed to be alone. There's nothing wrong with me. I promise."

"I'm not sure, Budd. I think you've had several really hard years where you put out a lot of effort, got little in return, and no pats on the back from anybody."

"Doesn't everybody?"

"Not necessarily . Your parents said you threatened them. Did you actually threaten them, or did you just run them off?"

"I told them to get out of the God-damned house and leave me alone for a while. I'd just been in a wreck. I have a concussion. All they do is nit-pick away at me, nit-pick away. If I was going to do something violent to them, I would have done it LONG before now."

"I think you're right. Your parents need for you to be ill if for no other reason than to take care of them in their old age. They have no intention of getting rid of you. It's a power play on their part. A pretty expensive one, emotionally and financially for you. After all, who's going to pay for this? They won't. They'll leave it to you and your work insurance to clean up what is part of a mess they created. Perhaps it has something to do with your humble beginnings. We'll get to that."

She looked around, then back to Budd. "I think you clearly have some problems and this is an ideal place to work them out. I can't see that you have any other option, at this point. Maybe you do. Maybe it is just a colossal power play on their part. At any rate, you're here. And, I am not going to spoil you. Remember that. I am your counselor."

"Yes Ma'am. You're the boss, Nicole. You always were."

"Okay. . ." She stared him straight in the eye. "I'll write orders for you to be put on the open ward today. You're not going to hurt anybody. You're just a loudmouth, always were. Funny, I've always thought you were basically a gentleman. We'll see."

The days went by -- good days bad, bad days good.

They didn't allow children as visitors on the psychiatric ward. However, Nicole thought it might be good for Budd to see his daughter and conversely. She bent the rules. She asked Budd's mother to bring Jennifer to the waiting room outside the psychiatric unit to see her father. Budd was allowed to go into the waiting room and visit. Nicole remained in an inconspicuously hidden corner of the room.

"She's beautiful! She certainly has some characteristics of her father," said Nicole after Jennifer and her grandmother had departed.

"Somehow, Nickie, her whole personality and looks remind me more of you than her mother."

After Jenny had gone home, the walls came up and engulfed him. Nicole and Budd walked back onto the unit. Suddenly he wanted to run, to hide anywhere.

"Dr. Dodd," he said as he confronted his administrative psychiatrist in the hall, "I want to go home. Just go home and read my books and be with Jenny."

"You run from closeness more than anyone I've observed," said Dr. Dodd.

"Who am I running from?"

"Nicole, for one. Look Budd, if you want to go, I'll write your papers at five p.m., this afternoon, and you may leave if your parents will have you. I pity what your life will be like if you go back home. You'll be their servant 'til they die -- then God knows what will happen to you. Or perhaps they may decide to send you to the state hospital now and get rid of you forever -- with the real possibility you'll never see them or Jennifer or anyone else from your life as you know it again. Frankly at this point in your life you don't have a lot of options. Right now, you're not grounded on much. You can't work. Budd, look at me: Before I write those papers I want to talk to you about your condition, because I think if you stay through this treatment program here you stand the possibility of having a good future. You're bright, and I think you have the intelligence to conceptualize some things that some people on this ward can't. Come sit with me." Dr. Dodd led Budd to a couch in the hall and motioned for him to sit down beside him.

"Budd, part of your psyche, I think, is missing. It's very important that you understand this part of your being so that you won't keep running into the same problems over and over."

" What are you talking about? I just want to go home and be with my daughter."

"Budd, now listen to me, please. Your ability to grow emotionally has been arrested. This is partially due to your heredity, but moreover, to your upbringing, your environment. I think you have a very strong personality, and I don't think that your father does. You've chosen to back away from growth at each step, and your father has not been assertive in pushing you forward. I think your personal growth as a strong, male child needed a strong father figure. The force in your family has been your mother.

"I just want to go..."

"Please, Budd... As a result, you have not acquired the structure to be a full, grown, productive male. As normal adults, we move forward at each growth step. Instead of forward, at each step you've moved backwards toward the womb. This may not make a lot of sense to you all at once.

"I just..."

"Budd, let's put it this way, it's difficult to maintain a love relationship when you can't maintain a job. You can't get very far. As for you, you latch onto some very powerful women to pull you through. But, in your case it doesn't work. Why? They ultimately sense you can't carry your own load, and when you lose at love you get ill and retreat into the womb. By most accounts, you cannot succeed without that mature male ego structure, and yours is so thin that when it's bruised, you bang from mood swing to mood swing, from job to job, and back to the womb. From what I've observed, you will not be happy without a special kind of woman who will participate in your success. I know that you want to work. I know you have tried countless times to hold a job. Maybe you are trying to do the wrong type of work, or maybe you are just getting too much flak from home when you try to be independent. I don't know. This much I think is clear: Your parents both want you to work, as long as you don't outshine your father's ego, which means you can't do a hell of a lot. They want you to produce money for their home, as long as it's not too much. If you produce a small amount -- but not enough to be independent, they have you exactly where they want you. God forbid you make enough money to be on your own! And if you do, I truly believe they'll do everything in their power to stop you, especially if you get involved in sales or business, as opposed to "the arts" or liberal government service -- as would be their choice for you. Budd -- pay attention -- when you do work, particularly if you are showing some signs of independence, they will do everything in their power to thwart you from succeeding, anything from something as mild as calling you a social climber, which I observe gets under your skin more than anything anyone could say to you, to maintaining control over the tools you use to work with, like their car. Why can't they make a down payment on a car and let you make the payments yourself out of the profits you make from working? Why can't they encourage you to be independent? Part of it is your own fault, Budd. You can out-power your father, coming and going. With all of your talk of 'The American Dream' and 'The Self Made Man' you're a little bit lazy. In some misguided way, you expect to have all the tools given to you to work with when you begin a job. Why can't you buy what you need for your job as you can afford it? I see that as part of the trouble with inherited wealth. You have no sense emotionally of what you're worth, what you've earned, and as we both have learned here, inherited wealth with you and your family has some pretty serious strings attached to it, especially wealth that your parents control, and they always make sure they have the ties to that money and how it is spent. I've confirmed that the Wilson family inherited a tidy some of money from your great aunt and great uncle, but not enough for all four of you to have everything you want. My notes show your father didn't inherit any of it, but your mother will make sure he gets his fair share. She'll fight you for that. But to have the audacity to relegate you to a position of being their servant in their old age, that's a bit too much. Somebody is going to get axed, and that someone will be you. That I"m sure of. You're the fall guy. It's no wonder they don't help you get your own car. They're firmly convinced you won't need one that long. Why, my notes show that your parents even try to control who you fall in love with, and when, and even almost how you should make love to her. No wonder you can't keep the woman you want! It's not a case of morality or immorality as your mother asserts. It's a case of control. They've got you tied so tight like a string, that when the string pops, here you are in the mental unit of Municipal Hospital and what you have are so many mixed signals that mentally you can't function."

"O.K., so..."

"Your case file shows that over the years, that force in your brain that allows you to work with stress just hasn't been developed, and what little it it has, has been twisted and confused by your parents' unyielding polarity. Budd, in any endeavor in life, if it's worth something, there is stress. If not, as in the case of underachievers, there's usually depression. You've grown up in such an environment. Your father, by all rights, had the potential and education to be a great classical composer. He settled for teaching piano lessons in the back room of his home on Olive Street. He is well thought of in Texarkana, but he could have been so much more. Perhaps he had his own demons to deal with. I don't know. Did you ever want to live in the real world Budd -- instead of hiding away in that house on Olive Street, or in your fantasy world as an unemployed, n'er-do-well playboy? As life goes on, and if you stay there, it's going to get depressing for you -- if it's not already. I hear you say you now have made the decision to join the world of the living. I think you've subconsciously made that decision through the outward manifestation of a recent car wreck in Mt. Vernon, Texas. That ultimately led you here. Perhaps life, or your higher power has intervened and has determined that you want out of this trap, out of this treadmill you keep running. You're a bright young man with the possibility of having a good future. Now, Budd, there's good news. There are now drugs on the market that will help you get away from that illness, and we'll deal with the use of these as we, or rather I should say, if we continue your treatment here."

"What are you talking about? I just want to go home and be with my daughter."

"I understand. I also know that people scare you to death, Budd, especially people you love. Think about it. Do you want to be an invalid or a responsible adult? You've got the rest of the day to think it over. If you still want to go, I'll write your discharge papers at five p.m. this afternoon and you may leave -- assuming your parents will have you."

Dr. Dodd walked out the door. Budd walked to the window of his room. Tears were streaming down his cheeks. He grabbed a long-playing phonograph record from the shelf and ambled blindly down the hall. Nicole was standing in the hall reading a chart. He turned to her. Then he walked into the meeting room. She picked up on his cue and followed him.

"That's her!" He pointed to the record cover he had brought in. He turned on the record player in the meeting room, and slipped the needle in the groove. "That's her! THAT'S JANE MITCHELL! When I've got her, I don't need anybody."

"Hum-m-ph," she said without emotion, "you certainly picked one, this time." For once Nicole saw in her own mind's eye some real competition in a female counterpart in Budd's life. She turned and started to walk out of the room. Then she stopped and immediately faced him.

"Do you know what an affair means to the woman who's being cheated on? Do you? Do you know how it destroys every bit of feminine ego she has left in her?"

"Your ego looks intact, Nicole."

"Yes, because I carry all the weight!"

"As for who's been faithful to whom, Nicole you have no right to talk."

"I won't address that one." She turned about face and walked out of the room.

Group was to meet in twenty minutes. Budd walked one way and she walked another. At one p.m., everyone converged in the meeting room. Nicole lit a cigarette and blew smoke out of her nostrils as her eyes swept the semi-circle of people sitting in front of her. They stopped for a moment on Budd. She blew out some more smoke, placed the cigarette in an ashtray, then crossed her hands in her lap -- regaining her composure.

"What did I do?" he asked.

Nicole rolled her eyes.

"Boy," said a lady in her early forties, slowly, softly, "you're so damned charming. It's disgusting. You're SO damned charming."

"Isn't he?" asked Nicole, icily. "Isn't he?"

"I didn't do anything. I didn't do anything at all."

"I know. You work at it, boy."

"Doesn't he?" Nicole responded.

"Now wait a minute. You two are relating to someone or something out of your past and not me."

"Damn it, Budd," said the woman. Both she and Nicole had their eyes right on him. "You sweep them off their feet, but it's never your fault because you're so God-damned charming."

"I didn't do anything. What did I do?"

"You make women angry, Budd," continued Nicole. "You don't show the real you. You're afraid to."

"Look, I am what I am. I mean -- I can't change. So I watched too many old Fred Astaire movies. Both of you are relating to something or someone besides me."

"We're trying to relate to a Budd Wilson other than the one you're showing. We're trying to relate to the real Budd Wilson."

"I am the real Budd Wilson. I am what I am. I can't help it."

There was a prolonged period of silence. Nicole lit a cigarette.

"What do you feel about me?"

"I loved you."

"I mean right now."

"I like you."

"You do not! You flash that picture of your latest paramour on the cover of that record. You don't like me at all."

"No, but I do."

She turned to the group. "I know this doesn't make sense to you, but bear with me, we're engaged in a form of role playing, a form of transference." Dr. Dodd had given Nicole complete freedom to employ whatever form of therapy she chose to use with her patients. Nicole was spontaneous and creative. She turned to Budd. "Look, Budd, you've washed up a marriage, you're washed up at thirty-six, you're mutually dependent on two pathetic old people whom you hate and who hate you. You sit behind the walls of that house on Olive Street living in a fantasy world as life passes you by."

"I have Jennifer."

"Yes, your beloved little Jennifer." She looked at Budd. "But why not? She's your reason for being, your raison d'etre. You speak of her as though I'm her mother. You programmed her to be my child. Poor Sissy, she can't win one way or the other. . . or can she.. . . ? It's no wonder she—"

"NO!"

There was a silence. . . then Nicole re-engaged in the interchange.

"The singer, the woman on the record, do you love her?"

"Yes, but more than that, I like her. She's my best friend."

"Would she marry you?"

"No."

"Why not?"

"Jane Mitchell has had many men and will have many men. Some whose ring she has worn. Some whose she will not. Jane Mitchell belongs to herself. However, throughout the years I will always be her friend -- her close friend. We'll always see each other on and off throughout life."

"How will you see her if you re-marry?"

"I will. I'll see her over the years."

"What will you tell your wife?"

"My wife doesn't have to know everything."

"Budd, did your spirit, your soul, die in a car wreck last month when you were being smothered to death on all sides, or did you really die when I left you in Austin in 1973?"

There was a long silence.

"It's not that I was trying to hide it from anyone,

It's that I wouldn't admit it to myself."

"I believe that, Budd," Nicole said. "I believe that. Go for it, Budd."

"I did love Sissy. Very much. But we didn't get along. We were so damned poor. I wanted everything for her, but we were so damned poor."

"You were sick."

"I worked so hard for nothing. It seemed like I was always getting fired. Then, Jennifer came along. I didn't even know how I was going to get Sissy in and out of the hospital. My parents had to pay for it."

He started to tear. Nicole handed him a box of Kleenex.

"Perhaps you invested your energies in the wrong directions, " she said.

"I was doing all I knew to do."

"Budd, I believe you have a hereditarily based mental illness that has been fed into and developed by your extremely controlling parents. Part of this illness is your inability to handle stress and be productive in the workplace. As for your loving one woman and feeling obligated and married to another, I think your family would have never accepted you if you had left Sissy directly for another woman. I'll touch on that later."

"I was doing all I knew to do."

"I understand the reality of your feelings."

"What are you saying, I'm a cripple?"

"On the contrary. Sir Winston Churchill considered himself a failure on the dawn of his finest hour, but he came back and led Great Britain to victory in World War II. He had times of great emotional heights and times of great emotional despair. He mastered a talent, a very simple talent."

"What?"

"Never give up! Look Budd, you're young. You're vital. You have a REAL future. I know it may seem trite, but remember the phrase, 'Pick yourself up. Dust yourself off. Start all over again'."

She paused.

"Your mother said you once told a customer at Brooks Brothers that their clothes weren't any better than those at J.C. Penny. Did you say that?"

"Yeah." He dabbed his eyes and wiped his runny nose.

"Why?

"'Cause they're not."

"Perhaps you don't have the right temperament for sales. Perhaps you're too honest."

"Well, if so, what does a nut like me do to make a living?"

"I happen to know that you're very talented in some areas you hide from the world. How many of you know that Budd, good ole' Budd Wilson, is a very talented jazz pianist?"

"In some people's eyes, not everybody's," responded Budd. Everyone smiled -- but no one raised a hand.

"How many of you know that Budd is a borderline genius who yearns to just be normal?

What all do you read, Budd?"

"Well, I read the Texarkana paper and the Dallas Morning News every day."

"From cover to cover?"

"Yes."

"What else?"

"Occasionally I read the New York Times when I can get it. Oh, and *The New Yorker,* and I just don't look at the cartoons and read the ads. I read the articles. It's amazing to me that F. Scott Fitzgerald and Dorothy Parker wrote for *The New Yorker.* I believe Harold Ross and Jane Grant founded it in 1925. It all began with the round table discussions at the Algonquin hotel in New York in the 1920s. My dad always called me `Gatsby'. I guess he's right. I guess I am somewhat of a Gatsby. Anyway, I read a lot of history and biography." He looked up and laughed. "Good tastes and a nickle won't buy you a cup of coffee."

"Budd does a good job of hiding his abilities behind his charm and glib remarks. But I don't necessarily agree with you here, Budd. Good tastes got you a job at Brooks Brothers, an American institution."

"Brooks Brothers, 'The Ivy League' since 1818. The clothier of F. Scott Fitzgerald, Clark Gable and Gary Cooper," Budd replied, without hiding his sarcasm.

"And of Presidents' John F. Kennedy and Franklin Roosevelt among others, and of countless professional and academic men across the country for generations. Budd, you always did have excellent taste. I always admired the way you dressed. You always wished you could have stayed at Brooks Brothers, didn't you? Maybe you can go back some day in the future," she added.

"Did you know that Abraham Lincoln was wearing a Brooks Brothers' suit the night he was assassinated at the Ford Theater?"

"Budd, I think you have a martyr complex, but let's deal with one issue at a time. You're excellent at changing the direction of a conversation. Let's keep it on line now. How many of you know that Budd has a photographic memory and wrote for newspapers at one time, anyone?"

"Swingtime," he started. 'Pick Yourself Up'."

"What's that Budd?" She started to chuckle.

'Pick Yourself Up. Dust Yourself Off. Start All Over Again' came from *Swingtime,* Fred Astaire and Ginger Rogers, RKO Pictures, 1936, directed by George Stevens, choreographed by Hermes Pan. The films were all in black and white, and the lack of color was perfect for the 1930s' art deco sets. All of the Astaire-Rogers movies were full of standards. In that particular movie, the music was by Jerome Kern and the lyrics were by Dorothy Field. Other standards in *Swingtime* included 'The Way You Look Tonight' and 'A Fine Romance'. There may have been a couple more. I get the songs of the Astaire-Rogers musicals and the people who wrote them confused. There were so many good ones."

"See! Everyone See!" she exclaimed "If Winston Churchill, or Abraham Lincoln, or Joshua Logan. . ."

"Joshua Logan. . . ." Budd picked up on it. "He was originally from Texarkana. His mother and my great aunt were good friends at one time. Their husbands were in competing creosote and timber businesses in Texarkana at the turn of the century. I understand my great uncle's company ran his father out of business. Story has it, Logan's father committed suicide and the family moved to Louisiana. But. . .he was, he was originally from Texarkana, his family was tied to mine in some sort of way."

"Who's Joshua Logan?" asked one of the group members.

"Tell 'em Budd. Tell him Joshua Logan's particular strengths and weaknesses."

"Josh Logan was a genius. He was a famous Broadway and Hollywood director in the forties and fifties. He was a manic-depressive, or bi-polar as they now call them, but between his ups and downs he made time to direct such American stage and screen classics as *Annie Get Your Gun, South Pacific, Mr. Roberts, Camelot,* and my favorite, *Picnic.* Geez, I'm in good company. Are you telling me I'm a manic-depressive, Nicole?"

"Let's just say you are a very creative and expressive person."

"No really, am I a manic-depressive?"

"Yes, but in a way you're lucky. Bi-polar illness, or manic-depression, is now being looked upon as mostly chemical in nature. As a result, it can be treated almost totally with proper medication. Through the usage of a drug, or rather an element, lithium carbonate, you may never have to come here again. I think you suffer from multiple, psychological illnesses. At this particular time you are bi-polar and because this is not a long term treatment facility, it is the illness component we choose to deal with. I imagine your life will always be a life of creativity, analysis and deep thinking. You've always been a little eccentric. I've always liked that in you. It doesn't necessarily have to be bad. Through proper treatment you may never have to come here again."

"Damm. Right when I was beginning to like the place."

"I know. That's why you wanted to run. Budd Wilson, I swear by the time you are ready to leave, I'll have to throw you out the front door. But not quite yet, you're just beginning. Admitting to your illness is the first step towards getting well. Do you remember when we were young, and you referred to us a 'Fred and Ginger'? When are we going to deal with Fred and Ginger, Budd?"

"Maybe one of these days," he said. "Maybe one of these days." He looked at Nicole.

"Okay, I guess you win. Tell Dr. Dodd he can tear up those discharge papers."

"Good!" She beamed.

The days went by, bad days good, good days bad.

She knocked on his door.

"Come in," he replied.

"May I have a seat?"

"Sure, Nicole."

She sat in the hospital chair. Budd sat on the side of his bed.

"Budd," she began, "you're adopted. What do you know about your real mother?"

"I know I must have loved her very much. I imagine she was very beautiful. I've always heard she was very wild and very beautiful. When I was born, my mother was a patient in the state insane asylum. Like me, I suppose, she was a little eccentric. too. She must have been a woman who tried to do too much alone. Perhaps her family wouldn't accept her the way she was, and she had no other place to go to. I certainly understand that. I always felt there was quite a bit of my real mother in me, and perhaps in Jenny, too."

"Budd, I want to try to explain something to you in an analytical sense, a kind of hypothetical thing. You're good at breaking things down, okay?' Perhaps your anger and depression began when your adopted parents took you away from your real mother."

"They didn't take me away. My mother had to give me up because she couldn't take care of me. She was in a state hospital. It was the only thing she could do."

"I know that, but lets talk about feelings, infantile emotions. Isn't it conceivable that you grieved for your real mother?"

"I still do."

"Okay. . , and isn't it conceivable that your adopted parents didn't knowhow to handle you and your grief from infancy on?"

"I suppose so. Momma said I used to stand in the play pin and shake it and scream. My father always resented any intrusion into his privacy. I don't think my father ever really wanted me. It was Momma who wanted a boy. All my life he hid from me. He felt threatened by me. He saw me as an intrusion into his privacy. He still does, as we well know. I've certainly intruded in his privacy over the years. She must have been one hell of a woman, my real mother," Budd continued. "I wonder if I'll ever find another one like her?"

"Budd, you've had three female role models in your family, your adopted mother, your real mother, and your great-aunt. Again, I observe that you've gotten some extremely mixed signals from two of them, your adopted mother and your great-aunt. Your adopted mother was exceedingly jealous of any of your girlfriends that weren't like her. Perhaps that's why she likes Sissy. Sissy is the only one like her."

"No. . . ?" He looked up. "Now wait a minute. . . You may be right. Sissy IS the only one like Momma."

"And what happened to you?"

"We divorced. Oh, my goodness. . . and what about my great-aunt?"

"Jane Mitchell, the beautiful, seductive older woman. There's a story there Budd, and perhaps if we have the time someday we'll uncover it. In Freudian terms it's called an Oedipus complex. Changing the subject while it's on my mind, I want to talk to you about your humble beginnings -- as I mentioned the other day. I think I now understand why your parents insist on your taking care of them in their old age. You were adopted from the state hospital. Would it be possible that when they adopted you they thought they would be getting a child who was, how do I say this, 'slow or retarded', one who would have no choice but to take care of them in their old age? A servant, so to speak? Unfortunately I guess none of you got what you wanted out of the other. You may have problems, but you're anything but retarded. Something to think about."

"Nicole, why did you come in here today? Now you've really got me confused."

"Me, too. I don't know. I came to talk about your family heritage. Boy did I."

The days went by, bad days good, good days bad... With a cadence in sight.

"Well, it's my last day."

"Let's give Budd some feedback on leaving the hospital," said Nicole. "Anybody?"

"You've really changed, Budd," said one group member, "but I guess what I didn't realize is that you were this way all along. When you came in here I thought you were a super snob but you're not. You're just like the rest of us, you put your walls up when you feel pain. You're okay. You're one of the guys."

"One of the guys. Did you hear that Budd?" Nicole asked.

"Thank you. Thank you, very much."

"Yeah Budd, you're okay," chimed another. "You really care about people. I mean you REALLY care about people."

"I always did. Maybe that's why I put up my walls. Caring sometimes can cause extreme pain. Well, I guess that's about it. Thank you all very much. I appreciate your acceptance and your patience."

"That's about all? Except for one issue," said Nicole. She smiled. "How about Fred and Ginger?"

"Jesus, can't we talk about it alone?"

"Go for it in group, Budd."

"Okay... ," he said slowly and deliberately, "I will. . . O.K. -- It's very difficult when you're single, divorced, and a male in your thirties to be confronted by a female on a daily basis with whom you have had a relationship with in the past and is now your present therapist."

"What are you saying, Budd?" asked one of the group members.

Budd looked at Nicole.

"I'm going for it, Nicole."

"You sure are."

"Why don't you say what you mean in plain English?" asked another group member.

"Let me help you a little bit, Budd," Nicole said and turned to the group. "Budd and I used to date. We cared very much for each other."

"Did you love each other?" asked a pudgy young woman who had never spoken in group before.

"Yes," Budd and Nicole said simultaneously

"Woah," exclaimed one of the young male group members.

"You think we didn't know that, Fred and Ginger?" asked another.

"You still love each other," said the pudgy young woman.

"I wasn't aware it was that obvious." Nicole blushed. "Budd," she continued, "tonight's Friday night. If you could have a fantasy for tonight, what would it be?"

"Watch out, Nicole," said another group member.

"An appropriate fantasy. I use the word `appropriate'."

"I'd be over at your parents' house, drinking Scotch and shooting the shit with your old man, and then you and I would take off to Shreveport and tear up the town from one end to the other."

"And then what?" asked the young male group member.

"After that, it's none of your business," responded Budd.

"I hope," began Nicole, "that someday you'll accept yourself for the true gentleman you are."

"Lady, I ain't no gentleman and you know it."

"I'm not so sure about that, Budd. I know from personal experience that you are." Nicole looked around the group, and at the clock, then back to Budd again. "You took a major risk just now. I'm very proud of you. Perhaps this time in group today is a fitting way to start bringing closure to something that has been festering in you for nearly twenty years. I'm very proud of you. What say you, group?"

They all applauded.

"Okay, times up. Budd, I need to see you in my office for a moment before you leave."

Budd met Nicole in her office. He had gone by his room and changed his clothes.

"Woah! Look at you! A new uniform!"

Budd was wearing tight jeans, sloppy polo shirt with the shirt tail out and white sneakers.

"It's sort of like your Mercedes and your eel skin briefcase."

"Gee, that's funny Budd. I always saw you with the Mercedes and eel skin briefcase."

"Nah." He smiled. "I'm more of a Cadillac, Lincoln man."

"Brooks Brothers all the way?"

"Yeah, Brooks Brothers all the way. Nicole, just a question. When I came in here and you had the option to choose me as a patient, did you do it because you wanted to treat me, or because you still loved me?"

"Whatever makes you think I'd do that?" She questioned him with all of her coyness and with that smirk on her face that he had remembered from their youth, then she broke into a broad smile.

"Both."

"That's what I thought. I love you, too. Good-bye Nicole."

"Bye Budd. I'm very proud of you."

The days went by, good days bad, bad days good.

Budd walked out of the door of Municipal Hospital into the world again. He was now 37.

He knew he had to work. He had marketable skills but he wasn't getting any younger. He knocked on one door, another then another. He kept knocking. Wherever opportunity was, it wasn't looking Budd Wilson in the face.

Even though his parents could support him for some time he knew the danger of relying on their help and of competing with them for the Devereaux estate. He felt guilty. HE HAD TO FIND A JOB. He looked at an advertisement in the local paper..

"Own Your Own Business—For An Investment of $300 to $1,000 You Can Start Your Own Jewelry Business"

Budd looked at the products. They were costume jewelry and priced to fit the budget of a working girl. They didn't look bad at all for the money. He got Arkansas and Texas sale tax permits, display mats for the gold plated necklaces, and trays for the cubic zirconia rings, some cases to carry them in and went on the road. By the end of 1987 he was buying from three wholesalers and traveling Northeast Texas and Southwest Arkansas unloading and buying costume jewelry as fast as he could. Then by March of 1988, business started to slow and things took a turn for the worse.

CHAPTER 8

It was an early summer afternoon in Diboll, Texas. He was sitting in a café peddling his jewelry, only no one was buying. He put the ring back in the tray and took a sip of coffee.

"Pretty jewelry. Nobody buying," said an East Texas oil redneck with a weathered face who was wearing faded denim coveralls and an old straw cowboy hat. He sat down next to Budd at the counter.

"No?" Budd looked up to him. "I can't figure out why. This stuff has always sold."

"Don't 'ya read boy?" the man asked softly as he stared straight ahead at his reflection in the mirror behind the Campbell Soup cans stacked across the back of the counter.

"Read what? Yes I read."

"It's the oil belt."

"The oil belt what?"

"Son, we're in a depression."

"A depression?"

"Get'ya a paper."

Budd walked over to the newspaper racks by the two swinging front doors of the café. He put a quarter in the slot and pulled out a Dallas Morning News. He walked back to the counter and sat down and began to read the headline.

"TEXAS CRUDE HITS TEN DOLLARS A BARREL"

He continued to read the accompanying story. "Ten dollars a barrel," he thought to himself.

He kept reading. "Texas is bankrupt." He turned to the man next to him at the counter. "No wonder nobody's buying my jewelry. Nobody can afford to buy anything."

"That's right," said the man. "People only buying what they have to and precious little of that."

"Jesus," said Budd, "I've been through everything. I've been through a divorce, a nervous breakdown. I thought the American economy had been stable since the end of the 1930s."

"I'm 59 years old," said the man. "I've worked for the same company for thirty-three years. Got laid off about a month ago. Now I just sit down here and drink coffee every day. How old are you, son?"

"Thirty-eight."

"Working for yourself?"

"Uh huh."

"Chances are neither one of us will ever have a job with a company again. For some reason they want'm green and stupid, right out of college. I don't understand that. I just don't understand it."

The man with the lined face and straw hat got up and started toward the cash register. He had weathered the work he had done for a lifetime.

"It's on me Frank," said the waitress from behind the register.

"Thank 'ya, Edith."

He turned back and positioned his focus somewhere between Budd and the waitress. "Well... Ya'll have a good day."

Budd paid for his coffee and nervously walked out to his parents' Dodge 600 that sat amidst the dust that lay between Highway 59 and the café. He put the jewelry cases in the trunk and started the ignition. He tilted the steering wheel down and pointed the car out towards the highway.

"I've got to keep this little son of a bitch on the road. Somehow I've got to keep this little son of a bitch on the road."

"A ring, name a price and we'll dicker."

The jewelry wasn't expensive. It was supposed to be putting the car on the road, paying for the food, the gasoline and maintenance, and making a profit. It no longer was. He sat in a familiar restaurant. The waitresses gathered 'round.

"Whad'ya want for that one?"

"What'll you give me?"

"You carry papers, Budd? You've always carried papers on me."

"No more. Cash only."

"I'll give you ten."

"Come on, fifteen."

"Twelve-fifty."

"Take it," he agreed. "Okay, sweetheart. What'll you give me for this little beauty?"

He emptied all of his cases in seventeen minutes. Meres, the head waitress walked up.

"You still got that necklace and earrings I like, Budd?"

"Sit down Meres. Want a cigarette?"

"I shouldn't. I'm on duty, but why not?" She looked around then went and sat in a back booth with Budd. She blew smoke up into the air.

"I've spent many an hour hustling jewelry in this place," he said.

"Yep."

"Well it's all over now."

"What'ya going to do Budd?"

"I don't know. Here." He pulled the necklace and earrings out of his pocket. "It's a gift."

She wrapped her arms around his neck and hugged him. "Take care of yourself, you old fool,"she said softly.

"Who's an old fool?"

"You are."

He packed his empty case and walked towards the door.

"Adios," he said and pushed open the door and walked out.

They sat there in the sunrise, Edgar, Mildred, Budd and Jennifer, waiting for the bus. For once, Budd's parents were not against his going to Dallas.

"Now don't' you cry when I leave you," he nervously said to Jennifer

"I won't Daddy. You coached me."

"Daddy HAS to go to Dallas and find a job. Do you understand Jenny?"

"Yes, Daddy. I understand."

He looked out the window of the bus station as though his watching could hurry it up. Then it came around the corner. The man at the counter announced the Dallas bus. They started to hurry.

He grabbed his bag and clothes and walked outside of the terminal

"Here." He pulled something out of his pocket and bent down to the little girl before he boarded the bus. "This is for you Jenny. Now don't you cry!"

She opened the little black box. There was a child's diamond pendant encircled by the man in the moon.

"I knew you'd do this Daddy. I knew it."

"Now don't cry!"

"I won't Daddy. You coached me last night."

He turned and walked rapidly towards the bus. Tears were streaming down his face. He never looked back. The little girl waved with one hand and clutched the black box with the other. She did not cry.

"Last call for Omaha, Naples, Mt. Pleasant, Mt. Vernon, Sulphur

Springs, Greenville and Dallas, Texas, with connections in Dallas for—"

The Dallas bus terminal was full of people not knowing where they were going. There were old people bumping into young people. There were people of all nationalities not speaking a common language bumping into each other. There were security guards barking orders to people in Spanish and English. People were waiting for buses that didn't show up and people were waiting for bus connections that didn't make. "GET INSIDE!" and "STAY IN LINE!" The guards ordered a mob of people who mostly did not understand what they were saying.

Trailways had just merged with Greyhound. The Dallas Trailways terminal had just closed and all busses were now being routed to the Dallas Greyhound terminal. It was pandemonium at the Dallas bus terminal. Budd weaved through the people with their dufflebags and suitcases into the coffee shop inside the terminal. He ordered coffee and looked for a seat.

"May I join you?" he asked. "There doesn't seem to be any other seat."

"Sure," said a tall, middle-aged woman.

"Where you going?" he asked as he sipped his coffee.

"Nowhere, anywhere I guess." She was quiet for a moment. "See all these people? They're people who've gotten screwed by the economy. Nomads. The so-called 'Oil Belt Crisis'. My husband is 62 years old. Been a petroleum engineer in Texas City for 30 years. Fired! After thirty years. Texas Crude bottomed out. Now all he does is sit at his brother's house and drink.

We lost everything. The house, everything. We lost it all. So I got on a bus in Houston.

I couldn't stand it."

"I'm so sorry," said Budd. "I'm so sorry. Where are you going to?"

"I've got a daughter in Connecticut. Hell, I'm going anywhere, nowhere."

Budd stood outside the Dallas bus terminal. She turned the corner in her little red Toyota.

"Hey good looking, want a lift?" she called from her car.

Budd had previously notified her of which bus he would be on and what time it would arrive.

He grabbed his clothes and bag and ran across the street. He got in the little red car. Her eyes looked straight at the road but darted to his every time one of them said something or made a response. It had been seven and a half years since he had seen Jane.

"I look horrible," she said.

"You look great, Jane."

"I took the afternoon off because you were coming. Kind of straightened up the house and bopped around a little bit."

"8001 Bryn Mawr," he said.

"Yep." She took a deep breath and slowly exhaled. She pulled into the driveway, cut the ignition, and they walked into the house. There was no furniture in any of the rooms but the master bedroom, the kitchen and the breakfast area.

"Been kind of strapped for money lately." She turned facing the bedroom hallway. "Had to get rid of some of the furniture." Books were stacked all around the walls. She turned again and faced Budd and shrugged her arms and shoulders. "Loneliness is the price you pay for solitude.

Oh well, how do I look for a woman who's getting old?" The change of life had a way of dealing with Jane the nightclub singer, and Jane the woman and person. A big part of her mystique had been based on her youth, her looks, and her sexuality. Now, though still beautiful, her features had become bolder and more stark, and her dark,dark hair with tiny threads of silver accentuated that fact. shel was still one of the most beautiful women Budd had ever known, but in a different phase of her life -- past one she could never go back to.

"You men get off the hook. It's easy for you. But for a woman it's a different kind of curse. I survive because I have to. I'm Jane Mitchell!"

"You look great, Jane. You're as sexy as ever. You look absolutely stunning. You look super.

Where's all of your furniture?" He changed the subject.

"Like said, kind of in a tight bind. I had to get rid of some of it. Say I've been saving up for this. Let's go out, tonight. Some place cheap and Dutch treat, okay?"

He walked into the kitchen and opened the refrigerator. "Jane, you haven't got anything in here but a can of tuna fish, a loaf of bread and a can of Hills Brothers coffee."

"That's what I'm good for right now—a can of tuna, a loaf of bread and a can of Hills Brothers coffee. I'm on a diet. I told you my life is changing!"

"I know that, but you need to eat."

"I am! I am!"

Budd pulled his father's gold Mastercard out of his wallet. Edgar Wilson had admonished him to use it for emergencies only. Rules were made to be broken.

"Look, where could I take you out to dinner?"

"Goodness. . . Have you seen the West End?"

"No."

"It's downtown. It's really neat. It's running Greenville Avenue out of business. Let's go down there and just look around from one shop to another. We'll get a bite to eat, huh?"

"Do you want a pizza, Jane?" he asked her as they passed one the West End eating places.

"M-m-m, I love pizza." She took his hand in hers and led him from one store to another, from one building to another never mentioning pizza again. "I want to show you something. Come on. Let's run!"

"Jane!"

"Come on Budd. What'sa matter, getting old?"

"All right."

She took his hand and led him through the open saloon doors of a crowded bar and eatery, Dick's Last Resort.

"You remember Peyton Park?" she asked.

"Yeah, I remember Peyton. He used to play at The Levee."

"He's got a Dixieland group in here and they're damned good."

"Can I buy you a drink?" Budd asked her as they sat down at the bar.

She laughed that golden laugh. "It seems to me you've asked me that before."

"Somewhere in my past I vaguely remember that," he said.

"Yeah." She smiled as she looked at the reflection of the two of them in the mirror behind the bar. She looked down. "Yeah," she said softly.

"A spritzer for the lady and I'll have a Budwiser."

"You always remember."

"Who could forget a drink called a spritzer."

"Budd, let's take our drinks and go down front and hear the band, okay?"

"Follow us with our tab," Budd yelled to the bartender. Dick's Last Resort was packed with people and noise.

"Peyton." She waved with her fingers.

"Jane! Jane Mitchell!" He got off the stand and walked to their table. "Come sing. Please, come sing."

"No-o-o. I quit the business. I'm a secretary."

"You're a born singer. Why?"

"I don't know. I just did."

"That's not right Jane. You should be up there behind the microphone."

"He's right Jane," said Budd. "Peyton, why don't you start a tune and maybe Jane'll come up and finish it."

"No. No. I really can't," said Jane. "Really I can't."

Peyton returned to the stand. The musicians conferred about what song to perform. They started and Peyton began to sing "If I Had You". Softly she began singing at the table. She turned to Budd. "I can't."

"But you are!"

"But I can't."

A waiter brought a tray of hot, steaming fried catfish and bowls of hush puppies and french fries to the next table. Jane kept staring at the food.

"How long has it been since you've eaten?" Budd demanded.

"Couple of days."

"Why, Jane?"

"I'm trying to lose a little weight."

He turned to the waiter, thought of his father's gold Mastercard and said, "Bring us the same catfish dinner for two."

"And a beer?" Jane smiled and asked.

"And two Coronas."

She smiled. "Our payroll hasn't come in yet for the week. Anyway, GOD, it's good to see you."

"So you ARE hungry?"

"I'm trying to lose a little weight."

"Jane you look great! Absolutely great!"

"For an old woman?"

"My, but haven't you changed," he said. "You were the one who was eternally young and sexy. I was the old one."

"I can still outrun you!"

"You can? We'll see. We'll see."

Their food arrived.

"Dig in," he said. She was already halfway through a catfish fillet.

"M-M-M. This is good. M-M-M. This is really good. Try one, Budd." She spoke with her mouth full of food. She wiped her lips with the back of her hand. "It's good to see you." She smiled and her hand slid across the table to hold his.

"I'm home," he said. "I'm finally home."

"Almost home," she said. "You're home is with Jennifer. Your home must always be with Jennifer."

"Well, let's don't think about that for right now," he said softly.

They ate and drank as the music played. Later that night after all the customers had gone, Budd, Jane and some of the leading musicians of Dallas sat and talked their trade as the bartender brought more drinks They were a privileged group at Dick's Last Resort and they'd retain that privileged status 'til they closed the place.

"So I'm too old, huh?" She started to run down the downtown Dallas sidewalk after the restaurant had closed.

"Jane, I never said that." He started to trot behind her.

"Too old, huh? I'll beat you to the car," she called.

"Jane, it's three o'clock in the morning in downtown Dallas. You're going to get us arrested!"

"Nah, I'm not. What'sa matter Sport? Can't you keep up with me?"

"Jane!"

"Sides -- I know every cop in this town."

"That I believe." He was running as fast as he could. She was tall, and her stride was longer than his. Suddenly she stopped and looked in the ground floor window of a downtown pub.

Budd caught up with her.

"Look Budd." She was smiling. "They're having a party. Look at all those highschool kids in their tuxedos and formals. They're having a prom party! Let me in! I want to come too!"

She started banging on the glass.

"Jane, for God's sake you're going to get us arrested." He grabbed her by the shoulders.

"Listen buddy boy, I can handle you."

"I believe that, Jane. Come on, the car is parked across the street. I better drive."

"If you must." She touched his cheeks. Then she smiled that Jane Mitchell smile.

She got in the car and leaned back against the seat and started laughing. "I haven't had so much fun in I don't know when. Huh, spoil sport? I have an idea. I want you to take me somewhere."

"Jane, it's after three in the morning."

"Past your bedtime?"

"Yes it is. It's been a long day, besides everything is closed."

"I can get it open."

"How? Bang on the window again?"

"Certainly. I'm Jane Mitchell, or have you forgotten?"

"How could I?"

"Go out Routh Street by the Quadrangle. Drive -- just drive!"
There was a blue door inconspicuously set in a tan brick wall.
There was a tiny neon sign that said "Raphael's". Jane banged on
the door and finally someone opened the peephole.

"Jane! Come in, my dear," said a voice with a thick Sicilian accent.

Budd walked into one of the most intimate and elegant restaurants
he had ever seen. In the middle was a tiny white baby grand piano
elevated on a tiny oval stage. Middle-aged patrons and debutantes
and their beaus in formal wear were dining at candle-lit tables in
parties of six to eight. Jane and Budd sat at the bar with various
local dignitaries. Jane began a conversation with an older
gentleman who was sitting at the bar.

"As I was saying Janie," said the older man who wrote a column
for the Dallas Time Herald, "ninety-nine percent of Jane Mitchell
is a Gershwin tune."

"Frank, how flattering."

"Or Richard Rodgers or Cole Porter ," Budd muttered in his
boredom.

"And who are you?" demanded the columnist of Budd.

Jane turned rapidly to Budd.

"This is my little brother. Aren't you my little brother?"

"No striking family resemblances. I'm her little brother, Red Mitchell. Or perhaps I'm her cousin. You know, Cuz like Prez. Yardcuz, that's me."

As the columnist dismissed Budd and started a conversation with someone else, Jane grabbed Budd by the head and turned him to face her. "You keep your nose clean down here. I know all of these people professionally. Besides, they all know Francois."

"But Jane, I thought you were a secretary? Who's Francois? He grinned.

"Oh! Go do something constructive."

Budd walked over to the piano. He started to play "I Should Care."

Jane's conversation stopped. Her eyes turned from the bar to the piano.

"My, your style's improved. My compliments."

"Jane, it's been nearly eight years."

"Little Brother. . . , you just graduated."

He smiled. "Who's Francois?"

Later that night they lay on the livingroom floor in the house on Bryn Mawr.

"You always did like younger men. Is Francois younger than me?"

"That's none of your business."

You always did remind me of Anne Bancroft in 'The Graduate'."

"Please don't get me too old ahead of my time."

"She's a very seductive, beautiful woman."

Thank you." She smiled and took a sip of his coffee. "Here, lie down and listen to the stereo and relax and be quiet. You're too tense...." Suddenly she threw herself over him and violently kissed him "I'm kissing you. I can -- not do this!" She put her fingers to her lips. "I AM kissing you. I can't do this. I am committed to another man."

"AHAH ! FRANCOIS! Now we get down to it. If you don't mind me asking, where is he, Jane?"

"He's in France on an extended business trip. Now look, I'm not going to let you get me into this."

"Is he younger than me?"

"He's younger than you."

"How much?"

"Again -- that's none of your business."

"Doesn't surprise me."

She went to the hall closet and pulled out an extra set of sheets and a pillow. She made Budd a pallet on the floor. "Now take off your clothes and go to sleep. Good night!"

She turned out the lights and shut the bedroom door behind her. It was ten, maybe twenty minutes. The bedroom door creaked open. She shut it behind her and walked into the living room. She stood above him in her Mickey Mouse nightshirt.

"Ah come on, you think I haven't seen a naked man before," she said as she grabbed his pillow and sheets. "I always was a sucker for stray cats." She led him to the bedroom and shut the door behind them.

When Budd was on the road he would get up early to have coffee and read the morning papers. It was a ritual he went through every morning to prepare for his daily trip. Jane, too, got up early to enjoy her solitude over a cup of hot tea. Since she quit singing, she'd awaken at 5 a.m., put on her bathrobe and had driven two blocks to steal an old boyfriend's morning paper. It was a game they both knew and played. Then she'd go home and read the paper and have tea alone. She was a creature of habit, and with Budd there it was more to her liking to get rid of him from 5 til 7:30 than to have him around. JoJo's was a twenty-four hour restaurant, a place he was accustomed to. After she'd confiscated the morning paper, she'd swing by JoJo's and drop Budd off at the sitters' for a while.

"Cup of coffee." He sat down at the long coffee bar and looked at his Dallas Morning News that he had bought from the rack outside. The waitress poured hot coffee in his mug. She was young and cute. She was small and had long, dark hair and lots of make up.

"You wanna menu?" she asked as she shoved the menu in front of him.

He looked at her nametag to get her name. "No, I'm a cheapskate Colleen. Just coffee."

She looked at her nametag. "You pick up fast."

"That's how I tell waitresses' names when I hustle jewelry to them in 24-hour restaurants."

"I don't see any jewelry. What do you do now?"

"Right now I'm a professional gigolo." He kept reading his paper.

"Gee, I'm sorry. Times are tough."

He looked over his paper and smiled. She had a smirky grin on her face. "Colleen," he said,

"I have found a true friend."

She winked at him. "Catch you later. I can't waste all my time on you. I got other tables to wait on." She looked at the manager who was giving her the evil eye.

"You better get back to work before you get in trouble. Besides, my lady friend will be here any minute," Budd said.

"Ah kind sir, your lady? Are you really a gigolo? How old is she? You're a gigolo."

"No -- I'm not.." He began reading the paper again.

"She must be awful hard up."

"Come on, Colleen. Get back to work," grumbled the manager.

The red Toyota pulled up in front of the entrance. Jane hit the horn solidly three times. Budd dropped two dollars on the counter and started walking toward the door.

'Snobby bitch,' Colleen said silently to herself as she served a table. 'She won't even come in. He is kept. She must not be too particular.

"Sausage and eggs," she said as she bent down with her knees to wait a table. "Pancakes and bacon." She lay the plates on the table.

He got off at the Dallas Transit System bus stop in front of the building that he remembered as Interfirst Tower. It was no longer the tallest building in Dallas and it was undergoing a massive reconstructive phase. The name had been changed to First

International. He entered through the lobby and looked to the right. There were plywood boards across the opening that had once been the ground level entrance to Brooks Brothers.

"Is Brooks Brothers still here?" he asked a stranger. The man kept walking.

"Is Brooks Brothers still here?" he asked a black man who was emptying an ashtray.

"Yes, sir. They're only on the lower level now."

"Thank-you. Thank you very much." He tried to think of how he had made it to the lower level. He turned right and walked down the corridor. He caught an elevator just as it was about to shut. Then it was in front of him. The "Golden Fleece" logo stood as a sign of solidarity. It hadn't changed much. He walked into his past.

"May I help you?" Larry Constant looked much the same -- only now his hair was greying.

"I'm Budd Wilson. Larry, don't you remember me?"

"I'm sorry. I'm afraid I don't. Perhaps you could refresh my memory. I'm certain I would."

"Larry, I used to work with you. Right here on this floor. I used to work right beside you."

"I'm . . . I'm sorry."

"I stole Mr. Miller's secretary from this place. Took her to Texarkana and married her."

"Sissy!" He exclaimed. "Yes I remember you. How long has it been?"

"Nearly nine years since I first went to work for Brooks Brothers."

"It has been a while. How is Sissy?"

"We're divorced."

"Oh I'm sorry to hear that. Look, many of the old crew are still here, Alma, Ruthie. They'd be delighted to see you," continued Larry as he led Budd over to the shirt counter. "Alma, look who the wind blew in."

The attractive middle aged woman whom Budd had first met when he walked into the institution as a young man looking for a job was now gray.

"Hello Alma." Budd smiled as he walked up. "Do you know who I am?" Larry Constant stood next to them. He was smiling, too.

"No. . . No, I don't. Who are you?" she asked. "Who is he, Larry?"

"This is Budd Wilson. He stole Sissy McGill from us some eight or nine years ago."

She put the shirt in her hand on the counter. She came around from behind the counter and hugged Budd. "It's good to see you. How's Sissy?"

"We're divorced."

"Oh, I'm sorry."

He pulled the wallet-sized photo from his hip pocket billfold. "This is Jennifer, our daughter."

Alma put on her black-rimmed half glasses. "She's beautiful. She's absolutely stunning."

All of the old gang at Brooks Brothers gathered closely around to see the picture.

"Looking for a job?" asked Alma.

"I believe once before you said I'd do," answered Budd.

She took him by the hand and led him to the manager's office.

"I don't think we're hiring right now but it won't hurt to get your foot in the door -- and you have worked here before. That's all a plus, but I don't think we're hiring right now."

"Mr. Miller still the manager?" Budd asked.

"Oh no, he's retired," answered Alma.

"Good thing, huh?"

"Good thing for everybody. You'll really like our new manager. He's very open and friendly," she said and smiled. She led him into the executive office area as she had done nearly a decade earlier. There was someone else sitting at Sissy's place. It seemed empty without her there. Alma knocked on the door and introduced Budd to the new, young manager. The two men greeted each other. Alma backed out the door, closing it behind her.

"I used to work here - soon after the store first opened."

"Mr. Miller was the manager then."

"Yes sir, I went to work just after the store opened. Mr. Miller was the manager."

"Yes." He smiled. "Mr Wilson—."

"Please call me Budd."

"Certainly. Budd, I'm not saying you won't get a job with Brooks Brothers. In fact, your chances may be much better than others. Judging from the way you are dressed, you understand the concept of the Brooks Brothers look, and you've worked here, though somewhat in the past.

Our products remain solid throughout the years. Budd, I'll be honest with you. Brooks Brothers in Dallas is in hot water right now. The big ticket retail clothing business in the state of Texas is struggling. The state of Texas is in big trouble. I'm not hiring now, and unfortunately I may have to let someone off. That's a very difficult thing to do. All of our employees have been here for years. It's like getting rid of one of our own family. All I can say is to keep trying. That's all I can promise you right now."

"Well thank you for your time and courtesy." Budd looked him straight in the eye, smiled and stood up and shook his hand.

"I wish I could offer you more hope," said the young manager. "Please keep trying. If an opening should arise, I'll seriously consider you."

"Thank you very much." Budd walked to the door, then looked back. "This place has always meant a great deal to me. The name Brooks Brothers has always been a standard for me since I was a teenager. It had something to do with an old coot named Fritz Cavanaugh, and Dixieland jazz, and Kentucky Bourbon. But then you wouldn't know that." He shut the door behind him forever.

The morning and afternoon pick-up place had become JoJo's. Jane would drop him off there early before work and pick him up on the way home. This would give Budd time to sit, drink coffee and figure out the city bus route schedule in the Dallas Transit System pamphlet while he waited for a bus to take him downtown. Once downtown, he would transfer to the appropriate bus he had found in the pamphlet, and that bus would take him to the basic vicinity of a job interview. Then he'd walk. He would try to get back to JoJo's in time to read the want ads before Jane picked him up after work. If he was late and she missed him, she'd run some errands and come by again. It was early morning after five and Budd sat at JoJo's reading a book.

"I swear, you've always got your head in some book," said Colleen.

"Yep," he said.

"Whatcha reading about, now?" she asked.

"Bout a bunch of sharecroppers from Oklahoma," he replied.

"Well, that's nothing special. I know. I'm one myself I grew up on a farm just north of Ardmore. Came south to Dallas to get rich, and I'm still broke. As a matter of fact, I-- ,"

Budd put his fingers in his ears to drown out Colleen and started reading softly to himself so he could hear the words.

"The tenant men looked up alarmed. . .But what'll happen to us? How will we eat? Pa was born here and Pa had to borrow money. . . but we stayed. . . . and we got a little bit of what we raised."

"Colleen, do you realize that land is still our most important asset? Do you?"

"You're weird, you know that? You're just... weird." She continued to wipe off the counter.

He looked in the refrigerator. He knew their money was running out.

"Jane, what are we going to do for food? We're running out of money."

She looked up from her book. "You'll find a job." She lay the book in her lap. "I have faith in you."

"Look Jane, one of the busboys at JoJo's says the cheapest flophouse in this town is some motel on Gaston Avenue. It's on a bus line. Take me down there and let me make it on my own. I'll find something in two or three days. I can't spend your money anymore."

She looked around and sighed. "Maybe so. Maybe so."

"Let's go down and see what it's like anyway, okay?"

"All right." She looked at the floor. "All right."

"I don't want to be a burden on you."

"You're not a burden!" she snapped. "You're not a burden," she repeated softly. "I'll get my keys."

They drove through a rough part of town to the motel.

"I don't like it," she said. "I don't like it at all."

"The only way we're going to make it now Jane is to function apart for a while."

She looked at the motel. "It's dumpy. It's a dump. Only stay here to sleep, Budd. Otherwise stay away from the place. I'm even scared for you to sleep here. Somebody will rob you or shoot you."

Budd walked over to the office. Jane watched outside as teenage girls were standing on stair steps displaying their wares to make a living. Younger ones were being taught the art of make-up and skin tight bluejean shorts to enter the trade, the trade of making a living with their bodies at the motel. Junkies were walking into their rooms after making sells that would support them and their habits for another night. Jane looked down at the sidewalk. There was a large patch of dried blood.

"This place is disgusting," she said to Budd as he came back from the office. They climbed the steps and entered the room. "I'm not going to let you stay here."

"Jane, I've just paid for a night. There are no refunds. We can't waste money like that."

He hung his clothes in the closet.

"It doesn't matter. Get your stuff. Get in the car."

They were silent for a moment, then she smiled from one side of her mouth. "I always did take in stray cats."

She broke into a full, warm smile and pulled him into her arms and hugged him. They looked at each other.

"Let's go home," she said.

He closed the door.

"Thank-you." He smiled. "Thank-you."

They walked down the steps from the second story of the sleazy motel.

The sign in the window of the Burger King said "Part Time Help Wanted". His job was to lay the patties in the automatic broiler and let them cook as he listened to the food orders given over the loud speaker by the person at the counter. When the order was called, Budd would place the number of patties in the broiler that corresponded with the order given by the counter person for the lunch and evening crowd on Mondays through Thursdays at the Burger King in Plano. He had to listen carefully to the orders so he would not cook too many or too few meat patties at a time. The culls or misshaped patties were to be thrown out. Although the misshaped patties were good meat, it was against company policy to serve them. Budd ate them. He wasn't supposed to, but it saved on their grocery bill. Later that evening he sat at the counter at JoJo's waiting for Jane to pick him up. It was a Tuesday evening. He drank coffee and read the Dallas Morning News classified ads.

"Goodson And Son Fine Clothiers Need Salesperson For Men's College Apparel Shop. Apply, North Park, Dallas, Texas."

"Jane! Jane!" he exclaimed on the way home. "Look at this in the paper. Look! Goodson and Son. They need someone in the college shop. Jane, I'm perfect! I'll see if I can go to an interview Wednesday or Thursday. I'm going to Texarkana Friday, Saturday and Sunday to see Jenny. I don't know if my boss will like me taking off half of Thursday to go to a job interview. Oh well, I'll tell him the truth. I've always known if I waited long enough and put out the right amount of effort, something would come along. I've always known!"

"You know, I hate to let my people go so much," said the manager of the Burger King the next day. "You have an important job in this place -- even if it is only part time. I get it -- you need a better job, but I need someone I can rely on to do your job. You want to be off Thursday, then take your regular days off Friday, Saturday and Sunday, right?"

"Yes sir."

"Well, all right. I'll let you go this time. Can't blame a guy for trying to better himself."

"And I'll still have my job?"

"Yeah, I guess so."

"Thank you. Thank you very much."

He sat in the executive suite across from the manager of Goodson and Son. The woman was cool but polite.

"Obviously your tastes and background are acceptable. However your tenure with Brooks Brothers was some time ago. Mr. Wilson, I don't know how to say this. We're looking for someone to run our college shop. Quite honestly we're looking for someone, well. ., more college age."

"Does that mean you're not going to hire me?"

"I'm afraid so, Mr. Wilson."

"Don't I look college age? Do I look thirty-eight?" He looked at her and demanded. "Do I? Do I?"

"No Mr. Wilson, you don't'."

"Do you realize I know as much about your lines as any salesman you've got on the floor right now? Do You?"

"Mr. Wilson, your tastes seem impeccable."

"And you won't hire me because I'm thirty-eight?"

"I'm sorry, Mr. Wilson."

"Hell!" He threw his resume on the office floor. "My girlfriend and I are barely eating now. How do you expect people to eat?"

"Mr. Wilson, there are a lot of people hungry in Dallas right now."

He turned and stormed out of the office and down the center isle of the department store. There were tears in his eyes but not one of them fell. They would fall later. He caught the bus and later he walked into the Burger King early in the afternoon.

"Budd," called the manager. "Budd, come on in the office. I want to talk to you a minute."

Budd walked into the cubbyhole office.

"Budd we've decided to replace you with Jimmy We need somebody who's going to be satisfied here and not wanting off to look for another job."

"But you said I still had my job. I wouldn't have taken off if I'd known I'd lose my job.

Jesus, two in one day!"

"I have to consider the best way to run my operation."

He sat at JoJo's trying to read his book. He heard the familiar honk of the red Toyota.

"How'd it go?"

"Just drive Jane. Drive. Get on the expressway and drive."

She obeyed.

"What's the matter? Did it go bad?"

"I want to cry Jane. I just want to cry."

"Then put your head on my shoulder and cry," she said softly. "Go on, put your head on my shoulder and cry."

"They said I was . . . I was too old, Jane," he said between the sobs. "Can you believe that? And then, I get back to the Burger King and I haven't got a job anymore. All in one morning! Can you believe that? All in one morning!?"

She stared straight ahead and asked, "What are you going to do?"

"Hell, I don't know. I've got three days off to go see Jenny. Maybe

I can figure something out then. At any rate, I'm going to interview with Neiman Marcus Monday. I saw the ad in today's paper."

"What time does your bus leave?"

"In about four hours. I need to pack my clothes first."

They went to the house and packed his bag. Then they put the bag in the car and headed south on Central Expressway towards town.

"I'm not supposed to use this credit card of his," she said of her absent boyfriend's in France, "but rules are made...."

"What are you talking about Jane?"

"I'm going to take you out to dinner before you leave for Texarkana."

"Remember my bus leaves in less than four hours."

"I remember. I remember." She smiled.

She pulled up in front of the door with the peephole on Routh Street-- Rapheal's.

"My," he said, remembering the first night at the beginning of this summer episode with Jane. "Why didn't you use this card earlier?"

"Because I'd get in trouble."

"And you're not going to get in trouble now?"

"Now, I don't care. Besides, you've earned it. You deserve it. Come on. Let's go." She parked the car. "The sky's the limit. After all, I'm not paying for it."

"Sure, big Sis." He broke into a smile.

"Oh stop that! You're not my little brother. You never were." They savored a leisurely meal. His spirits brightened. They enjoyed themselves. They were oblivious to time.

CHAPTER 9

After dinner, she backtracked the little red Toyota to Turtle Creek Boulevard, turned right on Lemmon Avenue, crossed the bridge over Turtle Creek and followed Lemmon Avenue to North Central Expressway. Then she headed north on Central.

"Wait a minute, Jane!" Budd exclaimed. "Where are we going? I 've got to catch my bus."

"You'll get there."

"At the Mockingbird Lane exit of Central Expressway, she U-turned over the Mockingbird Lane bridge and then went back south on Central Expressway.

"We've got a little time to kill." She smiled. "Let's sing some songs.

'You make me feel so young,' she began.

'You make me feel there are songs to sung,

Bells to be rung . . . and a wonderful fling to be flung.

And even when I'm old and gray,

I'm going to feel the way I do today,

CAUSE YOU MAKE ME FEEL SO YOUNG!'

I'm not that old, yet. Don't take me literally." She was smiling. She U-turned and headed north on Central Expressway. Several exits later, she headed south on Central again. The time was ticking.

"And that laugh that wrinkles your nose'," started Budd, "'touches my foolish heart,' What is it? I can't remember the lyric."

You'd make a lousy singer if you can't remember a lyric. Can't you sing at all?" she demanded.

"No!" he yelled back. "How about 'Embraceable You'?"

"Must I? You've worn that one thin."

"Story of my life." He laughed.

'The embrace that got away—'

'The road gets rougher.'

She picked up on it, and took the song.

'It's lonelier and tougher.

With hope you'll burn up,

tomorrow he may turn up.

There's just no let up,

the livelong night and day.

Ever since this world began,

there is nothing sadder than,

a one man woman. . .looking for.. .

THE MAN THAT GOT AWAY.'

They made several more trips up and down Central Expressway singing their songs.

"Jesus Jane, what time is it?"

"Oh my heavens, it's ten of eleven." There was a devilish grin on her face.

"We can't get down there on time! Shit, I'm going to miss my bus!"

"What time do you pick Jennifer up at Sissy's tomorrow?"

"Not until six p.m."

"Well, that means you can catch a bus in the morning and still be there in time to pick Jenny up. Besides, you don't want to be with your parents tomorrow, anyway." She took a left on Central Expressway and headed north.

"Where are we going?" he asked.

"Home."

Then he started to laugh. "Okay."

He walked out onto his parents' patio. Summer was passing and the first crisp winds of autumn were blowing in. The leaves were beginning to turn. He stood there alone, thinking. The back screen door softly opened and shut. His little daughter, Jenny, was keeping warm in a red coat and white mittens.

"What's a depression, Daddy?"

"It's when people are out of work and don't have enough to eat."

"Is there really a depression in Dallas?" she asked.

"Yes."

"And people don't have enough to eat and can't find jobs?"

"Yes."

"You never could find a job, Daddy."

He broke into a smile. "I know."

"But if you stay here at Grandma's, you can always eat. Grandma feeds you TOO much."

"If I stay here at Grandma's I'll always be a little boy. Can you see that, Jenny?"

"What's wrong with that?"

"Can't you see? I'm not a little boy anymore." He picked his daughter up and hugged her.

"I'm not a little boy anymore." He put his child down, then he took a crumpled napkin from his coat pocket and wiped his eyes.

"Well. . ," he said. "I'll give it one last shot, Neiman Marcus, Monday."

"Daddy what's so important about Neiman Marcus?"

"I don't know." He began to laugh. "I SWEAR I don't know. Come on, let's go eat lunch."

She picked him up early at the downtown Dallas bus station. He pitched his bag across the back seat of the Toyota and then got in the car.

"How's Jenny?" she asked.

"She's fine," he said, sensing that something was wrong. "Just fine."

They sat in silence.

"You're certainly being quiet this morning." He tried to make conversation. "Something wrong?"

"No, not really. We'll talk about it when we get home, okay?"

"All right."

"When is your appointment at Neiman's?"

"Any time this afternoon. It's a walk-in. Why?"

"Just wondered."

"Jane, what's the matter?"

"Really, let's talk about it when we get home." They drove in silence.

"We can sit at the breakfast table," she said after they arrived at the house. "I'll make some coffee."

"What's the matter? Why aren't you going to work?"

"I took the day off. I got a call from my friend Francois, the one in France. He's in New York. He's coming in, today. You must leave.

I'm sorry, but you must. I'm going to lose the house. I'm going to lose everything. I can't keep it all now on a secretary's salary."

"I thought this house was yours."

"It was, at one time. He took it over when I could no longer afford it."

"Some friend," said Budd.

"He's a good man. He has other obligations."

"What are you going to do? Where are you going to live?"

"I've asked for my old job back at The Seasons."

"Singing?"

"Yes."

"Alright!"

"Maybe they can advance me enough to get an apartment."

"They will," he said. "They will."

"You're going to have to leave."

"Okay," he said.

"Are you all right?" she asked.

"I'm all right. I'm just trying to figure out what I'm going to do. I'll take what I can now in my grip. The rest of my stuff you'll just have to stick somewhere until I find out where I'm going to be," he said. "Take me to JoJo's. I can walk to Neiman's from there."

"What?" she exclaimed. "You can't walk all the way out there! That's a suburban store. It's out in the middle of nowhere."

I'll make it," he replied.

Silently she picked his grip up and carried it into the bedroom and began packing. He changed into his suit, tie and trench coat as he prepared himself for the long walk, the weather, the interview.

"I hate this," she said as they walked to the car. "I hate it!"

She turned east on Walnut Hill Lane and then drove to the intersection of Walnut Hill Lane and Central Expressway. Then she U-turned back under the expressway into the westbound lane of Walnut Hill. She pulled the car into the parking lot of a shopping area on the corner of Walnut Hill Lane and the northwest side of the southbound access road of Central Expressway. JoJo's was up the hill on the access road. He picked up his grip and walked around the back of the car toward the driver's window.

"I can make it. I can walk. Pick yourself up, girl." He turned around and walked up the access road to JoJo's.

"You -- you can do anything!"

He turned around again. "It's all right. It's all right. Remember ninety-nine percent of Jane Mitchell's a Gershwin tune. Remember that."

"And a can of Hills Brothers coffee," she called back.

"Good-bye, Jane."

She waved her fingers good-bye. She looked down at the dashboard. "Loneliness is the price you pay for solitude," she purred. She put the car in gear and headed up onto Central Expressway. "Loneliness is the price you pay for solitude. Oh well."

He walked into JoJo's. He put his grip down next to a counter stool. Then he sat down and ordered coffee. "I've got to shove," he said to the waitress after gulping down his coffee. " If you see Colleen tell her I went for a long walk. Oh." He picked up the grip and handed it to the waitress. "Tell her to keep this for me. I'll be back to get it, tonight."

"Okay...?" The waitress looked questioningly , picked up the grip and took it to the back of the restaurant and went about her work. He walked down to Walnut Hill Lane and turned west.

It had been a misty morning, but by now the sun had burned the mist off. He passed Hillcrest and kept walking. It seemed the walk would never end, and he began sweating underneath the insulation of his trench coat and suit. He reached the intersection of Walnut Hill Lane and Preston Road. He waited for what seemed like an eternity. Finally the North Preston Road bus came. He boarded the bus and began the long ride out to the suburbs.

"I've come to apply for the job in men's clothing you have advertised," he said to the girl at the front desk of the human relations department of the suburban Neiman Marcus store.

She handed him an application. He filled it out.

"Here you are," he said to the girl. "Will I interview now?"

"We're just taking applications at this point," said the girl.

"Can't you make an exception, this time? If you only knew how much trouble it took me to get out here!" Budd was frantic. "I walked all the way from North Central Expressway to Preston Road to catch a bus to get here."

"I'm sorry." She looked at him rather strangely. "Just applications today. That's what the advertisement in the paper says."

"I must have read it wrong," Budd said.

He left the store and walked across the street to a small restaurant. He ordered a cup of coffee. He still had some change in his pocket but he broke his last dollar.

"Well, I've got to get back to JoJo's somehow. Can't sit here forever. Let's go." He mustered up all his strength and got up and walked to the bus stop.

"Walnut Hill Lane," said Budd as he eyed the familiar intersection from within the ingoing bus. He pulled the buzzer and got off when the bus stopped. "Okay." He sighed "Lets go for it, Central Expressway or bust." He put one foot in front of the other then put one foot in front of the other again. Each step was a decision.

The walk up the access road seemed interminable. It was around 7:30 p.m. when he walked in the doors of JoJo's again.

"Coffee," he said.

"Gonna read again?" asked the waitress.

"Yeah, I guess so."

"You don't look very well."

"I don't feel very well."

Colleen walked in a little after ten.

"Your buddy's down there," said the other waitress. "I think he's got the flu or pneumonia or something."

"What's the matter, Budd?" Colleen walked up to him and asked.

"I don't feel too good."

"You don't look good. Why don't you go home?"

"I don't have one, anymore."

"What happened to your fancy girlfriend?"

"She got rid of me."

"Snotty bitch."

"It wasn't her fault. She had to."

They were silent.

"Colleen, you always wanted this Rolex watch for your boyfriend. I'll give it to you in exchange for a place to rest for a couple of days and get back on my feet." He unfastened the clasp and handed it to her. " It's a fake, but it's still a good watch."

"It's a beauty all right." She examined the watch. "He's up East on a long haul right now."

She looked at Budd -- then at the watch. "Ah, okay." She dug into her pocket and pulled out her keys. "Here, I've got a '67 dark blue Mustang out in the back parking lot. There's a pillow in the front seat. Try to sleep it off. You look like Hell. I'll get somebody to bring you out some food."

"Colleen you don't have to do all that."

"I figure a Rolex watch is worth a place to stay for a couple of nights, even if it isn't real. Go on to the car. I'll cover your coffee. They told me your bag is inside. I'll bring it when I get back."

He heard the television. It was dark except for the glow of the television. He was in a mobile home, lying on a couch covered by an Afghan. Over her pantyhose she was wearing the official

JoJo's starched dress shirt. She was getting ready for work.

"Where am I?" He stirred.

"You've been asleep for nearly two days." She put on her skirt and went into the bathroom to put on her make-up. "I've washed your clothes. There's a fresh change of clothes here in the bathroom. Your suit and the rest of your clothes are packed in your bag. Come on. Get up.

"Budd. I've got to take you back to JoJo's. I've got to go to work. My boyfriend will be back tonight, probably. Here." She threw a towel and washcloth to him as she came out of the bathroom.

"Your underwear's on the clothes hamper. Take a shower and let's get going. I've saved you some lunch on the kitchen table."

He walked into the kitchen after showering and dressing. There was cold fried chicken and cornbread on a plate under a paper towel and black-eyed peas in a bowl.

"Colleen, you didn't have to do all this," he said as he sat at the table and ate.

"You paid me." She held up the Rolex watch. "You paid me. Come on. Eat up. Let's get going I don't want to be late."

They got in the Mustang. She started to drive.

"Where are we, Colleen?"

"North of D.F.W. airport."

"I don't remember coming out here."

"You were asleep. I had to practically carry you in the house."

"I don't remember any of that."

She parked the car behind JoJo's. She stuffed two dollars in his left pants pocket.

"Here, this'll cover you for coffee for eight more hours."

"Bringing your friend back again, Colleen?" grumbled the manager as the couple entered the restaurant. "That guy spends more time and less money drinking coffee than anybody..."

Her hands were firmly placed on the sides of her hips. "Leave him alone, Rusty! You hear me, leave him alone."

"All right Colleen." The manager backed down. "All right."

The sun was rising. It would soon be time for a shift change. Budd would have to leave.

She wiped the counter in front of him.

"What are you going to do, Budd? You can't sit here and drink coffee forever. When my shift's over they'll make you leave."

"I know."

"What are you going to do?"

"I don't know." He picked up his book and read. She stood in silence. He turned the last page and closed the book. He handed it to her.

"What are you doing?" She looked at the cover of the book, The Grapes of Wrath, by John Steinbeck. She looked at Budd. "I never heard of him," she said.

"Guy knew what he was talking about, Colleen." He took the two dollars from his pocket.

"This is for the coffee." He picked up his grip and headed toward the door.

"Be careful, Budd."

He looked back and smiled. "I can walk. If there is one thing I can do, I can walk." He stepped out of the restaurant onto the street. He walked down the access road to Walnut Hill Lane. The mist was turning into a cold, Autumn rain. He decided to step under the Central Expressway overpass until it died down.

He stood on the right side under the bridge. They stood on the left, a young Hispanic couple with a baby. All of their belongings were in a cardboard suitcase. All of were in his grip.

The mother wore a simple cotton dress and sneakers. The baby had on a diaper and a tiny cotton shirt. They were huddled together. They were cold; they were not prepared for the weather.

He looked at them. Then immediately he looked straight ahead. Then he looked down at his London Fog trench coat. He bit his lower lip and started to walk over to the couple and child. He unfastened the sash and unbuttoned the trench coat.

"Here," he said as he wrapped the coat around the mother and baby. "We're all in this together. We're all in this together."

"Gracias," said the father in amazement. "Gracias, amigo."

"You're welcome. Well, I gotta shove."

"Gracias Amigo, Gracias." Again the father thanked him.

Budd looked back and smiled again. "Adios. I got a long way to go. Oh well, follow the yellow brick road."

He picked up his grip and walked up Walnut Hill to Hillcrest. He turned south and walked all the way to Mockingbird Lane.

"Gee, I hope I don't get arrested for vagrancy." He felt a sense of vulnerability and nakedness, a paranoiac feeling about being out there all alone on the streets of Dallas.

He followed Mockingbird Lane, turned left on Lomo Alto and continued to walk down the blocks of Lomo Alto past the apartment in the 4300 block he and Sissy had shared years before.

At the corner past the apartment, he turned left on Fairway and right around the corner to the back of his sister's townhouse on Hawthorne. Budd knew his parents would come in sometime that week to see his sister. He also knew he wasn't welcome. He walked up to the back door of his sister's townhouse and rang the doorbell. She met him at the door.

"Budd you look horrible!" she began. "Budd, I can't put up with you right now. I'm having some people over for a dinner party. I just can't put you up."

"Let him go upstairs and put on some dry clothes," said his mother.

Budd changed into some old clothes from his grip. Colleen had done such a good job of packing his bag that once Budd pulled his suit out to get some other clothes he couldn't get it to fit back in his bag. Therefore, when he came downstairs from putting on some fresh clothes he was carrying the suit underneath his arm. They were waiting for him at the foot of the stairs.

"You've got to get out of here!" exclaimed his sister. "And, you've got to forget about your singer. You'll never be stable enough to have a real relationship with her, and we certainly are tired of footing the bills while you two play house here in Dallas. You've got to go home! I'll take you to the bus station now."

"You don't have to. I'll get there."

"HOW?" his sister demanded.

"I can take the Lemmon Avenue bus and get off downtown," he said. "Take the first Greyhound home."

"Here, then." She feverishly grabbed some bills from her purse. "I'm sorry. I just can't have you here."

He caught the Lemmon Avenue bus going downtown. He bought the ticket at the Greyhound terminal. He waited. Eventually, he boarded the bus and began the solitary ride back to Texarkana. It was in the middle of the night when he arrived. The rain was falling in torrents. The bus kicked up great waves of water as it came down Stateline Avenue to the downtown bus station. Budd got off the bus. The office was closed and he didn't have the right change for the pay phone to call a cab. He tried to stuff his suit in his bag -- but it didn't fit. He walked down Olive Street in the rain with his suit wadded up underneath his arm. He turned the key in the lock, opened the door and walked into his parents' house. He sat down on the couch.

"Why can't I get away from this place?" He sighed. "Why can't I get away from this Goddamned place?" Once again, was it fate or some misguided purpose or immoral desire that had put him at his parents' mercy or was he just a pawn? Perhaps he was just crazy. That's it, he was just crazy. Perhaps that was the reason for the whole thing, his whole life, he'd been ill...

He was too tired to think about it any more. He walked upstairs, draped his suit over a chair, the suit he had worn to Brooks Brothers to interview in years before, and fell asleep on his bed, still wearing his wet clothes.

Budd put himself through a regime of exercise to deal with his situation. He power-walked three miles daily. He kept himself in good shape. He used exercise as a way of coping. He kept to himself and spent most of his spare time with Jennifer. He was Daddy Longlegs and Daddy Warbucks both to his red-headed little girl. To Jenny HE WAS DADDY!

Budd and his parents got better at accepting each other for what they were. They helped him rent an old house down the street from their place. He called it "The Truman House". He became an excellent cook. He was always trying some new recipe on Jenny and his parents. Apparently, he was an adequate cook, for they never refused a meal. He stayed at home a lot. He read a lot. Even though he was an outgoing person, he was lonely. Sissy and Budd reached a working peace, also.

It was time Jennifer met her godmother. Jenny's eighth birthday present from her daddy was to take her to Dallas to meet Jane. They drove to Dallas on Interstate 30. They talked about everything along the way. The Interstate merged with I-75, North Central Expressway, on the edge of downtown Dallas. They headed north on Central Expressway, passing the skyline of the city.

"Doesn't it look like the Emerald City?"

"Daddy, Dallas sure is big," Jennifer responded to her first encounter with the metropolis.

They drove out North Central Expressway and stopped at the same JoJo's where Jane, Sissy and Budd had gone to breakfast years before, the same JoJo's from which he'd left Dallas in defeat. The hostess showed father and daughter to their table.

"Is there a young lady working here named Colleen?" Budd began. "She used to work the night shift."

"Colleen? Sure. She's on days now. She ought to be back there rattling around somewhere. You'll hear her."

"Could you get her for me?"

"Sure, just a minute."

Budd waited for a few minutes. Out came Colleen. She hadn't changed. "Some guy?"she asked the hostess, then peered over to Budd.

"Well I'll be damned." She walked over to their table. "You still alive? I can't believe it. This your little girl? You're much better looking than your dad." Jenny smiled. "Course that ain't sayin' a hell of a lot." Colleen turned to Budd.

"You got enough money to get out of here? I was always having to bail your daddy out."

"Colleen," barked the manager, "haven't you got any tables to wait on?"

"Yes sir." She bent down close to Budd and Jenny. "Been here three years and he hasn't fired me yet. I'll see ya' later." She took off towards the counter.

"Daddy, how come city people look different from people at home?" asked Jenny after looking around the restaurant.

"Well there are a lot of people from different places living here. Dallas is an international city. Look at that little old lady sitting there by herself. She looks like she's from Beekman Place."

The elderly woman had on a tailored, medium green raw silk suit with a matching pillbox hat, a small strand of pearls, and white framed, cat-eyed prescription bifocal sunglasses. Her face was covered with white powder and red rouge, but the battle of age had been lost long ago. She delicately sipped on a small bowl of soup using a large round soup spoon. An unfiltered cigarette with bright red lipstick stain on the tip sat burning in an ashtray by her, and her white dress gloves were placed on the table.

"Do you know who she is?" he asked.

"She's Shirley Temple."

"I was thinking more like Norma Desmond " He pictured an instantaneous fantasy of the woman being dredged up from some gigantic old Highland Park castle.

". . . Oh well, every little girl should be taken to Neiman Marcus at Christmastime," said Budd after they left JoJo's. Jenny agreed. They observed the beautiful lights and decorations that adorned North Park Mall at Christmas. They fought for a parking place -- then they made the grand tour starting with Lord and Taylor, then Neiman Marcus and every specialty shop along the way. After they'd seen the sights, they went back and checked into their adjoining motel rooms and rested up for the evening.

"Dad, what'ss Jane like?" Jennifer later asked.

"Jane. . ? Well, she's very attractive."

"Yeah, but what's she like?"

"Well, Jane's kind of hard to describe. She's a loner who thrives on being around people. At first you'll think she's cold, but she's not. She's a very warm person. She'd do anything to help you."

"Is she always dressed up like on her record cover? Like maybe in a fur coat from Neiman Marcus?" Jenny had toured the fur section of Neiman's earlier that afternoon.

"Nah, not really. I guess Jane's most at home in a pair of jeans and an old sweatshirt."

"I can hardly wait for tonight, Daddy."

An evening on the town with Jenny in Dallas began with a hamburger and french fries at McDonald's. Then they went straight to The Seasons. They took the elevator to the tenth floor. Rather than going into the restaurant this time, they went into the club. As was always his tradition, they were early. For an hour, Jenny sipped on Shirley Temples and her father drank coffee.

"Hello, Sport." He felt her presence, heard her throaty voice.

"Aunt Jane!"

"Jennifer Lee! I swear, you're beautiful! You look just like Sissy."

"Hello, Baby," said Budd as he stood up and hugged her. " How are you? Jenny, how did you know she was Jane?"

"She's wearing black, Daddy, like on her record cover."

"You look great, girl," he said. Jane's return to singing had been good for her.

She had a capacity to re-invent herself over and over. It kept her youthful and alive as she grew older.

"Scoot over Sport, let me sit between you two. Jennifer, did you know your mother and father used to come in here all the time?"

Jenny nodded a big 'yes/'.

"That was a long time ago," said Budd.

"It wasn't that long ago," Jane replied.

"Eight or nine years ago."

"Yes, I guess it was. My -- time flies."

"I wish I could say the same,"said Budd,

"WILLIAM GEORGE WILSON. . . I have something to say to you." Jane pointed at Budd.

'Travel a new highway.

Travel a new road.'

"Auntie Mame!" cheered Jenny. "You're Auntie Mame!"

"You're right, my beloved. I'm your Auntie Mame " She laughed. "Now Budd, as I was saying, 'The person you want to be is three-dimensional'. Her pianist sat down and doodled on the piano. She looked at her watch. "I've got to start. My pianist is signaling me. I've reserved you and your father a table right down front. It was your mother and father's table 'a long time ago', as your father would say."

She walked up to the stand, settled herself on the stool, flashed a smile at Jenny and began. "I have a little friend here tonight, a beautiful little girl, Jennifer Wilson. I've heard that whenever she falls down and skins her knee, her father has a special song for her. I'd like to try to do it.

"One two, one two three four----

'Nothing's impossible, I have found,

when both feet are upon the ground,

so pick yourself up—'

"Daddy!" yelled Jenny. 'Pick Yourself Up'!."

'—dust yourself off,

start all over again.'

"Daddy, isn't it neat?! It's like you say to me."

"I say to myself," he concurred.

'Work like a soul inspired,

til the battle of the day is won.

You may be sick and tired,

but you'll be a man, my son!'

'Can you remember the famous men,

who had to fall to rise again?

so pick yourself up,'

(She went up a half step)

'take a deep breath,'

(She went down a half step)

'so pick yourself up, dust yourself off,

START ALL OVER AGAIN.'

Budd and Jennifer applauded loudly. They were somewhat conspicuous. It was early in the evening. The crowd was small.

"Now Jenny, here's one for your father." She began to half sing and half whisper.

'Embrace me,

my sweet embraceable you.

For years,

you irreplaceable you.

All this time,

my heart still grows tipsy in me.

You and you alone,

bring out the gypsy in me.

I love, and will always love

the many charms about you.

Above all,

I do miss my arms about you.

Don't be a naughty baby,

come to Mamma, come to Mamma do.

My always sweet embraceable you.'

"Thank you Mr. Wilson." She looked down and smiled as she finished. "Miss Wilson, thank you."

'I remember you.

You're the one

who made my dreams come true,

a few kisses ago.'

* * *

'When I want rain,

I get sunny weather.

I'm just as blue as the sky.

Since love is gone,

can't pull myself together.

Guess I'll hang my tears out to dry.'

* * *

'Somewhere there's music,

how faint the tune.

Somewhere there's heaven,

how high the moon.'

* * *

'It is only a paper moon,

hanging over a cardboard sea,

but it wouldn't be make believe

if you believed in me.'

* * *

"We've got to go. I've got a little one. Getting late."

She looked down from the stand. "Can you find my place?"

"6306 Shady Brook Lane, #2107. I think I can. If not, I'll call you. See ya' tomorrow."

"Bye, Jennifer Lee!" Jane smiled, crossed her eyes, then winked and laughed.

"Good-bye, Aunt Jane."

It was ten-fifteen on a Saturday night in Dallas, Texas. Budd and his daughter walked to their car. They stopped at Denny's for a bite to eat and then went back to the motel. It had been a long day and night and new territory for the little girl, Jennifer. They both were tired. The next morning they met Budd's sister at La Madeleine on Lemmon Avenue for a late Sunday breakfast. Budd's sister was afraid the city might frighten Jennifer. On the contrary, Jennifer was having a good time, and making her first value judgment in favor of a large city over a smaller one like Texarkana. It was a conclusion that would stay with her for life. They had coffee and croissants. They visited during what was left of the morning, then Budd and Jennifer excused themselves and headed in the direction of Jane's apartment.

After one call for directions they found the place.

"Come on up!" she called from her second-story apartment window. "Here I am!"

"Hi Jane!" Jenny exclaimed. They climbed the stairs.

"Hi, Baby." She embraced Jennifer. "Well, it's not Bryn Mawr, but it's comfortable and it's home."

"Jane, it's lovely," he said. "Look at all the paintings. I didn't know you were an art connoisseur."

"Well -- on a low budget. You know my life has taken many turns."

"What's his name Jane, the artist?"

"Sit down, Jenny." She chose to ignore Budd.

"Where?" Jenny eyed the empty room.

"Well, let's sit on the floor." Jane shrugged and smiled. "Budd, what are you doing?"

"Thumbing through your records."

"I never listen to them anymore.

"Anita O'Day ," he said as he picked up the album. "It's autographed with a personal note to you. Did you copy Anita O'Day?"

"Well, yes to a certain extent. She came in to hear me once at the club when I was singing. We had a few drinks. She liked my style." She shrugged. There was a silence. "You know, I started in folk music in coffee houses in the early sixties, then I heard people like Anita O'Day and Chris Connor and June Christy and they were so swinging and so sensual that I had to get into jazz. In retrospect, it wasn't a bad move. Jennifer," she changed the subject, " how about a coke?"

"Yes, ma'am."

"Budd, let's have hot tea."

Budd flipped on the Anita O'Day record. They sipped their drinks.

"I know," Jane said. "Jennifer I'll show you my scrapbook. It'll probably bore you to tears."

"A scrapbook?"

"Yes, of all my years of singing." She went to her hall closet and pulled out a large album. She sat down on the floor with Jenny.

"Oh, this Dallas Times Herald article and picture of me were taken about the time I met your father and mother. Oh, and this was me in 'Profile' in the Dallas Morning News. Look how skinny I was. I was thirty-nine at the time."

"Aunt Jane, you're a celebrity!"

"No, not really. I might have been one but I started too late and I had children, a family here in Dallas. You have to go to New York or L.A. to really make it big in jazz to get the exposure. You've pretty much got to be on your own. I had other obligations. I don't really regret it. At least, I don't think so."

"Speaking of that, let's drive over to Bryn Mawr and see the old house," said Budd.

"Well, okay. . . Everybody put on their jackets and wraps."

"Jane, you drive. I don't even know if I could find the place anymore."

"Both of us," she replied. "Hop in the car, Jennifer. Everybody in? Seat belts?" She adjusted the mirrors. "Let's go."

"Lord, they've changed this place," she said as they parked in front of 8001 Bryn Mawr. "I can hardly recognize it."

"Daddy can I get out and look around?"

"Yes honey, but stay right here in front. I want to be able to see you all the time. And don't bother anything. This is somebody else's house now."

Jennifer looked around the front yard.

"We had some good times here." Budd looked at the house sentimentally.

"We sure did," she said softly, "Right or wrong, what we've had has been good.

Did you ever regret it, Budd? What we've had, what affect it had on Jenny, or Sissy, or on your own life?"

"No, never did. You're the best woman I've ever known."

"Am I?" She was gently amazed. "I'm afraid I've never fit a mold."

"That's what I love about you."

She looked at the house on Bryn Mawr and all its memories....
"Come on, let's go. We mustn't live in the past."

"Living in the past isn't bad if we live there together."

She smiled. "Let's go."

They drove back to Jane's apartment and walked up the flight of steps.

"We've got to go home," said Budd. "Monday comes. At least once a week, Monday comes."

"Yeah I know. I've got to take off tomorrow. I've got a doctor's appointment. Routine mammo."

It was though Jane had saved the remark for the very last thing to be said to Budd before he left.

"Are you okay?"

"Oh -- yeah, sure I'm okay."

"You're positive?"

"I'm okay. Really I'm okay. Nothing to worry about. Routine. Piece of cake."

"Okay. . . Honey, go kiss your Aunt Jane good-bye."

Jennifer ran up to Jane Mitchell. They hugged each other.

"Au Revoir, mon petite," Jane said to the child as she kissed her.

"How do you say, 'Auf Wiedersehen?'" he questioned.

She looked at them both. "You don't. Farewell, my beloved."

And they both left Jane at the place Budd couldn't easily find.

Budd went his own way alone. He still flirted with waitresses, but they were getting younger and he was getting older and they all knew it. He maintained the Truman House and he still cooked. Jennifer was constantly making a beeline between Budd's and his parents' homes bringing books and games from one house to the other.

'Budd Wilson,' he said to himself as he sat on the front porch swing after doing the supper dishes, 'I swear you're becoming an old maid bachelor. Listen Buddy-boy, you need to find some foxy ole' mare here and settle out to pasture.' There was more sadness than hope in what he said because for whatever star struck reason or extra sensory impulse he knew that the chapter of his life in Dallas was in the process of closing, and that his life would soon be taking some strange twists from the past and into the present in Texarkana. His instincts would soon prove him right.

One night, as he was sitting on the porch Steven Brantley stepped out of the dark.

"Say!"

"Hello Steve. Have a seat."

"Don't mind if I do. . . Say you don't know a Nicole Smithson, do ya?"

"Nicole Smithson? Lord yes, Stephen, I know Nicole. I've known her for twenty years, rather intimately at one time."

Thirty-eight led to thirty-nine.

A dialogue between two neighbors began...

CHAPTER 10

It was not until the week-end after the fire that Budd came out in his front yard and ventured across the street to look at the charred ground. Two of Budd's neighbors sat next door on their front porch.

"Hey, Budd," the young man called. "Come here."

"Did you see who did it?" asked Budd. "Where's Steve?"

"Steve went to Dallas," the other neighbor said. "I know who did it."

"Who?" asked Budd.

"You saw it," responded the neighbor.

"And I'm afraid of what I saw."

"A German car." The neighbor spat on the sidewalk.

"Have you seen it before?" Budd asked.

"I might have."

"Where?"

"'Bout south three blocks, over two."

"Then you went down there with him?" Budd asked again.

"Stephen's a Vietnam war veteran, ain't he?"

"You just answered my question. I saw it all and I know both of them. Who did you see get out of the car?"

"Tall guy, long hair, beard."

"Me too. What about you, Dan?" Budd asked the other neighbor.

"Same."

"Who is he?" asked Budd.

"Drives a white van."

"The white van... Describe this van."

In the many conversations Budd had engaged in with Steve Brantley before the fire, Steve had often mentioned that Nicole was having an affair with a long-haired, Vietnam group member with a questionable drug background who drove a white van with a red continental kit on the back. According to Stephen, Nicole and the group member had met at late hours in her office and at her home. Budd had always defended her right to have such a relationship saying to Steve it was her business. Steve was a rigid moralist. Budd wasn't. He had lived through a deteriorating marriage. He knew that in some times of crisis, woman and man must seek each other's comfort, if for no other reason than to prove that they are still alive.

Dr. Allen Tomlinson was not considered one of the best psychiatrists in Texarkana. However, he was the last of the original psychiatrists still practicing in the city. It was a generational concern and the older generation still governed the behavior and ethics of the younger group by age and experience. Nicole belonged to. Dr. Tomlinson's office. It was located in the Main Street Doctors' Plaza, although it was in a different suite and independent from Nicole's and the Vietnam War counseling office. Budd had an appointment at 1:30 p.m. Dr. Tomlinson's waiting room was full. At four p.m., Budd was escorted by the receptionist into the doctor's office.

"Mr. Wilson, I understand you want to be in therapy."

"No sir," Budd started. "I want to tell you about a fire."

"Don't know anything about a fire. Don't want to know anything about a fire."

"Someone in Nicole Smithson's car set my neighbor's yard on fire. There were enough explosives in this person's house to take a couple of blocks with it if had it ignited."

"Now Mr. Wilson, I find that a little hard to believe. Think you're suffering from a slight delusion. You ever work for a living?"

"Yes sir, I have," said Budd.

"What's the best job you ever had?" The doctor chortled under his breath.

"Brooks Brothers, 201 Field Street, Dallas, Texas."

"That's Fort Worth?"

"No sir, Dallas, Brooks Brothers."

"Is this Brooks Brothers the same as the Brooks ladies' shop in our mall here?"

"No sir, it's not." Budd was getting angry. "Look, there are explosives in that house. That fire put a lot of people in jeopardy including my parents and my little girl."

"Mr. Wilson, you're talking to the wrong person. You need to go down to the police, if what you say is true. I'm just an old country boy . . . you know. . . from the farm." The doctor smiled and looked over his half glasses.

"The trouble with people in your profession is that you are always trying to trip people up some way."

"Did Miss Smithson try to trip you up some way?"

"Not to my knowledge, at this point."

A call came in for Dr. Tomlinson. He talked to a friend about bulls and cows for roughly twenty minutes.

"Phone call." Dr. Tomlinson smiled beneath his half glasses after he hung up.

"I'm paying for this!" Budd was angry.

"Why would Nicole Smithson burn your neighbor's yard?"

"I didn't say she did it. I said it was her car."

"Where else are some of these Brooks Brothers stores? Never heard of them."

"Oh, New York, Chicago, Los Angeles, the major cities. If I

remember correctly, we carried your size." Dr. Tomlinson was a rather portly man-- "a Fifty-three regular."

"That's a pretty good guess. Mr. Wilson, you've been sick in the past?"

"That's right."

"Mr. Wilson, I believe you belong in a state hospital. You're definitely suffering from paranoid delusions. I think you're dangerous."

"Why would I be? I have nothing against Nicole."

"But you're accusing her of setting your neighbor's yard on fire. You're saying that a nut has enough explosives in his house to blow up the block. You're down here telling me all of this and you say you don't have any anger against her? Mr. Wilson, I find that hard to believe. It doesn't make any sense."

"If only you knew how much I do care for her," said Budd softly.

"That's even more reason to have this distorted story -- revenge for a lost love. It would be better for you to be away for a while."

"BUT I'M NOT CRAZY RIGHT NOW. I'm telling you the truth."

"Founded in Philadelphia, wasn't it? Brooks Brothers! Where was Brooks Brothers founded!?"

"Lower Manhattan. New York City."

"Where in lower Manhattan?" the doctor demanded. The tension was accelerating very rapidly.

"On Katherine and Cherry Streets!" Budd shot back.

"When!?"

"In 1818!" Budd yelled .

"You're right." The doctor backed off. 'The Golden Fleece'. I am a size fifty-three regular. Your memory for detail is very good Mr. Wilson, but I think you have two personalities, a very normal one, and a very sick one."

"I know I'm sick. I always will be and I've had to learn to live with it. I take my lithium."

Dr. Tomlinson buzzed the receptionist on his phone. She came in.

"Take him to the lab. Get a lithium blood count on him, right now please," the doctor demanded.

"I don't mind. I take my lithium."

"Well, we're going to find out, aren't we?"

"Okay! That's fine!" Budd started to roll up his sleeve. "All I'm trying to do is to keep a lot of people from getting hurt. I give up! I quit. This has been a waste of time and money."

"You think so? We don't."

Budd offered no resistance. He followed the lady to the lab.

For four days, Budd tried to get the results of his lithium blood analysis. Each time Dr. Tomlinson's receptionist was too busy to give it to him.

"This is Mrs. Edgar Wilson, Budd's mother. He has been unable to get his lithium blood count from your office for four days. I'd like to know what it is."

"We gave him the results of his blood test."

"No, you did not!" Budd's mother knew the receptionist's statement was not true.

"It's..." The receptionist put Mrs. Wilson on hold. There was a long wait. "It's normal."

"Thank you... very much," Mildred Wilson answered in a quiet seethe.

Budd called Stephen on the phone. "Come on over, Stephen. I need to talk to you."

"I'll meet you on your patio in the back yard," Stephen replied.

Budd asked his mother to join the conversation. All three of them met on the Wilson patio.

"He didn't believe a word I said Stephen, not a word. I got a royal screw job."

"Well you should'a never gone down there in the first place. What do you expect, Buddy?

People in that profession stick together. He may have told you you're crazy, but he knows you're not, and figures your parents are spiteful enough or you're dumb enough to fall for it and he could put you away. Fortunately, he's wrong on both counts. Never-the-less, he heard you, Budd."

"His lithium level is normal," said Mrs.Wilson.

"Mrs. Wilson, regardless of what Budd said to him, or he said to Budd, the Doctor heard him."

"I've never dealt with anything like this before," replied Budd's mother.

"Me either," said Budd.

"We-a-ell," Stephen squatted down and rubbed a stick in the dirt on the Wilson patio, then he looked up. "It's the shrinks over the nuts, two to zero.

"Who's going to win, Stephen?" asked Mrs. Wilson.

"I don't know."

"She betrayed me! Again, she betrayed me!"

"You're catching on. Now calm down, flyboy. Calm down. Don't want to get your silk scarf dirty. He may've tried to convince you you're crazy, but he knows you're not. He clearly heard you."

It was the first time Stephen used the nickname 'flyboy" for Budd.

Mrs. Wilson smiled at her son and her neighbor.

"I'll get you boys some iced tea."

Budd decided to move back into his parents' home. If they were going to protect themselves and that block of Olive Street, they were going to protect it as a family.

Budd's illness was a biochemical illness. He knew, that with proper medication he could remain virtually symptom-free. Lithium carbonate had been accidentally discovered for the treatment of manic depression. At that time, a patient who was being treated for a physical illness and was also a manic depressive was given lithium carbonate for the treatment of his physical symptoms. Amazingly enough, both physical and emotional symptoms disappeared. To insure one remained within the normal range of lithium effectiveness, one had to take a routine blood test to give a measurement of one's lithium blood level. Budd had done this every month since he'd begun taking the medication, and once a month, he'd had the lab forward the results to his pharmacist.

One day in early summer, soon after his visit with Dr. Tomlinson, Budd was running errands with his mother, which included stopping at the pharmacy and refilling his prescription for lithium carbonate.

"We'll give you three or four more pills on this lithium," said the pharmacist. Budd had never had problems with his pharmacy. He looked at his mother.

"I smell a rat."

"I do too."

Budd had taken his medication as prescribed by Dr. Dodd from the day he had left the hospital. He believed in it. He religiously believed in it. It was beneficial, if not tantamount to his sanity.

"You either fill this prescription or I'll sue you."

"Sue me for what?" the haughty, dumpy little pharmacist questioned.

"Denying a patient access to life-sustaining medication."

"Listen Budd, Dr. Dodd is dead. We don't even know this Dr. Carter you've been using."

"He's on the staff at Timberview in Dallas, will that do?"

"I'd have to talk to him."

Dr. Carter had been Budd's therapist in the early seventies after his problems with Nicole at the University of Texas. Budd and Dr. Carter had a bond. He knew he could trust Dr. Carter. Dr. Carter was independent, powerful.

"Come on Mother, let's go." Budd felt the greatest fear he felt during the whole ordeal that day.

"Where are we going?"

"We're calling Dr. Carter in Dallas."

When Dr. Dodd had died, Budd had been without a psychiatrist. At that time he had conferred with Dr. Carter who, in turn, represcribed Dr. Dodd's medication until Budd could find another doctor. Now it seemed it might be becoming a battle between the local psychiatrists, who was trying to protect one of their members, and with the distant judgment of a prestigious out-of-town doctor who was concerned about the treatment of one of his former patients whom he trusted.

Dr. Carter returned his call at noon. Budd went through the whole story from before the fire to the present.

"Do you think I'm paranoid?"

"Yes, but it's justifiable paranoia. It's real. Unfortunately what I am saying may make you more paranoid. It seems to me you're caught up in the middle of something dangerous.

If there is a fire, get your family and get the HELL out of there. What is the name of your pharmacy and it's phone number? At least I think I can clear up your medication issue. Call your pharmacy at 1:30 this afternoon and ask for your prescription to be refilled. Take care, Budd."

"This is Budd Wilson. I'm calling for the pharmacist to see if he had a call from Dr. Carter in Dallas."

"Mr. Wilson, there has been some misunderstanding, I assure you."

"Will you refill my prescription?"

"Mr. Wilson, Dr. Carter has given us a standing order to refill your lithium for the next three months."

"Thank God." He turned to his mother and softly said, "Outranked her."

"Good." His mother shook her head in defiance.

"Deliver it," Budd coldly finished.

Every night, Budd would call Steve at around nine-thirty.

"How's the weather report?"

Sissy Wilson Harrington, Budd's former wife had been tremendously supportive. She knew Budd. She knew what he was capable of and what he wasn't capable of. They both had decided that at best life would go on for Jenny, her father and grandparents as ususal. They all knew Jennifer's presence at the Wilson home would create an added extra responsibility and they would have to be extra careful when she was there

"How's the weather?" Budd asked Stephen that familiar question on Jenny's visitation night.

"Ah-h, it's going to be okay. Least I think so. You flyboys worry too much."

"Steve, I've got a little one over here."

"Well, just keep a close eye."

He tucked Jennifer into bed in his mother's room, the bedroom below his. He listened to her prayers. He went upstairs to his room, opened the front window, sat in a Windsor chair and looked out the window. He had no firearms nor any knowledge of firearms. He had only shot a gun once in his life when he was thirteen years old, shooting at ten cans with a friend. His only hope if something happened was to see it coming, hit 911, and get Jennifer and his parents out of there. He put on his walkman, flipped on a Glenn

Miller tape and began his nightly vigil. His daughter was sleeping in the bedroom below.

"Moonlight Serenade." Dancing in Austin years ago. He sat down in the Windsor chair and stared out the window.

"Why, Nicole, why?"

"In the Mood" came on the tape.

"I can outlast you. Damn it, I can outlast you."

Around six in the morning he awoke. He sat up in his chair.

"We made it another night. We made it another night." He walked downstairs and fixed a pot of coffee for the family. "Yes sir, we made it another night." He passed his father's room and walked into his mother's room while his mother and Jenny were still sleeping.

"Hello, my little one. Daddy loves you," he said softly as Jenny slept. About seven-thirty he heard her.

"Daddy! Daddy! Hi Daddy! What are we going to do today?"

"Let's go out to breakfast, honey."

He took her to what Jenny called, "the green seat place" which was about a half mile from Municipal Hospital. The closer he got to the vicinity of the hospital he realized he was being followed by the city police.

"Let's just go in here and eat, okay?" The walls were coming up.

"Sure Daddy."

Later as they were going home, the same police car appeared and followed them again. Budd was silent. He kept driving.

"Daddy, in school they teach us the police are our friends. They are, aren't they Daddy?"

"I certainly hope so." They continued home. No one stopped them.

"How's the weather report tonight?"

"Ah-hh, we're going to have a quiet one tonight."

"Again, I got a little one over here, Stephen."

Around two a.m., an old Chevrolet pick-up truck slowly passed by, weaving from one side of the street to the other. It was rumbling with a bad muffler. It went up a half block then stopped, just sitting there in the middle of the street, rumbling. Budd picked up his flashlight and beamed it towards Stephen's bedroom window. "DOT DOT DOT—DASH DASH DASH—DOT DOT DOT." The S.O.S. was returned. The truck slowly passed again and stopped in the middle of the street in front of the house next to Budd's, directly across the street from Steve's.

"Hit it!" Budd yelled in a whisper. He flew down the stairs to the phone and dialed 911. Then he ran up to his mother's room. She was already on her feet and holding the sleeping child in her arms.

"Take her into the bathroom!" He ran upstairs and threw on his robe and slippers and ran down again. He stood at the front door with it cracked open. The truck was still sitting there, rumbling. The police came and the man left. Budd crossed Olive Street at 2:20 in the morning.

"What was it?"

"A guy looking for some girl's house," said the officer.

"Close call," said Stephen nonchalantly.

"No kidding!" said Budd as he stood in the middle of Olive Street in the middle of the night.

"You flyboys worry too much," said Stephen. The officer excused himself after his job was done. "You worry too much, flyboy," Stephen reiterated.

"Jesus Christ, Stephen! You've got a house full of explosives and I've got a little girl and two old people lying over there asleep! What are you trying to accomplish, huh Stephen, what are you trying to accomplish?"

"See who blinks first. In any war there are those who suffer from collateral damage. That's just a fact of war."

"But Stephen, don't you see, this is not a war! This is just a bunch of people on Olive Street trying to get through the middle of the night!"

"You worry too much, flyboy. Let's go to bed."

"You're not even upset, are you Stephen?"

"A good soldier must always keep his composure. That's the first rule of the jungle."

"But Stephen, this in not the jungle. It's Olive Street. Jesus, you're crazy!"

Budd Wilson walked back to his home from the middle of Olive Street.

By October 1989, the resentment for Nicole was building up in Steve Brantley again. It had the same tone and fervor it had before Saturday, April 1, before the fire. There had been no communication at all between Budd and Nicole since the night of the fire. He worried about her. He had heard all kinds of second hand information about her. Most of it was from Steve, and it wasn't good. Budd was beginning to wonder if Nicole was involved in the fire at all. If Steve was involved in it there was a chance that he might have a partner, Charley Smithson.

Three days earlier, Budd had been sitting in the Burger King at five in the morning writing a paper of propositions and conclusions of the events and people surrounding April third. Each proposition had a different answer. To his knowledge, there were only three men he knew who had feelings for Nicole. Although his feelings were strong at this point, he was not involved with anyone.

He was dealing with the knowledge that Jane now had cancer. He called her every afternoon to check on her health and give her a report of what had happened between Stephen and Nicole and on Olive Street for the previous 24 hours; if anything Jane looked forward to hearing the reports each day. It gave her something to think about other than her illness. Budd didn't realize how sick she really was.

'There are other women in my life besides Nicole. I'm single. It's not inappropriate for me to have various women friends because of that,' he thought to himself.

"Even though Steve Brantley is single, there is only one Nicole Smithson in his life -- and the relationship is strange, to say the least. Charley Smithson had been married to Nicole, but he had other women. This in part had led to his and Nicole's divorce.

Steve probably loved Nicole more than anyone, but only because of his illness and the fact that he was being treated by her as a patient; and, he had no appropriate way to achieve the personal love he desired. Nicole had probably been the only beautiful woman who had ever cared for Stephen -- but in a therapeutic way, until both of their tempers had gotten out of hand.

When he had given her roses at the Vietnam war veteran's group in 1987, she had told him that she could'nt accept them because she was his counselor. Steve interpreted it as rejection and went into a rage. She countered with her own anger and fear, then she called the police and had Stephen ejected from the counseling group. The exterior seeds were sown then. Budd, however, felt that there was antagonistic behavior on both of their parts before that night in group that led to the exclusion of Stephen from Nicole's Vietnam veterans' group.

Budd wrote his analysis early that morning at the Burger King:

Budd Wilson—Single. Positive feelings for Nicole Smithson. Dealing with grief for Janel's illness, his friend, his lover, not reaching out to any other women at this time because of that.

Charley Smithson—Married to Nicole Smithson. Unfaithful. Had other women in front of his wife, which, in part, led to their break-up.

Stephen Brantley—Single. Dealt with anger issues in his life. Conflicting feelings for Nicole, his therapist, the only beautiful woman who had cared for him but with whom he was unable to have a fulfilling relationship with—CONFLICT.

Budd looked up through his reading glasses. He felt sure it was Nicole's car. However, Nicole said she was at home alone reading a book that night, and that her Mercedes was in the driveway at that time. Budd was not concerned about the car, but who was driving it, and why. In his excitement on that rainy night that Stephen Brantley's yard was set on fire could he have mistaken the person who got out of the car? Could it have been Smithson or Brantley, both of whom he had instinctively thought of from the outset? He still believed the incident and all of its trappings had a tremendous amount to do with a man who drove a white van with a red continental kit. At any rate, Budd knew it was a male who got out of the car. Stephen had always claimed he was on his mother's front porch during the fire. The tremendous lightening would have shown him if he was there. Budd never saw him, and he was out there for forty minutes before the fire. No one knew he was out there except his parents. He had no idea where Charley was that night. What were the underlying motives for the fire, other than the fact that Steve and Nicole were fighting? Who were all the players in and surrounding the fire on Olive Street when it occurred, and what role did they all play in it? And then the thought occurred to Budd that this episode was just the tip of an iceberg.

Budd was frightened and confused. He tried to organize his thoughts. He put them all on paper early att morning at the Burger King. Then he dashed over to Captain Prichart's office at 7:30 in the morning and left them on his desk.

Budd was exhausted. He was a social drinker. However, through the entire experience he had not had one drink. He wanted to keep his head as clear as possible. That night he decided to go out to his cousin Jim Beutner's who lived in the country and have a bourbon and water or two and unwind. He needed it. Many times Budd relaxed from the world at his cousin Jim's and had a drink or two However, this time there was another reason. Jim, Budd's cousin, had played golf with and was a friend of Charley Smitihson's. Charley had moved to Houston following his and Nicole's separation.

Budd and Jim had a few drinks. When Jim's wife excused herself and went to another part of the house to do some chores, Budd opened up to his cousin.

"You and Charley Smithson are pretty good friends, aren't you?"

"Yeah, he just got divorced. He's a pretty good guy. Says he's glad to get rid of her. He says Nicole was always talking up to him about how she was a professional and made more money than he did. She's really a bitch."

"She is in a lot of trouble, Jim," Budd said.

"Yeah, I understand you're right in the middle of it."

"Yeah, I am." Budd was silent for a moment. "If what I hear is correct, she's so jumpy she could shoot someone. I've heard she's got a .22 revolver in her purse. She's so paranoid she could go for anyone who scared her."

"Why do you care so much about Nicole, Budd? You've always loved her. Hell, Budd, she messed up your mind years ago in Austin. She isn't worth it. What DID happen that night in front of your house?"

"I'm not sure I know." Budd proceeded to tell the entire incident including the information he had written in the Burger King and had left for Captain Prichart earlier that morning. About three days after Budd had visited his cousin he received a phone call from Steve.

"I didn't know you had a cousin. You been writing too many papers lately, Buddy. There's a husband down in Houston that don't like you too much."

"Who do you mean, Stephen?"

"Well, somebody's been saying to a cousin or someone that a husband might have been behind some incident or fire or something."

"What are you talking about?" Budd tried to keep the conversation going in order to encourage Stephen to elaborate. However, it did not work.

"Well, of course, that's just what I hear."

"Hear what, Stephen?"

"Well, I gotta go Buddy...gotta go."

Budd knew that there were only two people who knew the information he had given to Prichart several days earlier, Prichart and his cousin Jim. Budd assumed his cousin had contacted Charley right after he had talked to him. The irony was that Budd had found out about the interchange between he and his cousin from Stephen. He called Captain Prichart the next morning and checked it out.

"Captain Prichart, that information I turned into your office the other morning, did you show it to anybody else?"

"What do you mean? That paper has never been beyond my desk."

"That's what I'm trying to say, Captain Prichart. I, in no way, have any reason to mistrust you."

"Okay. Go on."

"I told my cousin about all of this. He's a friend of Charley Smithson, who is now in Houston. Here's the kicker, the one I heard about it from was, of all people, Stephen Brantley. The whole thing was wired kind of funny-- from my cousin, to Charley Smithson, to Steve Brantley, to me. WHY WOULD STEVE BRANTLEY TELL ME?"

"You mean you think Stephen Brantley and Charley Smithson are tied together in this?"

"Exactly!"

Budd continued thinking about it for several weeks. He had both negative and positive feelings.

Somehow he felt he had to do something. He called Municipal Hospital.

"I'm trying to reach Nicole Smithson."

"She isn't on the staff anymore."

"Well, this is Budd Wilson."

"Mr. Wilson, we'll try to put you in contact with her."

Four minutes later, Budd's phone rang.

"Budd, this is Nickie."

"Hi! Are you all right? I've been so worried about you! You're not at Municipal Hospital anymore?"

"No. I'm in private practice."

"Oh. . Okay."

"Do you know anything?" she immediately asked.

"No, not really. Could it have been Charley?"

"No. Charley's in Houston... has been for nine months."

"Nickie, I have some information that leads me to believe Charley played a role in this."

"Go on."

Budd proceeded to explain about the paper he had written at the Burger King and had given to Captain Prichart and the unusual trail the same information went through from his cousin, to Charley Smithson, to Steve Brantley then back to Budd.

"Budd, it gets so confusing, more confused and more confused."

"Doesn't it?"

"Why did you call me, Budd?"

"Because I love you."

"Budd!"

"Don't analyze it. Just accept it."

"All right."

"I'm trying to help you."

"Budd, can you see when Stephen comes and goes?"

"Yeah, I live right across the street from him."

"Can you tell me every time he leaves his house in that old car? What kind of car is it?"

"It's a Plymouth, '71 or '72."

"Do you know his license number?"

"I can get it."

"God, Budd, you're doing great! You're doing great!"

"Where can I reach you Nicole?"

"Call me at home."

"At home?"

"It's okay." She gave him her phone number.

"Nickie, what are you doing for a living?"

"I told you, I'm in private counseling."

"How do you eat?"

"I make some money. I get by. Remember, Budd, get a license number on that old heap."

At 9:30 p.m., Budd heard Steve crank up the old Plymouth. He called Nickie, as requested.

"Nickie, he's airborne."

"Did you get a tag number?" she asked.

"It's 837-ENR, Texas."

"Great, Budd! Great! Call me every time he moves."

Twenty minutes later, Stephen returned, and Budd called Nicole back.

"He's just been making his nightly round on Main Street Plaza."

"Oh yeah. My watchdog. . . There's nothing I can do, Budd. Nothing I can do." She sounded flat, distant and soft. "He'll never do anything to me."

"Listen Nicole, a year and a half of this is enough for me. I'm getting old."

"Try three years, Budd."

"In six months, I'll be forty. Can you believe that Nicole?"

"He'll never do anything to me. . . What do they say? Life begins at forty?"

"I certainly hope so, Nicole. I certainly hope so."

"Happy Thanksgiving, Budd."

"Happy Thanksgiving, Nicole."

He knew he had to go do Dallas to see Jane no matter what was going on in Texarkana. He took off just before Thanksgiving and hurriedly went there for the day. Jane was living with her daughter, Julie, who now had a family and home of her own. Budd got directions from Julie and drove straight there. Jane was sitting up in a reclining chair in the living room when he arrived. The room was hot and stuffy and it was though there was a cloud that oppressively held itself over her's and everyone else's heads there promising a darkness soon to come. Her hair had turned gray and a dirty shade of white and her features were sunken and sallow. She was breathing oxygen from a tank through a clear plastic tube in her nose. In the house there was an odor of stale urine, and of a leaking colostomy bag. It was the odor of death. Her breathing was very quick, very short, very shallow. She looked up.

"Hey Baby," He gently put his hand down on her shoulder -- then he kissed her cheek.

"Hey," she softly said. "Glad to see you."

"How are you?" he asked.

"Seen better days," again she softly replied. "Seen better days. How come you're not in Texarkana? You need to be in Texarkana, taking care of Jenny and your parents."

"They can spare me for one day."

"You needn't have come. I'm okay. I'm okay." Her voice kept getting softer. "You remember when that man said that ninety-nine percent of me was a Gershwin tune? You remember?"

"Yeah."

"Well, it isn't anymore. It isn't anymore."

"Jane, you're the greatest, the only authentic jazz singer I ever knew."

"Not anymore. Not anymore."

"Don't say that."

"I paid my price."

"Maybe I should stay here, Jane."

"No. I'm in good hands. I have good doctors, Southwestern Medical School. I have hospice care; Julie is taking good care of me. I'm in good hands. Good hands."

"I need to come more often. I couldn't tell your condition by phone. Why didn't you tell me?"

"I didn't want you to worry. You have enough to worry about with that neighbor and that nutty shrink. They say I'm dying, but I'll make it through the holidays. I'll make it through the holidays. You've got to take care of Jenny and your parents. You go now and be careful. I'll be here for the holidays."

He stood up and bent over to embrace her.

"I'm getting sleepy now. I must rest. They have me on so many pain killers. I just want to sleep all the time. We'll be together again."

Tears were running down his cheeks. He wiped his tears, then looked at Julie, then back at Jane. She was asleep.

"We'll be together again," he said softly.

"I hope Mother does make it through the holidays. She always loved the holidays when she was singing. All the beautifully dressed patrons at the club. All the flowers and decorations. I hope so."

Julie walked him to his car. He looked back, then headed home for the holiday season.

On Thanksgiving Eve, Budd sat with his parents in the kitchen as his mother cooked for the next day.

"I miss Jenny," he said.

"I do, too," said Budd's mother. It was Jennifer's year to spend Thanksgiving with her mother. "Thanksgiving just doesn't seem the same without her."

"A little sherry, Mother?"

"Yes, I believe so."

Budd and his father sat at the kitchen table sharing a bottle of sherry with his mother as she cooked.

"Well, nine-thirty, guess I'm going to bed." Budd begged off.

"So early?" his mother asked.

"Yeah, I'm gettin' tired. Hadn't got anything better to do. Read a little while. Besides I'm going to church in the morning."

Budd was upstairs sleeping soundly. About two minutes after midnight he heard a car screech around the corner of seventeenth and Olive and hit the accelerator. The car was loud and sounded like an older American V-8 with a bad exhaust pipe. There were four rapid shots, followed by a fifth lone shot. Budd lay in silence. He heard it go north on Olive for what sounded like three or four blocks. Then he heard a distant screech of tires. He heard it come back on Wood Street, one block east, parallel with Olive. He could hear the exhaust pipe. At eighteenth and Wood, he heard the pattern again only softer--four quick shots followed by a fifth lone shot. The engine noise of the car he was sun!

"They've hit Stephen's car, or was it a recording? They couldn't have a sound system in that old heap that good? But I heard it twice, the same pattern, very softly the second time, the next block over. Let him call the police this time."

In the dark, he plugged in his small coffee pot by the bed. He drank two cups of coffee. He turned off the coffee pot and rolled over for het thought was for about two hours. Then he went back to sleep, again. He met his mother in the kitchen around eight in the morning.

"Mother did you hear five shots last night? Four in a row followed by a fifth lone shot?"

"Yes, I did." She looked at Budd hesitantly.

"And then a few minutes later did you hear the same pattern of shots, only real soft?"

"Yes."

"What time?"

"Around midnight."

"How 'bout three minutes after midnight?"

"That's close enough."

Budd got dressed for church. He backed the K-car out of the garage and came around the corner out onto Olive Street. He slowly drove down the 1700 block towards town. He glanced at

Steve's car. There were bullet holes in it.

"My God! They DID shoot Steve's car. I wonder when it was actually shot."

He headed downtown for St. John's Episcopal.

Two days later Budd called Nicole again.

"Nicole, get this. Someone shot up Stephen's car with, I think, an automatic rifle, three minutes after midnight, I think, Thanksgiving morning."

"Who!? When!?"

"You heard me."

"They shot up his car? Oh my God."

"Nickie in no way do I think you're responsible for this."

"Look Budd, you musn't call me again. You've been a tremendous help but they mustn't know we're communicating. Do you hear me? THEY MUSTN'T KNOW!"

"I'm sorry, Nickie. I'm sorry. I was just trying to help."

"I know. I know. Good-bye Budd."

"Good-bye."

All around and everywhere it was the Christmas season. He and his parents were having Jennifer visit for the holidays. At church and everywhere he was feeling the true meaning of Christmas. He prayed for Jane Mitchell, not really knowing what to pray for except for her to have as much comfort and the least amount of pain as possible. He prayed for her peace, knowing that at this point it was unrealistic to pray for her continued life. He had never dealt with the approaching death of someone he loved so much and he did not really know how to pray to God about it, or what to pray for. He prayed for his parents and Jenny, the heart beat of his family. And he prayed for Nicole, that somehow God would untangle the mess she was in. He missed her presence that Christmas, but he never called her at her wish. He sent her a card. "Peace on Earth. Good Will Towards Men."

"Jenny, what are you doing?"

"I'm memorizing my part for the Christmas pageant at the church. You want to hear me?"

"Yes, I do." Budd sat down next to his daughter.

"And suddenly there was with the angel, A multitude of the heavenly host, Praising God and saying, Glory to God in the highest, And on Earth, PEACE, GOOD WILL TOWARDS MEN'."

"That's real good Jenny! Would you like for me to coach you? Give you some pointers?"

"Yeah, Daddy."

"When you say 'GLORY' that should be a real important word. Emphasize it. Also emphasize 'AND ON EARTH, PEACE, GOOD WILL TOWARDS MEN', Okay?"

"Uh huh."

"Go for it again."

"And suddenly there was with the angel, A multitude of the Heavenly host, Praising God and saying, GLORY to God in the highest, AND ON EARTH, PEACE, GOOD WILL TOWARDS

MEN'."

"That's super. You wanna do it again?"

"Yeah.

`And suddenly. . .'"

It was Christmas Eve day. Although snow was forecast, it was a bright, sunny cold day. That morning Budd had done some yard work for one of the members of his church. He had just finished lunch at home with Jenny and his parents when the phone rang.

"Nickie?" He was surprised at her calling.

"Budd.. . . Thank you for the card."

"You're welcome."

"Could I talk to you? Could we talk?" she asked.

"You're sure...? Yeah, go for it."

"No, not on the phone."

"Well, what do you want to do, meet me somewhere?"

"I don't know. O.K., yes I do."

"Where?"

"I don't know."

"Jesus Nicole, do you want to meet me or not?"

"Yes. . . Yes I do."

He thought for a moment of a discreet place from his days of peddling jewelry to waitresses.

"Meet me in the waiting area of the restaurant in the Flying `J' truck stop at Mandeville, Arkansas at two o'clock, okay?"

"I don't know. Okay, I'll be there."

He drove up at 1:40 p.m. The Mercedes was sitting in the parking lot. He was a little afraid, but then, he'd been a little afraid for over a year. He pulled the K-Car into the space next to the Mercedes. He got out of the car and looked down at the right front hubcap of her car.

Nicole was sitting on a bench in the waiting area in the front of the restaurant. She was smoking. She had lost weight. She was wearing dark sunglasses, a black turtleneck sweater, black slacks and a waist length silver fox jacket.

"Hello, Nickie."

"Hello, Budd." She looked down, then up to him.

"Well, here's Budd the walker." Gracie, the hostess, grabbed two menus. "Gee Budd, I didn't think you could pick up someone this classy. She's the real thing."

"Shut-up Gracie," he whispered under his breath. "Take us to a booth -- way in the back."

"I hear you. Table for two in the back."

"Hi, I'm Crystal. I'm your waitress."

"What d'ya want to have, Nickie?"

"Just coffee." She fiddled through her purse for a cigarette.

"Me, too. Here." He handed her a cigarette.

"Thank you."

He lit her cigarette and she took a deep draw. They were silent for what seemed like an eternity.

"Budd, why do you care? What's in it for you?'

"I want to tell you what I think happened. Then I want to listen to you, but I guess I just want to affirm you, right or wrong."

"I know that. I appreciate that."

The waitress brought the coffee.

"Thank you, Crystal. Leave us alone for a little while, okay?" He paused. . . "Nicole, had you been having an affair with a prominent businessman in this town?"

"No."

"Are you sure?"

"Yes."

"Okay. . . let's take a different approach. Were you having an affair with a questionable guy in your Vietnam group, a guy who drives a white van?"

"Yes," she said hesitantly. "It could have cost me my license if Steve had let the right people know. He had to be shut up and we knew he was talking to you."

"What difference would that make?"

"Weren't you angry with me? Didn't you want revenge? Haven't you been angry with me for years?"

"No, Nicole. No."

"But you called Municipal Hospital and put the blame on me the night the fire happened."

"Because I thought you had broken the law. In retrospect Nickie, after all we've been through in the last year, I don't care what you did."

"But from the night the fire happened, you accused me."

"Again, it was because I thought you broke the law."

"Do you, still?

"It doesn't matter, now."

"Yes, it does! Yes, it does. Look Charley had deserted me. He was out on the road on tours all the time. I was alone. He was bringing home other women -- young, beautiful women. I'm nearly 39. Budd, I was alone. We were in debt, growing more in debt. I needed someone. I needed money." She looked down and paused.

"Money from a wealthy lover? Only he didn't come through, did he? He found it more expedient to stay with his wife, at least for the time being. How sad. Nickie, did you falsify insurance vouchers for hypothetical group members that didn't exist to make up for some of that debt after you realized you were own your own?"

"No! No! No! Please no, I didn't. Please believe me. Budd, no."

"All of this was related to time spent after hours in your office and home with a guy with a questionable drug reputation, the man who drives a white van. Wholesaling from one hand to another, so to speak."

"You're smart."

"You could have gotten in big trouble."

"I could have. I nearly did."

"Steve Brantley told me about your insurance fraud. I'm not sure he knew the scope of the entire deal, but he was an excellent and dutiful scout, and he had a masterful ability with a camera and license plates."

"What are you talking about?"

"Nicole, with me, you were setting yourself up for failure all along."

"How, other than what you think you know happened?"

"'Observe. Observe everything'. THE SIGNAL FOR THE STORM."

"What are you talking about?"

"Monday, April third, your call to me."

"Did I tell you to observe everything?'

"Yes, you did. . . and what was I doing that night?"

"Standing on the porch in a storm, obeying orders. . . observing."

"You got it. Nicole, only from a distance... I've observed a lot of your behavior and words."

"Such as?"

"Nicole, why would a 38 year-old woman want a Volkswagen?"

"What?"

"The night of the fire. You told me while we were discussing the merits of a Mercedes and a fire that you wanted a Volkswagen."

"Maybe I'd just like to have one."

"Or maybe you'd like to be young, beautiful and carefree again --
like back in 1968, huh?'

"Maybe."

"Now run the night of April third from the start to the end, all the
way through, and leave nothing out."

"All right," she was silent a moment. "Brantley had gone to
Charley. He'd shown him some pictures of the van at the office."

"Whose van?"

"My friend's."

"The same friend who lit the fire?"

"How do you know he lit the fire?"

"OBSERVE. I was standing on my porch. Did he show Charley
any pictures of any other vehicles on the Main Street Plaza lot over
a period of time?"

"I don't know what all he showed Charley. Why do you ask me all
these questions?" She looked up in fear, fatigue and pain.

"Nicole, I've always felt you had a soul, a conscious. I still do.
That's why I think you met me here today. Who set the fire,
Nicole?"

"You!"

"What? No, I was home with my parents and my daughter who
saw the fire being set by a man in a silver Mercedes Benz, or does
he drive a white van?"

"When you called on Saturday night before the fire I was

convinced it was a conspiracy. You and Steve had enough on me to press for an investigation."

"Investigation of what, Nicole?"

"Steve had gone to Charley. They were blackmailing me."

"For what, Nicole?"

"Having an affair with a client. . . I could have. . . lost my license."

"The same client who drove down Olive Street on the night of April third? The same client who drives an old white van with a red continental kit, a man with a questionable past and ties to illegal drugs?"

"You had to be in on it!" Her eyes were piercing as she looked him straight in the eye. "You knew everything!"

"Nicole, after twenty years of loving you?"

"But -- you had reason to get even with me. I was unfaithful to you. I left you in one of your greatest crises in Austin for Charley. Then I broke the therapist-client bond after your treatment at Municipal Hospital."

"Now wait a minute, Nicole. What happened with Charley in Austin was twenty years ago. I was sick. It was a normal response on your part. When your boyfriend, or partner, or WHOEVER he was drove down Olive Street on April third, I was no longer your client."

"You don't hate me?" she questioned.

"No, Nicole, I don't hate you. Never did."

"Oh, Budd." She looked down. Tears were streaming down her cheeks. "I'm sorry."

"You don't have to be. . . Nicole. . . ? Who shot up Stephen's car?"

"Probably my former husband was behind that one."

"I have a tendency to agree with you. Stephen had talked to me too much about his relationship with Charley. I always figured that he'd better shut up or realize I could put the whole picture together. After all, Charley WAS your husband, for better or worse. I still wonder what time of day or night Stephen's car was shot up, and what kind of stereo system they were packing, if they were. What people will do for money. I'm blessed. I don't want it anymore."

"What?"

"It doesn't matter."

"What are you going to do with me, Budd?"

"It's Christmas Eve, Nicole."

Each booth had a phone in it for truckers. It was a long distance call from the phone in the booth of the Flying "J" Truck Stop to Texarkana. Budd keyed in his A.T.& T. calling card number and keyed in the number.

"Captain Prichart, this is Budd Wilson. I'm out at the mall. You know I said on the night of the fire and afterwards that I thought the Mercedes on Olive Street had wire wheels. Well, I just saw Nicole Smithson drive down Kennedy Lane. She's got disc hubcaps on that car, like all other Mercedes. Now I don't think she'd change hubcaps on that vehicle."

Nickie's eyes grew as big as dollar pancakes.

"Yeah. Well, Stephen did make a lot of enemies and he is a colossal snoop. You know, if I could have just gotten a license number off that car the night it happened it would have all been over in ten minutes. Yes sir, well have a Merry Christmas now."

"What is my license plate number?" she asked.

"207-MJS Texas."

"How long have you known that number?"

"Since the night of April third. Merry Christmas Nicole." He held up two fingers and made a "V". *"Peace,"* he softly added.

"Merry Christmas," she stammered. "What are you going to do?"

"Pay the check, walk you to your car, get in my car and go home."

"Then what?"

"Celebrate Christmas with Jenny."

They walked out of the truck stop.

"Well, it's over. It's finally over. Do you feel better?"

"I don't know. It doesn't seem like it could be over." She looked down the sidewalk, then up to Budd again. He lit a cigarette.

"May I have one?"

He gave her a cigarette and lit it. She took a deep drag, then said, "You once told me - the last day in group when you were

leaving the hospital - that if you had a fantasy it would be to take me out for a drink. Does that offer still hold."

"Well Nickie, I don't know." He was squirming. "It's kind of like going out with your ex-wife. All I've thought about for over a year is Nicole Smithson. I'm kind of tired of it."

"I understand."

He walked a way down the sidewalk, maybe ten feet, came to a halt, then turned around. "Ah-h. . . What right do I? Who am I to. . . ?" Then he smiled. "Get in the car." He started the motor and began to back out.

"Okay, Nicole."

"Yes, Nicole."

"Okay, Nicole."

Then she whispered something in his ear.

"Nickie, you haven't changed in twenty years. Let's go for it."

Peal upon peal of laughter broke forth from both of them. He put his car in drive and put his foot on the accelerator, knowing full well the last laugh was his.

—THE END--

COPYRIGHT NOTICES

Mitchell Paris, Edgar Sampson, Benny Goodman

Copyright 1938

"Alice's Restaurant"

Arlo Guthrie

Copyright 1967

"Muskrat Ramble"

Ray Gilbert and Edwards "Kid" Ory

Copyright 1926

Can't Get Started"

Ira Gershwin and Vernon Duke

Copyright 1936

"When It's Sleepy Time Down South"

Leon Rene, Otis Rene, Clarence Muse

Copyright 1931

"Blowin' in the Wind"

Bob Dylan

Copyright 1963

"Drearnsville"

Henry Mancini

Copyright 1959

"Prefude in D Minor"

Serge Raclunaninoff

Public Domain

"Take the A-Train"

Billy Strayhorn

Copyright 1941

"Satin Doll"

Johnny Mercer, Billy Strayhom, Duke Ellington

ubsidiary of All Belo Corporation

508 Young Street

Dallas, TX 75202

The Wall Street Journal

1211 Avenue of the Americas

New York, N.Y. 10036

The New York Times

The New York Times Company

620 Eighth Avenue

New York, NY 10018

The New Yorker

www.newyorker.com

Annie Get Your Gun

Herbert Fields and Dorothy Fields

Irving Berlin

1946

Mr. Roberts

Frank Nugent—Joshua Logan

1955

"Open a New Window"

Jerry Harmon

Copyright 1966

"I Remember You"

Johnny Mercer and Victor Schertzinger

Copyright 1942

"Guess I'll Hang My Tears Out to Dry"

Sammy Cahn and Jule Styne

Copyright 1945

ABOUT THE AUTHOR

Born in Terrell State Hospital, in Terrell, Texas, Bob was adopted by Dorothy and Edward Walters, of Texarkana. He grew up in East Texas, living in a home where music and teaching were celebrated and practiced daily.

Bob's success as a writer began in High School when he wrote a theme on a series of unsolved murders that had occurred in Texarkana in 1946. His popular "Phantom Killer" piece hooked Bob as an author for life.

His father, a devoted reader of novels by American literary giants, gave him a solid grounding as a reader of important literature. Bob's biggest influences include Hemingway and Fitzgerald.

He attended Texarkana College, the University of Texas at Arlington and the University of Texas at Austin, where Bob studied journalism. While pursuing early coursework at Texarkana College, the author enjoyed his first job writing for a city newspaper.

Bob tells us he has suffered various forms of mental illness since his high school days. He says he draws upon his personal struggles, triumphs and experiences to write and live. He is relieved his medications work; and, his motto is testament to a positive outlook on living and a sanguine plinth that anchors this writer's life and shapes the central characters in his novel:

"...nothing comes easy, nothing comes overnight. If you want to be successful, you must be willing to pay the price."

www.ingramcontent.com/pod-product-compliance
Lightning Source LLC
Chambersburg PA
CBHW031253170626
46807CB00001B/125